THE MACKEREL PLAZA

PETER DE VRIES was born in Chicago, Illinois, in 1910. After attending Calvin College and Northwestern University, he had a number of jobs, including vending-machine operator and radio actor. He also worked for *Poetry* magazine, as an editor, before moving to New York in 1943, when he became a regular staff contributor to the *New Yorker*, with which he has been closely associated ever since. He has published many novels and short stories and is a member of the National Institute of Arts and Letters. He lives in Westport, Connecticut.

FREDERIC RAPHAEL was born in Chicago, Illinois, and was educated at Charterhouse and St John's College, Cambridge, where he was a Major Scholar in Classics. He is the author of fourteen novels, including *Lindmann* and *Richard's Things*, and of many short stories, essays, screenplays and translations. His screenplay for *Darling* won an Academy Award in 1966. His television series, *The Glittering Prizes*, gained the Royal Television Society's Writer of the Year award in 1976. His most recent book is a biography of Byron.

D1332092

PETER DE VRIES

The Mackerel Plaza

INTRODUCED BY
FREDERIC RAPHAEL

OXFORD UNIVERSITY PRESS
1984

For Gus Lobrano
In Memoriam

Oxford University Press, Walton Street, Oxford OX2 6DP

London Glasgow New York Toronto
Delhi Bombay Calcutta Madras Karachi
Kuala Lumpur Singapore Hong Kong Tokyo
Nairobi Dar es Salaam Cape Town
Melbourne Auckland

and associated companies in
Beirut Berlin Ibadan Mexico City Nicosia

Oxford is a trade mark of Oxford University Press

© Peter De Vries 1958
Introduction © Volatic Ltd.
First published in the UK 1958 by Victor Gollancz Ltd.
First issued as an Oxford University Press paperback 1984

British Library Cataloguing in Publication Data
De Vries, Peter
The mackerel plaza. – (Twentieth-century classics)
I. Title   II. Series
813'.54[F]   PS3507.E867
ISBN 0–19–281471–0

Library of Congress Cataloging in Publication Data
De Vries, Peter.
The Mackerel Plaza.
(Twentieth-century classics) (Oxford paperbacks)
I. Title.   II. Series.
PS3507.E8673M29 1984   813'.52   83–23718
ISBN 0–19–281471–0 (pbk.)

Printed in Great Britain by
Richard Clay (The Chaucer Press) Ltd
Bungay, Suffolk

INTRODUCTION

BY FREDERIC RAPHAEL

' . . . who needs no introduction from me,' is probably how Dale Carnegie's *Hints To Introducers*, should such a volume exist, would advise that no introduction should begin. But then how shall we define a Modern Classic save as a book so well known that it has to be introduced? Good wines get a lot of bush these days, when all they really need is a corkscrew. As for *The Mackerel Plaza*, it does not even require a bookmark: allowing for a fair share of the usual delays, due to modernization, and a signals failure somewhere along the line, any self-respecting commuter who has not forgotten his glasses will manage it easily at a sitting, or a swaying. And he will be comforted to know that when the first De Vries has been absorbed, there are plenty more. Someone once said of Ivy Compton-Burnett, 'When you've read them all, you've definitely read one.' De Vries would not, I suspect, faint at that kind of praise.

His comic gifts are, the blurbists can fairly burble, prodigious. His capacity for heaping one unlikely effect on top of another (and one unlikely character on top of another) is almost chirrigueresque, as numerous critics have doubtless observed. Yet however grotesque his invention, his plots come out as neatly as a quadratic equation set for a school exam. Indeed, like Compton-Burnett, he builds a cruel kind of comedy out of the logical consequences of often very simple *données*. Like the same author, he is a pitiless moralizer and he never lets anyone off. Dialogue is used not to depict character – something for which Creative Writing pundits reproach him –

but in order to squeeze the last drop of acid from any forbidden fruit that happens to be on the sideboard. The desires of married men, like Bob Swirling in *Madder Music*, may be perfectly understandable, but that doesn't mean they are going to get away with them. Equally, when the Reverend Mackerel, recently widowed, chances to meet a peerlessly pretty girl to whom, it seems, he appeals as much as she does to him, fairness would seem to require that they be allowed to live happily ever after. Mackerel is technically free to marry and the girl is more than willing. Greek tragedy, we were always promised, results from a fatal flaw in the protagonist's character; De Vriesian comedy results from a fatal virtue, usually honesty. The course of true love is full of bunkers, and lost balls. The suburban image, like the *double entendre*, is bread and butter to De Vries: he is at home in the kind of places which fancier citizens prefer to pass through as quickly as may be. The pun, an addiction beyond treatment, announces the duplicities of normal life, the two-facedness of the ordinary. (It also gets a lot of laughs, which can't be bad.)

Peter De Vries was born in Chicago in 1910 and educated at Calvin College, Grand Rapids, Michigan, a place famous throughout the States for its torrents of office furniture. The influence of Calvinism on De Vries's fiction is so marked that only a critic writing an introduction would feel obliged to allude to it. He is unquestionably one of very few writers in English who have succeeded in making Dutch origins a subject for jest. But then humourlessness makes him laugh and laugh. Farce, on the other hand, is no laughing matter: the elegant joinery of his plots cannot conceal the man's constant sense of tearful reality behind the ridiculous veneer, or the ridiculously mixed metaphor. However lapsed a Calvinist may be, there is always further to fall. God is not mocked, and when He is, we know Who is liable to have the last laugh. 'It is the final proof of God's omnipotence', says the Reverend Mackerel, 'that he need not exist in order to save us.' Or in order to play us a dirty trick. The comic possibilities of the Liberal Pastor are exploited here with an exuberance which is cunning enough to stay within the bounds of the plausible. Individual characters may indeed not be conspicuous in De Vries's *œuvre* for their 'size and complexity', as one carping eulogist has complained, but the character of American Suburbia is delineated with puncturing attention to specifics. In *Madder Music*, for example, Swirling, the hero who has metamorphosed himself into Groucho Marx, stoops to sweep up some scraps of window-pane, 'using a shirt cardboard for a dustpan', a caressable detail which furnishes the story with a typically sweet stroke of accuracy. The Reverend Mackerel might, in an English novel of comparable intent, be little more than a comic hypocrite. De Vries plays fairer than that: Andrew's libidinous liberalism is consistent and cant-free. The humbugs are his parishioners, on whom, unfortunately, his living depends. When he complains that the proposed monument to his supposedly saintly wife will lose something if it becomes an excuse for business enterprise, tight-lipped questions are asked about this apparent hostility to 'business', no dirty word in Avalon, Connecticut. De Vries knows commuter-land like the back of his hand, and the back of his hand is what he is often tempted to give its inhabitants.

De Vries was a Chicagoan for the first forty-three years of his life and the capital of the Midwest made a deep mark on his style. His home-town is the most American city in the Union. Its architecture, after the great fire, announced that it owed nothing to Europe. Louis Sullivan and Frank Lloyd Wright initiated the tradition of the new. Chicago's newspapers showed little deference to New York, less to the old continent. England, and English manners, might intimidate the snobs of Manhattan, but Chicago bowed neither left nor right. Its writers found their inspiration in life, not in libraries. Most of them began as journalists. The success of men like Ben Hecht and Charles MacArthur, in plays such as *The Front Page*, proved that local talent could take on all comers. Hemingway's idea that a good story was one which no sub-editor could prune was typically Midwestern. Yet there was a Bohemian side of Chicago which indeed looked to Europe, however furtively. In the Twenties, Montparnasse came to the near North Side in the form of smuggled copies of *Ulysses*. Arty rooms were lined with silver paper and racy young men came and went, speaking of Eliot and André Gide. Modernism was taken seriously. Peter De Vries, in the intervals between being a vending-machine operator, a toffee-apple salesman and a radio actor, became an associate editor of *Poetry*, the long-running highbrow magazine which still proves the vitality of Chicago's cultural ambitions. De Vries was thus exposed both to intellectual finesse and to the cruder aspects of American life, where he found the material on which 'heroes' like Stanley Waltz, in *Let Me Count The Ways*, could be based. He too moved furniture, not an activity to be taken lightly. It was his good luck to grow up in a period when the tiro could not make a living from Fellowships and Grants. The varied sources of his early income were a privileged humiliation from which he continues to draw benefits.

In his position as a member of *Poetry*'s editorial board, he was responsible for luring James Thurber to Chicago, to give a benefit lecture, in 1943. Now if it is true that Chicago never willingly accepted its status as the 'Second City', it must be admitted that no chic Chicagoan could look at the *New Yorker* without a twinge of envy. When the visiting celebrity offered the modest security of a staff job on the *New Yorker*, his temporary host was not slow to follow him eastwards. There followed, one would guess, a period of acclimatization, perhaps institutiona- lization. De Vries had already published a novel or two, but his great period did not begin until 1955, with *The Tunnel Of Love*. Thereafter, for something like twenty years or more, he gave birth to novels with the regularity of an exemplary Catholic mother. The influence of the *New Yorker* can scarcely be overestimated: S. J. Perelman's compulsive word-play and his mixture of literary knowingness with streetwise one-liners clearly inspired De Vries, though he never lacked a personal voice. It may be, however, that being one of the in-house crowd inhibited him, for longer than he might have liked, from abandoning the comfortable uses of derision. *The Blood Of The Lamb*, published in 1962, embarrassed his laughing audience by dealing with a dying child and her father, for whom the lack of a God proves the cruelty of man's liberation from delusion. The continuity between De Vries's comic ideas and his sense of Godless modern tragedy proves that his vision of the world has an obsessive unity. There is always guilt on his ginger-bread.

The Mackerel Plaza was published in 1958, the high summer of the Eisenhower era. The conformities of the commuting communities were never more demanding, the complacency of America never more apparently justified. Sex in the suburbs, and sects in the suburbs, offered De Vries a target full of bulls'-eyes and a field full of bullshit. *The Mackerel Plaza* is a modest novel about a good and modest pastor. Its hilarity has a professionalism which another writer can only hope to emulate: the laughs are not stinted and they are seldom procured by the kind of coterie smugness which English comic novelists of the period so often displayed. Yet the book has an obstinate decency which transcends the premeditated contrivances of routine funnies. To call a preacher Mackerel, and to open him to the minor comedy of being called both Flounder and Halibut, might seem rather juvenile stuff, but Serious Issues are raised, and not shirked. De Vries is scarcely an autobiographical writer, but Mackerel's first-person narrative seems now and again to be indistinguishable from his author's own voice:

. . . I came of Dutch immigrant Calvinist parents. We lived in Chicago, in one of several such communities which still dot that city, hermetically sealed from the American life around them and the Middle West at large. I was taught the Bible at home and in a parochial school, but my parents became a bit dismayed when I began to show signs of appreciating it as literature. They labored with me and prayed for my soul. To keep peace, I recanted the heresy that the Bible was literature, agreeing that it was just God's word. The Dutch Calvinists thrived on schisms, being themselves, of course, the product of many. They were hairsplitters the like of which an ordinary human being in our time is totally unlikely to hear. 'One Dutchman, a Christian; two Dutchmen, a congregation; three Dutchmen, heresy,' was the charge levelled at us by more Americanised people, who boasted, for instance, of belonging to denominations that hadn't had a schism in a hundred years. To these my father always had a ready reply: 'Rotten wood you can't split.' We multiplied by dividing.

An epitomizer could fairly claim that he had isolated the essence of De Vries in this far from facetious paragraph. Candour can, of course, be just one of the masks which a writer adopts, but a New Yorker might be impelled to remark that the above is striking evidence that you don't have to be Jewish to be an immigrant. Come to that, he might add that you don't need to be a Jew to be Jewish. The wry joke about the hair-splitting habits of Dutchmen reads like the transposition of a standard Jewish crack about Jews. De Vries's manic tendency to pun his way out of any charge of po-facedness (the last sentence of the quotation is a neat instance) owes something to the immigrant's characteristic blend of smart-alecry and sad-sack anxiety. No one is keener to prove that he is at home in a language than the man who was not born in it. (In *Lolita*, Nabokov established his credentials by the same kind of nervous ostentation.) The

Dutch immigrant is a particularly vexed case, of course, because he has come to a land which his own forefathers founded and where no names are more manifestly Yankee than Vanderbilt and Roosevelt, for showy example. Yet De Vries's America sometimes verges on Kafka's Amerika, a place full of astonishingly complacent people in a great hurry to do crazy things which they never suspect to be anything but normal. The omelette with *bones* in it that Mackerel eats with Molly Calico belongs to a world in which surrealism has been made available on a franchise basis. Molly's own remark, on a different occasion, 'I've always been a good judge of horseflesh and this is horseflesh', is another bite at the same cherry, as well as being an example of the Grouchoing habit that can sometimes lose its head and dwindle into mere ouchoing. (De Vries must endure with what fortitude he can muster the captiousness with which creative largesse is so often greeted: he makes so many good jokes that some of them are bound to be less good than others.)

Well, folks, now for the fellow you've been waiting for. I've told you some of the plot of the story he is going to tell you and I've made free with a quip or two from the same source. I'm sure you would dearly like me to delay your pleasure a little longer, because as the preacher once said, a pleasure postponed is the best way the Lord can think of to get us to do the right thing in the meantime, but I can't rightly think of anything useful that remains to be said. Truth is, the proof of De Vries is in the reading. I rest my case. Frankly, he can perfectly well carry his own.

Lift up thine eyes,
And let me read thy dream.

Shelley's *Prometheus Unbound*

THE MACKEREL PLAZA

One

LIKE most irritable people I rarely lose my temper (a dog that's let out for regular exercise isn't as apt to run away when it does escape), but I was losing it this morning. I said into the telephone, "Office of the Zoning Board? This is Mr. Mackerel. Reverend Mackerel — of P.L."

"?"

"People's Liberal."

"Oh, yes. That church." The voice at the other end was a female one. "What can I do for you, Reverend Mackerel?"

"I want to report a billboard in the Mobile Bay section," I said, glancing out the window over the treetops to an intersection where the offending object was plainly visible. "This is a residential area, where I need not remind you public hoardings are strictly forb —"

"Yes, I know. You're triple-A out there. Please don't get upset, Reverend Mackerel. Go on." The woman — or more likely, girl — was audibly eating something, a fact not calculated to sooth Mackerel's nerves or cool his pique.

"I assume a waiver was granted by the Zoning Board or the signboard wouldn't have got as far as it is," I went on.

"How far is it?"

"It's up! I can see it now from my study window, over there on Cooper Street. And I don't like it."

"What does it say, Reverend Mackerel?"

"It says —" I craned my neck to look out the window, as though I had again to verify the testimony of my senses. "It says, 'Jesus Saves.'"

"Oh, yes." There was a silence at the other end, except for an act of deglutition, and then a faint crackling noise which I could believe was that of a successor to a swallowed caramel being unwrapped. "I only work here," the girl declared at last, "but I do remember something about the board deciding that wasn't strictly commercial."

"Commercial! That's not the point. It's vulgar. And the lettering is that awful new phosphorescent stuff — green and orange. No, this is a blight on the landscape and I protest."

"I know what you mean, now that you mention it. You're not the first to complain. The Presbyterians are appalled. The Episcopalians are sick. All the better element there, with property values at stake —"

"Oh, property values! Please get that out of your mind, miss. Do you think I own the parsonage I live in? I'm talking about spiritual values. Spiritual and aesthetic ones. How do you expect me to write a sermon with that thing staring me in the face? How do you expect me to turn out anything fit for civilized consumption?"

"I know. It's terribly *de trop*. And in that part of town — the Mobile Bay section!" There was another silence, but a thoughtful one this time, and unbroken by any of those annoying sounds. Then she said, "But do you think you're entirely right in opposing this? I know this man is a cheap huckster of religion — your religion — but it's the form his faith takes, and don't we need all the faith we can get today?

4

Doesn't the crisis of our time, the mess in which we find ourselves, come from our not having any *belief*?"

"Nothing concerns me more than the crisis of our time, Miss —"

"Calico."

"Miss Calico. Nothing concerns me more than the crisis of our time, but, believe me, nothing concerns these people less. They're content precisely to let this life go hang for the sake of another, which you and I know doesn't exist."

"Well . . ." she said, worriedly.

"Oh, come now."

"But the world needs restraint. Some moral order. And that should be on any level the given person can grasp. What does the Apostle Paul say?"

"I have no idea, but Oscar Wilde reminds us that while crime is not vulgar, vulgarity is a crime. Jesus doesn't save any of these people, because all they want to do is boost their paltry souls into heaven, while completely shirking the obligation to *evolve*. What we see around us these days is not a revival at all but a kind of backsliding, and I do mean that — a failure of taste as *well* as nerve." To make my point I had resorted to a phrase from my last Sunday's sermon, and I felt it only fair to the girl to favor her with the entire passage. I therefore continued, "Let us think and do according to our *time*. Let us graft on the Christian principle of self-lessness, as Auden so cogently urges, the Freudian one of maturity, and come up with an ideal suited to our era. Thus two people, each bent on pursuing a different one of these two systems, would die having lived identical lives: one of consideration for others."

"Put it under the phone book so it won't blow away." The girl had evidently moved her head a little to address a fellow worker in her office, but now her voice resumed

5

more clearly, "I'm sorry, Reverend Mackerel. What were you saying?"

"Nothing. Just tell me whom I see or how I go about filing my complaint."

"You can send a letter of protest or stop in at the office here and get yourself on record," the girl said. The faint glutinate noises reappeared in my ear. "Any time."

"I'll be there this afternoon. I have to go into town anyhow."

"That will be fine. We're in the city hall, of course, second floor. Same office with the Beach Commission. I'm here till like five o'clock."

Bouncing the three miles to town in the plastic bubble my congregation had given me to commemorate my fifth year as their pastor, I mused on the infinite varieties of human belief and on the no less infinite variations within a given belief. Mobile Bay — so named by some anonymous wit because of the numerous wire and scrap metal sculptors who infested the area — is a special section of a city that is itself a rather special jewel on the exurbanite strand. Avalon, Connecticut, lies forty miles out of metropolitan New York on the New Haven commuting track. It is a community where tired successes flee to enact the old charade of seeking roots, knowing they will never have them but must and will, like the fabled mistletoe, live and die without them, suspended between the twin oaks of home and office. They live a kind of hand-to-mouth luxury, never knowing where their next quarterly instalment of taxes or the payment on a third car is coming from. It is a community where the cleaning women have washing compulsions; where lawn benefits are given for folk singers who have escaped from jail; where an Old-fashioned Christmas consists in truly drinking

6

it otherwise than on the rocks for a week. There, Max Kaminsky, Messy Williams and other noted trumpeters come up from New York to play at Easter services. There, one overhears conversation like, "After each divorce, Monica's disillusioned, and then she goes and gets married again." There, I once heard a woman say, "I've read *Billy Budd* four times and hate it more each time." A special culture, with special and terrible needs, which one tries to meet with all the compassion in one's nature.

Our church is, I believe, the first split-level church in America. It has five rooms and two baths downstairs — dining area, kitchen and three parlors for committee and group meetings — with a crawl space behind the furnace ending in the hillside into which the structure is built. Upstairs is one huge all-purpose interior, divisible into different-sized components by means of sliding walls and convertible into an auditorium for putting on plays, a gymnasium for athletics, and a ballroom for dances. There is a small worship area at one end. This has a platform cantilevered on both sides, with a free-form pulpit designed by Noguchi. It consists of a slab of marble set on four legs of four delicately differing fruitwoods, to symbolize the four Gospels, and their failure to harmonize. Behind it dangles a large multicolored mobile, its interdenominational parts swaying, as one might fancy, in perpetual reminder of the Pauline stricture against those "blown by every wind of doctrine." Its proximity to the pulpit inspires a steady flow of more familiar congregational whim, at which we shall not long demur, going on with our tour to say that in back of this building is a newly erected clinic, with medical and neuropsychiatric wings, both indefinitely expandable. Thus People's Liberal is a church designed to meet the needs of today, and to serve the whole man. This includes the worship of a God free of outmoded theological definitions and palatable to a mind come of age in the era of Relativity. "It is the final proof of God's omnipotence that he need not exist in order to save us," Mackerel had preached. (I hope I may be indulged these shifts into the third person in relating things about which I am a trifle self-conscious.) At any rate, this aphorism seemed to his hearers so much better than anything Voltaire had said on the subject that he was given an immediate hike in pay and invited out to more dinners than he could possibly eat.

I parked the car four blocks from the city hall and continued my trip on foot. As I walked along the sidewalk, I found my eye drawn to a form swinging loosely along ahead of me in a belted polo coat. I was unmarried at the time, and prolonged physical denial had made me more than normally susceptible to attractive women.

The one of whom chance had put me in view was a young lady I should have judged, from there, to be in her late twenties. She was a shade above medium height, walked with an easy, fluid stride, and carried a book in one hand. She had finely tapered calves and well-molded flanks, enhanced, of course, by the rhythms of locomotion. I often find relief, when publicly exercised, in the notation of a bad feature or disillusioning trait. It's something that I imagine most men do to some extent, at least unconsciously, but I had developed it into a kind of technique for stanching useless stimulation. It was therefore in hopes that a plain profile or something of the sort would balance out the ravishing form and thus, so to speak, get me off the hook that I now hurried to overtake this creature.

Shuttling through the noonday crowds like a broken field runner, without breaking into too conspicuous a trot, I drew abreast of her. Then I turned to look. The profile was a good one. Indeed, it quite lived up to the view that had provoked my quest. I thought, "Damn." Well, fine profiles do not always survive stern frontal inspection, so I quickened my pace further to avail myself of that. I scuttled on past her, and then, idling abruptly at a shop window, glanced back. Blue eyes swimming in luxuriant lashes met my own. Her complexion was like flawless amber, and her hair was a cloud of honey.

Seething with rage, I stopped in my tracks altogether to get a look at the book she was carrying, cradled in one arm. Surely deliverance lay there. Surely you couldn't be all that beautiful and intelligent too. Of course — the volume would be a trashy romance, or something in the current vein of inspirational pap. Maybe even just a picture book. That would undo the creature in my eyes, and get me off the hook.

She swung on by and I caught a glimpse of the title: Parrington's *Main Currents in American Thought*.

My hands plunged into my pockets, I stood watching her trip out of sight. The place next door was a sandwich shop, into which I presently turned and, after waiting a moment for a stool, sat down at the counter and had a cup of coffee. I drank it moodily, thinking of the girl. When I had finished the coffee, I dropped in at a florist's to order some flowers for a bedridden friend, and then set out for the city hall.

It's a nondescript building of four stories, so pervaded, even to its stairways, with the smells of worn varnish and unventilated records that comprise the odor of officialdom that I was grateful not to have to mount more than two. I found the office jointly occupied by the Beach Commission and the Zoning Board, and stated my business to the girl in charge. She told me the clerk I wanted had stepped

9

out but would be right back. I sat down on a bench to wait. Wandering around the room, my eye was caught by a book lying on a desk. Its title was *Main Currents in American Thought*. There were two desks in the office. The girl on deck sat working at one. The book was on the other. I sat revolving my hat between my knees, my mind a hash of resentment and dumb, preparatory gloom.

The door opened and she swung in. She was wearing a red and blue plaid wool dress. Her eyes were as blue as I remembered them to be. The hair that had seemed like a halo in the bright sun turned out, at close view, to be an abundance of chopped curls worn in the current tossed-salad mode.

"What can I do for you?" she asked, when the other girl pointed a simple finger at me.

"I've come about the Jesus Saves sign," I said.

"Oh, *you're* the — ?" She recoiled a step in surprise, then laughed and said apologetically, "But you're young. You can't be more than like thirty-five. And you certainly don't *look* like a preacher."

This pleased Mackerel. Mackerel so disliked the term preacher, and so abhorred the term brother, as designations for the clergy that he was always grateful for assurances of their inapplicability to himself. It was not merely the wish to elude prototype that lay at the bottom of this, though that wish did exist in Mackerel to an exquisite degree; it was, more cardinally, a fear of quarantine, a desire to belong to his species — in which even the deferential "Reverend" tended to blur one's membership — that made him want ever so much to be known simply as Mister Mackerel. The familiarity of "Hi, there, Mackerel" would not have unduly alarmed him. Just beyond that, however, lay the comic marshlands of "Holy Mackerel," a nickname under which he had smarted in student days and which he lived in cold fear of some local wit's reviving even here in Avalon, three hundred New England miles from the seminary where he had been trained. But so far so good. For the decade or so since his ordination, fair winds had carried him safely between opposing caricatures: neither Brother Andrew nor Holy Mackerel, but his own dear human self alone.

He murmured some grateful acknowledgment of Miss Calico's notation, and smiled floorward.

"Well, all right," she said, passing through a gate in a railing to her place behind the counter, "you're a taxpayer and you have your rights, but . . ."

Miss Calico pursued the argument she had over the phone, briefly and good-naturedly, and not without a charming self-disparagement. She was no fanatic herself, she laughed, and certainly no "mental heavyweight," explaining the Parrington, when I pointed inquiringly at that, as something a more intellectual friend had given her. "I'm only groping for answers, like the rest of us," she said. "Not enough watts up here though." She tapped her skull. She picked up the book and thrust it at me. "Here, you can have it. I mean it. I'll never finish it. No, I insist. It'll go to waste here. My speed is like the Overstreets or Will Durant. Something you can read at lunch."

"I'll take it on one condition," I said. "That I return it."

She stooped to pick up a wad of paper from the floor and drop it into a wastebasket.

"Conscientious type," she said, glancing nervously at the other girl as she straightened up. The other girl smiled wanly without raising her eyes from her work, as though amused by some detail in the day's chores.

It was the principal upshot of my call, and established the main track of my interests for some time to come. But a sequel more directly connected with the business that had

11

brought me came about when Miss Calico said abruptly, "If you want to file that protest, I'll put you down and make sure you're notified when the Zoning Board has its next meeting. But I'd go easy. I mean I hear the fellow's a religious crackpot, and they can be dangerous."

"Then it is a private party?" I said. "I thought it might be some new tabernacle come to town, or a crowd of Jehovah's Witnesses moving in."

"No, it's a private party. Name of —" She snapped her fingers, unable to recall, and went to a filing cabinet. She rolled open a drawer, tipped a Manila folder partway up and slanted her head to read something in it. She tucked the folder back down and slid the drawer shut. "Turnbull. Frank Turnbull. He lives over there on Massasoit Drive. What's the matter?"

I gripped the book I had in my hands and made an effort to control myself. I must have paled. The crank was a parishioner of mine. A member of my own congregation! A man exposed each Sunday morning to what were taken to be among the more urbane dissertations available at that hour in Avalon, and this was the fruit of it. He puts up evangelical billboards. It had all come to that.

"Nothing," I said. "The name just sounded familiar. Thanks a lot for your trouble. You've been very kind. I won't file. This is something I've got to handle myself. I'll return the book in a week or so. I'm very scrupulous about those things."

I said good-by and headed back uptown in the runabout, making straight for Turnbull's house and driving her faster than I yet had. I could feel myself losing my temper for the second time that day. And after this, off on another mission of some delicacy. I had to call on a woman bent on visiting hospitals and organizing hymn sings among the patients, and to discourage her.

The problems of running a congregation were getting to be too much for me. I ought to have an assistant.

Two

___

RIDING along in the plastic bubble, I thought some more about this business of my temper. At least in that respect I was resembling our Lord, who was forever losing his. It took very little to rile him — Scribes and Pharisees, his family, even a fig tree.

By the time I reached Turnbull's house my anger had pretty well subsided, and I felt ready to deal with him objectively, little realizing what new irritant lay in store for me. It was a puzzle what made old man Turnbull tick. He represented what any minister will tell you is the bane of parish work: somebody who has got religion. It's as embarrassing to a cleric of sensibility as "poetry lovers" are to a poet, and in much the same way. Besides being a nuisance it can be very time-consuming. Turnbull expected me to be on tap at all hours like a doctor, not scrupling to rout me out of bed in the middle of the night to ask about some spiritual point that had come up in his mind or some doubt that was vexing him. Lately he had become obsessed with a sense of sin — which had undoubtedly touched off the Jesus Saves thing.

I saw his shaggy head watching from the window as I parked in front of his house, a damp, cavernous place in which he lived alone, and he opened the door before I could touch the bell.

"Thank God you've come," he said, taking my hat. He plucked it directly from my head, which struck me as odd, even by his rather weird standards of hospitality. Indicative of tension.

"Then *you* called *me?*" I said, closing the door behind me.

"Yes. Your housekeeper said you were out and I left the message. Isn't that what brought you?"

"No. I'm just dropping in for a call."

Turnbull was a rangy man in his late sixties, with a mop of sulphurous red hair. He usually dressed in loose-fitting tweeds, which usually smelt of cigar smoke. He had a nasal, not unpleasant, twang to his voice, rather reminiscent of a jew's-harp, or that sound that is produced by placing tissue paper over a comb. His teeth were still white and sound, though of assorted lengths. I watched him hang my hat on a peg under an elk's head with one eye missing, a fact which gave the remaining one a look of baleful awareness it might otherwise have lacked. Then he led the way into the living room.

I appraised him warily. His call meant that he would want to unburden himself confessionally again, and then be prayed with. The latter was not an aspect of pastoral life to which I took, supplication being something I felt to be in its nature private and not best realized by an intermediary. Further hazard was heaped on the office in this case by one's being hysterically enjoined to one's knees. Penitents always gave me the willies, but Turnbull was the end. The living room was long and comfortable, filled with deep leather chairs and sofas, and the heads of beasts slightly more unusual than elk, shot in bygone years. Turnbull

15

waved me to a chair and took one himself. I opened the conversation before he could.

"Well, I see you're not satisfied with the preaching in this neighborhood," I said. "You feel you've got to pitch in and do a little yourself."

He glanced at me, taking a cigar from a leather case. Turnbull was a very heavy smoker, and his cigars were enormous; almost like the splats of chair legs in size. He patted his pockets looking for matches, and I rose and reached for a box of them on a table near me.

"You mean the sign?" he said.

"That's right."

"I wanted to surprise you with that." He gnawed the tip from his cigar and sucked on it to confirm its draft. "How do you like it?"

"I'd like to answer that question by asking another. Just what does that statement mean — 'Jesus Saves'?"

"What do you mean, 'mean'?"

"What does Jesus save us from?"

"From our sins. What else?"

"I see."

I struck a match on the side of the box and extended the flame to him. He took a few puffs and emitted a cloud of smoke, which he dispersed with a wave, as though from some points of view he deplored the habit.

"And what will happen to us if we aren't saved from them?" I inquired. "What then?"

"Why, we'll go to hell," he answered, and lapped at a tatter in the side of his cigar.

"And where will we go if we are?"

"To heaven."

I sank into my chair and dropped my arms over the sides. "Another backslider," I thought wearily. It was this damned religious revival. They were everywhere, these converts, defecting to pie-in-the-sky from the hard-won positions to which they have been urged and hauled by rational and honest men. Looking at the codger, I thought, Can this man be educated? Or is he beyond salvation? I remembered that prior to his retirement he had owned a factory in which, it was said, he had given out report cards to his employees.

I leaned my head back and blew out of my lips, turning the matchbox end over end on the arm of the chair. I looked at him sadly. "You going to put up others?"

"A few maybe, around town." He mused a moment. "They won't all be the same. Some will have texts on them. On one I thought I'd put just 'John 3:16.' Nothing else."

"Well, that'll drive the commuters back to New York. It'll accomplish that much."

"That's not my purpose." He reached for an ashtray and settled it on his knee. Then he smiled in a modest fashion and said the thing that blew me out of my chair. "The reason I wanted to surprise you, it's all a little something I thought I'd do in memory of Mrs. Mackerel."

It was one of those situations to which nothing in the range of known facial expressions is adequate. The man needed to be dealt with charitably, and that was a demand I was determined to meet. At the same time, the gesture was so appallingly inapt, so grotesquely out of line, that some glimmer of that fact must be got through his head if it meant boring a hole in it.

"That's awfully nice of you, Turnbull, it really is," I said. "It's the sweetest thing in the world of you, but . . ."

"But what?"

"Well, it's not precisely the sort of thing she would have cottoned to, in life."

"Why not? Wasn't she a Christian, a fine upstanding

17

woman always doing good? Social work, organizing that clinic with her own two hands —"

"I know. For which she is now known as the Jane Addams of the East. I realize all that," I said with more heat than I had intended. I got to my feet and stood before him with my hands spread. *"But she was more of an intellectual than I am, man!* It's fine for you to memorialize her, but I really think you might have consulted me about it. When you give a living person a present you take pains to make it appropriate. The dead deserve as much."

He was swinging a slipper on his great toe, but his manner became sullen and sulking. "Oh, all right," he said at last. "It's still anonymous. I'll think of something else." He fell silent again. Then after a few more puffs on his cigar, he asked rather aggressively, "Didn't she believe in Original Sin either?"

"Not in that sense, no, Turnbull."

"If I may say so, I think that's what's wrong with our world — no sense of sin. Guilt feelings, sure, that's very fashionable. But a sense of sin, no. Well, I believe in it. We're all sinners, of which I am chief."

"Aren't you rather giving yourself airs?"

"I'm quoting Saint Paul."

"You're no Saint Paul."

"I am a sinner," he persisted stubbornly. "A miserable, guilty, life-long rotten, damnable sinner."

"Prove it."

It was the wrong thing to say. He had been itching to do just that, and my challenge opened the sluice gates. He fell to it with relish.

"Have I ever told you about the woman I met in Naples in 1927?" he said.

"No, I don't believe I've heard that one," I said.

18

Turnbull sought a more comfortable position in his chair. He studied the coal of his cigar, and rather a gleam came into his eye. "Well, she was traveling without her husband, and we met on the Bay there at a time when I happened to be knocking about alone myself. It was 1927, or maybe '26 — no earlier. We were both at loose ends and one thing led to another. I was the only man who ever led her off the straight and narrow," he said, his eyes tending abjectly downward, "ever succeeded in that feat. O Lord, the sins of my youth, remember them not . . ."

Something dawned on me. It was that all of these tortured disclosures of Turnbull's — and this was far from being one of his more graphic — dealt with carnal peccancies no longer open to him. Was he regretting, thus, not the acts themselves, but the time of life when they were possible? I remembered Freud's having defined melancholia as grief at the loss of libido.

"When I think of the sheer *number* of sins," Turnbull bragged away. "I mean in one night. I wouldn't care to say how many times. And that isn't all. I had two going at once," he confided, and hung his head.

"Two *affairs?*"

"Yep. We toured the Abruzzi together," he said, now quite recovering the tone of anecdote, which added to the illusion created by the leather chairs and potted greenery that we were in a club, "and one evening as I was sitting alone in the lobby of a hotel in Aquila, I saw walking out of the dining room thee — most . . ."

The story flowed on and the cigar wore down. I studied my host's face with interest. It was large, handsomely molded, like a monumental ruin of good looks, and while I had no doubt that my penitent was bewailing more than had occurred, I had little trouble seeing a blade of thirty years ago knocking the ladies for a loop. That would have put him in my own present age bracket, roughly the middle thirties. I was not free to let my attention wander, for as he made a clean breast of this particular conquest, he fixed me with a vitreous eye: an almost colorless gray eye behind which one glimpsed emotions still turbidly boiling, like coffee under the glass knob of a percolator. I kept my ear cocked for discrepancies, however, wondering for example whether Aquila was actually in the Abruzzi. I made a mental note to look it up later (and was punished for my churlishness by finding it to be quite the case). But Turnbull needed a good psychiatrist and that, alas, People's Liberal did not have. Von Pantz had been hired for the clinic in the belief that since it was church-sponsored the appointee should be devout, as though that has any more to do with a psychiatrist's skill than it does with a surgeon's. How much wiser the Catholics were in these matters! They had hired Matisse to do the chapel at Vence on the stated principle that "an unbeliever with talent is of more value to the church than a believer without it." I had failed to make the trustees see that point, and so now we were saddled with this seedy Jungian who read the Bible to patients, to say nothing of traipsing off to Madison Square Garden to hear Billy Graham! It seemed I had to fight the revival singlehanded, besides being in and out of the clinic trying to give the patients a little insight . . .

". . . times in one night."

Turnbull's wanderings in the Abruzzi had come to an end. He sat back with an air of accomplishment, the corners of his mouth coming faintly into play as he regarded me.

"Now do you say there's no sin?" he said. "Now do you believe in it?"

"Not in the Mosaic sense, no."

"Well, I do. I believe in it. And in the Law — forever handed down."

"In convenient tablet form."

"I shall pray for you."

"And I for you," I answered levelly.

I knew this was not the tone to take with Turnbull — not if he was to be won over. "A little resilience, please," I had often to remind myself, in the need to curb my youthful idealism. This was a caution doubly urgent in the case of Turnbull, if he was to be brought in check before he went off and disgraced us with something worse than Jesus Saves hoardings. It would be all very well to point out to him later that what lay behind his present cycle was a kind of inverted libido protest — but not now. Now, I must be diplomatic. So I began to speak more tactfully, even buttering him up a bit. I allowed it was all a matter of terminology and that the world was full of what no one could deny was plain human deviltry, recognizing his testimony as impressive evidence in point, if, indeed, I had ever heard of a wider swathe being cut by a man in his prime. Turnbull took these reproaches with eyes modestly lowered, thanking me for my patience in hearing him out and promising, for his part, not to put up any more of those depressing signs, at least not in memory of my wife. I suggested he was doing enough by contributing as faithfully as he did to the clinic that bore her name, but he said no — he wanted to give her a specific memorial of some sort. I little dreamt that this was the theme round which the symphony of my entire life was, so to speak, to be abruptly and violently woven. Now in the long, dreaming harmonies of resolution, I can look back and see myself sitting there in the quiet afternoon, talking to Turnbull, unaware that the motif was being "stated," and that I was about to be snatched up and whirled away, helpless as a straw in a cyclone, in its contrapuntal furies.

Turnbull would continue to put his mind to the problem, he said, and was confident that he would think of something suitable soon, but he would, without fail, consult me about his choice before doing anything about it, or even making a public announcement of it. He promised me faithfully.

All that agreed, I took my leave — suffering the replacement of my hat on my head — and bustled off to complete my day's rounds. Then I went home to a good dinner, and immediately afterward hurried upstairs to my bedroom study, carrying my coffee in one hand and *Main Currents in American Thought* in the other.

I was eager to get to the book as fast as I could.

Three

I PHONED Miss Calico when I had finished the book, three days later, and arranged to meet her the following evening at a restaurant on the edge of town, in order that I might return it. "I feel I owe you a dinner," I said.

The idea was agreeable to her and so was the place I suggested, an Italian restaurant run by a couple named Chimento. We had a fine meal, with a bottle of wine, and later went for a drive across the river to an industrial town there named Chickenfoot.

"Why are we going here?" Miss Calico asked, as we rattled over the bridge in the bubble.

"It's full of wonderful old bars," I said. "Not any of your 'swank' Avalon cocktail lounges. You don't want any of those, do you?" Another thing in its favor was that it had no congregation of mine in it, with members out seeing their leader riding around in the glass house they had given him (not without a certain cunning, I now realized).

Taverns devoid of fashionable décor were not hard to find on the street — dominated by closed fish houses — on which I parked the car, even for a person not gifted in slumming, and as we walked by several, making our selection, I sensed that my friend had begun to lose what stomach she'd had for the enterprise. It had turned cold and snow was falling, the first snow of autumn. Flakes so huge they resembled small doilies fluttered dreamily down on her hair and her lashes, where they turned to tears, to stars. A nap of white had already collected along the dingy pavement, and I executed a few steps in it and flapped my arms to suggest that we were having more fun than might otherwise have been supposed.

"Let's go in this one," Miss Calico said. "My feet are getting wet."

We stood a moment sizing up the tavern before which we had come to a halt, and went in.

A bartender wearing an overcoat and three men roosting on stools watched without expression as we stood inside the door stamping our feet. "Snowing," I said with a conciliatory smile. I piloted Miss Calico past them to a row of empty booths and settled her in one that seemed more securely moored to the floor than most. The silence putting me on edge, I walked to a jukebox in the corner and asked out in a hearty voice, "What'll it be?"

"Number seven," a voice answered from the bar.

Number seven it was. Without pausing to read its title, I dropped a dime into the slot and pressed the button. Before I had rejoined Miss Calico in the booth, the strains of one of the more tiresome religious ballads then high on the Hit Parade billowed through the tavern:

> His hand is on the wheel
> When Life rocks my boat;
> He will steady my keel,
> He will keep me afloat.

There were no customers in the booths other than Molly — which was Miss Calico's name — and myself, and only the three men at the bar. The verses came on with murderous volume:

> He watches from the bridge,
> He rules the briny deep . . .

"Who he?" I muttered under my breath, which was visible.

"You don't believe in a personal deity, do you?" Molly Calico asked.

"Would it make any difference?"

"No, I suppose not. But keep your mouth shut in here or you'll get us both thrown out on our ear."

I turned and, sure enough, eyes bright with menace watched from the bar; eyes whose owners quite sensed the disesteem in which their set of criteria were held. Ranged, under a shaded bulb, in a composition to which the bartender lent a loose background, and motley in the sense that one or two wore switchman's caps, the group had the grubby solidity of drinkers in Post-Impressionist paintings.

"You don't look as though you enoyed that, Jack," one of them asked when the "Top Ten" tune was at last over. He was a barrel-chested man with a face like a broken crock, under a visor bent limp by a decade of truculent fidgeting. He fingered the peak now as he put his query.

"Oh, sure, I liked it all right," I said. I spoke with a large tolerance, which the other was quick to detect.

"But what?"

"Don't you think it's a bit maudlin?"

Broken Crock set his glass down and, very deliberately, walked over to the jukebox and put in a coin of his own. The strains of "My Skipper" were heard all over again.

I asked Molly Calico what she would like and she said, "A brandy." That sounded about right for me too, and I signed

25

to the bartender and called for two brandies. He clarified his position immediately. He was willing to pour them but not to deliver them. I went to get them, giving as wide a berth as possible to the three traditional theists, who remained sullen and even belligerent, as though their tastes were still on trial, and one of whom, it was impossible to tell which, smelt violently of creosote. I took them back to the booth where we drank with no delay. I made a face to Molly as I tasted the brandy, to point up the hilarity of unfolding events, and to imply that this would never be "our" place. When the song was finished, I smiled and raised my glass to the men at the bar, in a sort of hope, or trust, that some one enveloping reality bound our natures into a coherent whole, and to suggest that meanwhile, certainly, we might consider ourselves united in the assumption of a First Cause. The bartender, who had been following with interest the course of some animate thing along the bar's edge, removed his shoe and brought the sole down on the target.

"This place is getting a little too wonderful for me," Molly said. "Let's go."

I tried to pay with a twenty-dollar bill, which brought grumbles and delays from the bartender (as though the question of denomination were one that would always plague me here) and Molly had to fish two singles out of her own purse. I pushed back a fifty-cent tip for the bartender and we hurried out, skirting the theists as we made for the door. As it closed behind us, we heard the half-dollar hurled against it and go clanking away along the floor somewhere inside.

"Well, that was nice," Molly said, hitching up her coat collar.

"Can I have another chance?"

She tiptoed through the snow to keep her slippers from

filling up with it, clinging to my arm. She didn't answer, and when we were sitting inside the bubble — made a snug igloo by the falling snow — I offered to kiss her. "We're not at my door yet," she said, drawing away, no small feat in those quarters. At the door of her home she did hold her face up to be kissed good night, and I asked, "How about some evening next week, or the week after that?"

"Well," she said, digging into her bag for a key, "I'll probably see you in church before that."

I drew back to give her the full value of my grateful surprise. "*When?*"

"Like next Sunday? I'd like to find out what you *do* believe."

Preaching my way into a woman's heart was a new challenge to me and I met it eagerly. I was glad to see the worship area full, which put me in at least that good a light. I had no trouble spotting Molly toward the rear, wearing a blue tweed coat and a fetching blue hat of the sort that is known, I believe, as a pillbox.

The service had something special to it. Torrential storms had struck the state during the week and flash floods had all but wiped out a small river town a hundred miles from us, all this close on the heels of destructive windstorms farther down the coast. The Connecticut relief program included the donation of canned goods by members of various congregations, ours included. Offerings were to be laid on a table below the pulpit this morning in a kind of family processional just before the sermon. During the choir number my eye ranged round the audience, and I must say I was a bit taken aback by the foodstuffs some of the better-heeled commuting members of my flock were clutching: vichyssoise, artichoke hearts, smoked clams and even trout *paté* were visible among the more standard and more rational donations of canned beans and peas, and peaches and pears. Cocktail snacks for flood victims. One could not restrain the image of groups partaking of these essentials on the roofs of floating homes, nor repress an affectionate smile for the exurbanite givers in their pews.

My own simple outrage at the spectacle of senseless human destruction was so characteristically acute that I was hardly able to keep a civil tongue in my head when I rose to offer the invocation.

"Let us hope," I prayed, "that a kind Providence will put a speedy end to the acts of God under which we have been laboring." I cocked an eye open and saw Molly raise hers, as well as her eyebrows. But it was von Pantz I wondered whether the irony had gone home with. I looked his way and, sure enough, his shaggy head was lifted momentarily in surprise. Good. I realized how much I hated his woolly Mama Bear *Reader's Digest* optimism. Good old Turnbull of course suspected nothing; he had heard two pious phrases used in rapid succession and that was good enough for him.

"We know thou hast a difficulty for every solution," I went rather dryly on, "but also that the obstacles put in our way are in the end to our spiritual good — stumbling blocks which, if we cannot convert them into stepping stones, leave us unworthy to be called sons of God, much less to be saved, even by the skin of our teeth. But do give us relief from the troubles and calamities under which we have been groaning, for Christ's sake!"

After the prayer we had the family procession with the canned goods — which piled up three feet high on the altar table, the Bon Vivant brand of vichyssoise looking just as good as the Del Monte peaches there, each playing its part in the whole — and after that came the sermon. I chose for my text a passage from Havelock Ellis in which he speaks of how flaws and faults increase our affection for one another, rather than the contrary. "He is thinking of the narrowly sexual sense, but I think we all agree it has its broader application to human relationships as such," I said. "We often love people for their very frailties and absurdities." As I was finishing, a jar of calf's-foot jelly toppled off the altar and rolled into view in the aisle.

Afterward I hurried to the vestry to meet Molly and hear her opinion.

"You were very amusing," she said.

"Thank you," I said. "How about dinner?"

"Well—" The door opened and a little boy wandered in, crying and carrying a can of tomato aspic. Had he lost his way and been walking around the church building ever since the procession? It turned out that his parents had left their offering in the car and had sent him in after the service to put it on the altar. I took care of it for him, dried his tears and saw him to the side door where he had come in, and where his parents were waiting for him.

"Cute," Molly said. "Why, Wednesday night would be O.K. I mean I won't rest till I've got you figured out, and I certainly haven't yet."

"You mean what makes me *tick*?" I said, leaning back at the dinner table Wednesday night.

"Well, what do you *believe*? Don't make it too long, and not too heavy on the theology. I'm no de Tocqueville."

I was delighted. My first wife had been an intellectual, so I'd had that. I moved a hand impulsively toward hers across the table. She picked up her pack of cigarettes and smoked one.

"I mean you puzzle me — why you went into the ministry. It certainly can't be for the money," she said.

"No. There's no jack in the pulpit."

"Then why? What goes? You're always knocking religious things. In fact they're all I ever hear you knock. I know
— two shades of the same color sometimes clash more than
two different colors, and let's clean house and all. But there
must be more to it than that. You've got something in your
craw. Always racing your motor. So let's have it. What *do*
you believe and why ever did you go into the ministry?"

A fair enough pair of questions, which have probably occurred to you too, so I'll answer them here out of quotes, including for your benefit what I may not have told Molly
Calico, at least not then.

I believe in belief. I believe that some binding ethic and
some informing myth are necessary to any culture, the
myth being to the morality what the wooden forms are to
the concrete that is poured into them, in building construction. When the concrete is hard you can remove the forms
(or they will rot away) and the walls will stand of their own.
Has Western man reached the point where his ethical walls
will stand without the forms of his faith? You tell me, after
thinking a moment about our sexual, drinking and crime
records, our political and business practices, and the present
behavior of a crop of teen-agers raised without religious instruction. But I believe that a faith is a set of demands, not a
string of benefits, that a man is under some obligation to
better himself, not sit around as he is and wait for Jesus to
save him. Thus my going after this billboard thing was an
honest act of war, not just a dilettante beef, as Molly, and
maybe you, too, thought.

Now as to why I became a minister.

I became a minister because my mother wanted me to.

30

She made me promise on her deathbed that I would go to divinity school and become a clergyman. I promised her because there was nothing else to do under the circumstances. When I got into divinity school, I became genuinely interested in church history and religion, then fascinated by it, so that what began reluctantly continued agreeably. It took only Toynbee's argument to convince me that ours is *the* religion. Of course the cleric I became is rather a far cry from the one my mother had in mind, but that's something else again. After all, a Calvinist in Connecticut . . .

For I came of Dutch immigrant Calvinist parents. We lived in Chicago, in one of several such communities which still dot that city, hermetically sealed from the American life around them and the Middle West at large. I was taught the Bible at home and in a parochial school, but my parents became a bit dismayed when I began to show signs of appreciating it as literature. They labored with me and prayed for my soul. To keep peace, I recanted the heresy that the Bible was literature, agreeing that it was just God's word. The Dutch Calvinists thrived on schisms, being themselves, of course, the product of many. They were hairsplitters the like of which an ordinary human being in our time is totally unlikely to hear. "One Dutchman, a Christian; two Dutchmen, a congregation; three Dutchmen, heresy," was the charge leveled at us by more Americanized people, who boasted, for instance, of belonging to denominations that hadn't had a schism in a hundred years. To these my father always had a ready reply: "Rotten wood you can't split." We multiplied by dividing. The very thought of a new sect in the wind thrilled our folk. In my adolescence, when flarings of more genuine revolt began, I said to my father one evening, on hearing that a splinter of a splinter had split off again and started another church around the corner, "Instead of all this bickering and contention over nonessentials, why can't people emphasize the central truth on which all Christians can unite?" My father took his pipe out of his mouth and said, "Stop talking like a crackpot." After a screed on his pet subject, the Total Depravity of man, I exclaimed, "Oh, come now, people aren't all that bad. Take you, for instance. You're a good sort. In fact I think you're quite a nice guy." He looked at me and said, "You're wearing me thin."

Molly smiled and nodded when I finished, and slowly relaxed the rather tense position I noted she had assumed while listening. She withdrew her forearms from along the table and leaned back. "That's quite a story," she said. "Quite a story."

I now considered her with the same expression with which she had, when asking her questions, considered me. This was, roughly, the head-cocked-a-little-to-one-side expression with which one looks at a picture to see if it is hanging straight.

"Now that I've unbuttoned myself," I said, "don't you think it's your turn?" I saw her look over her shoulder toward the kitchen door. There was a delay in our dessert, which was a Baked Alaska I'd ordered, and we had been drinking coffee without it. "There's time. Anselmo won't rush. So how about you? Where do you come from? What are you doing in that office? And so on."

"I come from here," she said, tapping the table top. "I was born in Avalon. I left home at the age of eighteen — ran away from there *and* business college — to become an actress. New York, of course. I've come back ten years later, which gives you my age too. And I guess you know how I made out."

"Well, New York's loss is our gain," I said gently. "Didn't you get anywhere in the theater?"

"Oh, sure. I'd get like second ingénue leads in plays that ran three weeks, or the maid in ones that ran three performances. Or I'd get like bottled-up as understudy in long runs. Nothing that encouraged Molly Calico's belief that she had anything on the ball."

"How did you live?" I asked, leaning forward with my elbow on the table and my chin in my hand, trying to purge from my heart the churlish possession of her failure.

"Radio and TV parts. Once in a while a commercial modeling job, and there I'd be in some magazine saying good-by to old-fashioned methods or cutting carpet costs in half. You've probably seen me. I got engaged to a guy who had a job in a publishing office, where he made like eighty dollars a week? Not the down-to-earth type. He'd sit in the dusk with the phonograph going, listening to like Berlioz's 'Harold in Italy' and eating strawberries. His name, need I add, was Martin. After nearly a year of this, I asked him point-blank when this was going to end, if any, in matrimony, but it developed you weren't supposed to ask him that. You were just supposed to come on him in the dusk eating strawberries and listening to 'Harold in Italy.' When pressed to name the day, he said we were all endearing mixtures of good and bad, and that he had a nervous sister in like Terre Haute whom he had to send money to every week, and so he couldn't take on the financial burden of a wife just yet. So that was the end of that chapter and I pulled out."

"And then what?"

She paused in the act of getting out another cigarette, to give me a slow burn. Very professional. When Molly looked at you like that you knew you were withered by the best. "You mean and then *who*, don't you? You've got that look a man gets when he wants to know who he's got to outshine. You're like dentists in that respect, have to know who your predecessors were. All right, I'll tell you All, on one condition. That you forever after hold your peace. Agreed?"

"Agreed," I said, in some surprise, for a sexual dossier had been the last thing I'd had in mind. But I listened attentively to what she seemed so eager to have over and done with.

"There were three in all," she said, lighting her cigarette from the match flame I extended, before getting back into my listening slouch. "Martin was the first. The second was a long-hair too, besides being bald to boot. But he had dazzling teeth, as so many men have who don't have hair, if you've ever noticed. I often thought to myself, I'd give my eyeteeth for a smile like that. What are you laughing about?"

"Nothing. The idea of you envying anyone their smile. You have a lovely smile. Go on."

"Anyway, he had the idea that life is for the discerning few? That what we have to develop in this country is an aristocracy of taste? So he'd go out and buy some liquor and throw a party, and you'd get there and there'd be like Cole Porter and Ida Lupino and maybe one or two others, and after that it would dwindle away to just people talking. There'd be little groups discussing like Kierkegaard and herb cooking and which were the places to go in the Touraine. These parties would last till like three o'clock in the morning, with the place looking like the Aeolian stable. There'd always be an aristocrat of taste or two to carry home. It was four o'clock before you got the place cleaned up."

"Did you live with these men?" I asked, burning in the fires of hell.

"Well, I mean it's all a question of semantics really." She waited while the waitress refilled our coffee cups, announcing that the Baked Alaska would be a minute yet. "All he ever did was talk, but he did that in great detail. My breasts were two brioches, warm and steaming from the oven. And so on. But he never did anything about it. Just talk. When he saw me with my clothes off he'd launch a violent attack on surrealism or go cook something. He'd whirl up a batch of shish kebab, denouncing everything under the sun and waving the skewers around. I saw no woman was safe in there, and got out. He never did anything — just weave poetic compliments by the hour. My two —"

"Who was the third?"

She smiled ruefully and drank a little coffee.

"The third," she said, "was the opposite extreme. This guy was your pipe-knocking globe-trotting man of action. Literary, but the *active* sort? He fancied himself the foreign correspondent and went around in a dirty trench coat chewing a *match*? But all he ever wrote was those 'as told to' articles for sensational magazines. Articles with titles like 'I Had Myself Committed' and 'I Profaned a King's Tomb.' The idea was that he would one day settle down and write novels flecked with French, and any woman smart enough to stick with him would end up at the rail of an ocean liner holding a pair of dogs and wearing a mink coat. I brought in a little money with what bit parts I could get, meanwhile enrolling at an actor's lab which was like the Studio, only more so. I went to the meetings with a friend who was also an actor. Mike was sweet, in that mad Rumanian sort of way? He loved to ride with the top of his convertible down so much that he'd do it in cold weather too, so that we'd be riding around with the top down and the heater turned on both. You'd love him. Cocky with everybody because he lacked confidence?"

"Well, now, wait a minute," I said. "You said there were three. This makes four already, doesn't it?"

"Well, I mean it's a matter of mood, actually. Sometimes he'd be dark and glowery and you couldn't get near him. I had a string of slave bracelets I used to like, and he'd look up from a brown study and say, 'Pliz don't wear so many bracelets at once. It gives me a sense of shower curtains.' He wasn't anything in my life. We just went to Ivan's Lab and around town and into the country looking for dear little inns and all, but getting back to Analysis — this 'as told to' journalist was a Greek named Analysis, though actually only his parents came from Greece, he was born in like Omaha or Salt Lake City or somewhere around in there. Months passed and he wasn't getting to his serious work. He brooded about it a lot but that was all. Couldn't get started for fear of failure? At that, he was better than Robert, painting his damned unicorns, with flies on them for realism. He was so hard to get along with that periodically you'd blow up and tell him off, and always get the same answer. That defects were basic to the artist's make-up, and it was by the tarnish that you could tell it was silver? At such times you were better off alone in the flat with Terwilliger."

"Who was Terwilliger?"

"His dog. A foxhound who clattered all around the place chewing things up, but very devoted. And Robert was devoted to him. Robert would get down on all fours and play with him. He'd take the dog's bone in his teeth, and the dog would take the other end of it in *his* teeth, and they'd tussle around the room together, trying to get it away from one another. Robert did that a lot, that sort of thing, to show

36

that he could be warm and human. But getting back to Jack Analysis. One day he wrote an article entitled 'I Got Women For Stalin,' and when that came out with both the man who told it to him *and* him anonymous (to protect the innocent or something), when I saw that, I knew there was no future with him either, and I packed my things and cleared out. And that's the story of my life up to now."

However, as she drank from her coffee cup again, I knew there was more to come. She set the cup down and said:

"There's a little postscript about this Actor's Lab that Ivan the Terrible ran. Stanislavski wasn't *in* it, the way he could use the Method. By the time you were through with the course you could be a gate with a broken hinge, or not just grapes *but seedless grapes* — you could be anything like that he told you to be, up there in front of the class. The only thing wrong was that you were unfit to portray anything resembling a human being in recognizable circumstances. A few more months of pestering producers in vain and Molly Calico realized she just didn't have it. And home she came to Avalon, Connecticut — to find that in her absence her little old home town had become the chic place to move to." She put up her hands and smiled. "That's all there is."

I removed my chin from my hand and my elbow from the table and sat up.

"That's quite a story too," I said. "All I can say is, I'm glad she came home. And I hope she's glad I'm glad."

She drank coffee again, rolling a grave eye at me as she gulped.

"She's glad all right enough," Molly said, setting the cup down in the saucer as though it were a most delicate piece of china, "but I can tell you one thing, after all those ex-

37

periences in New York, next time it's damn well going to be with bell, book and candle. That or nothing."

There she sat, blue-eyed and honey-haired, more than a little absurd, thinking de Tocqueville was a theologian and carrying Parrington in the noonday sun. My loins constricted, and I felt as though my chest were filling up with smoke. I saw the kitchen door kicked open and the waitress bearing toward us with our dessert on a huge platter. It was flaming, and looked as big as Alaska itself. I suddenly felt a little ridiculous, seeing other diners turn their heads and smile. Anselmo had done me proud to the point of parody. We couldn't possibly eat all that.

Quickly, before the waitress could reach us, I said to Molly:

"How about dinner next Saturday?"

My own experiences with the opposite sex were, having been limited to one member of it, much less bewildering and apparently much more satisfactory than Molly Calico's. My wish to remarry was proof enough of that. I would never give the world reason to suspect my first marriage by resisting a second, or even by delaying to contract it. Indeed, it was a measure of the void that had to be filled that plans for its replenishment were afoot some three months after the commencement of my widowhood.

This involved a complex of civic and private niceties best met, the new lovers both felt, by their meeting, for the time being, secretly and in towns other than Avalon. Most of our rendezvous took place therefore in nearby Chickenfoot, to which I fled on all nights when pastoral duties did not claim me. So named because of the resemblance its fanning streets bore to a splayed hen track, Chickenfoot was a sizable city of a hundred thousand, but still only ten miles

38

from home, and to spare no pains in avoiding premature discovery, we met in one of the more disreputable quarters along the river front, where my parishioners were certain never to wander. This was the Ninth Ward, notorious in municipal politics as "the Disturbed Ward," and our favorite, or at least customary, haunts were beer halls in whose smoky booths we might linger by the hour safe from molestation, or movie houses in whose even gloomier depths we could hold hands with even greater impunity.

"We can't go on meeting like this," Molly said one evening in one of these cinemas, scratching an ankle. It was a remark she had made so often that it had acquired for me the nature of an endearment rather than a threat of discussion, and I merely smiled in the dusk and drew her closer. She brought the subject up again as we were having a bite of supper after the show. The dives into which discretion drove us were a far cry from the restaurants in which I had begun my courtship, but having become serious about one another we cared about what people "thought," and so resolved to steer clear for a while of places like Anselmo's, where there was a danger of being seen. The one where we now sat was called the O.K. Grill, and from my chair I could read in reverse a sign pasted to the window with the legend "Franks and Beans 30¢," flanked by the warning "This week only."

Molly said, "That new Van Druten play is opening in New Haven next Thursday. How about that? We could have dinner at the Hofbrau."

I chewed thoughtfully, nodding.

"Don't tell me we have to worry about being seen there? I know there's lots of Avalon in the audience, but the chances of anybody from your congregation on a given night are so slim . . ."

"I just remembered. There's this ceremony Thursday night. A dinner where they're turning over all of Ida May's papers to the clinic for their library. It was in her will."

"Then let's go Friday. Or Saturday."

I frowned uncertainly. "It wouldn't look right. So soon . . ."

Molly bent over her food. She remained busy with it for a while with her fork, not eating it so much as selecting elements from it for possible later consumption, laying them to one side of her plate. "There's a melon seed in my turkey," she said.

"I know. It's a tough situation," I said, "a delicate situation. It isn't as though Ida May were an ordinary woman, and consequently it isn't as though I were an ordinary widower. Let's face it — she's the town heroine."

"In fact let's face it, she's its patron saint. I even heard about her in New York. The Jane Addams of the East."

"Right. And a certain *noblesse oblige* is expected of us in this case — of me, anyway. Call it grace under pressure," I said, taking in with a straight gaze the beautiful girl before me. Breasts like brioches . . .

"I never knew her, of course, but, Andy, aren't I right in my feeling she'd be the first to understand?"

"Oh, absolutely! But it's not her we have to reckon with, it's the townfolk. This may be Avalon but it's also New England. The commuters are only floating on top — underneath is the Yankee hard core . . . Can I order something else for you?"

"No. I'm not hungry." She put her fork down and smoked a cigarette.

"I know what you mean. This is the first omelet I've ever had with bones in it."

I laid my own fork down and told a story that I thought might cheer her up.

"It seems there were the inmates of this penitentiary who had become so familiar with one another's stories that they no longer bothered telling them but gave each story a number, and when a prisoner wanted to get one off he simply said the number. A newcomer heard them being swapped this way in the yard one morning. 'Number twelve,' a convict called out, and everyone laughed. 'Nine,' chimed in another. Guffaws. 'Twenty-eight,' said a third. Roars. Finally a small, somewhat ineffectual-looking prisoner piped up from the rear of the group, 'Thirty-two.' It was greeted by a dead silence. The newcomer asked his cell partner, a seasoned inmate who had just got through explaining the system to him, 'What's the matter? Isn't that a good story?' 'Oh, sure,' the cellmate answered, 'but he don't tell it right.' "

She put down her cigarette and burst into tears. I stared at her miserably.

"I suppose it is a little special," I said, apologetically. I drew a handkerchief out of my pocket and started to give it to her but quickly put it back, realizing that it was black-bordered. She produced one of her own and twisted her nose with it. I thought about my housekeeper. It was she who put the black-edged handkerchiefs in my pocket every morning. She was Ida May's sister and appeared to set a great deal of store by these outward symbols. She had even for a while sewn dark bands on the sleeves of my coats. I had acceded to them, not because such props meant anything to me — they had no more connection with the flesh and blood woman I had lost than did the plaster saint into which public oratory was now busy converting her — but out of a kind of feeling for my housekeeper herself.

Molly had quite regained control of herself and apologized as she put her handkerchief back into her bag. "But why must we always meet in fleabags?" she said.

"I have my reputation to think of."

We called for our coffee, found it not bad, and each had a brandy with it — this place being an annex of a bar. After a few sips, I set my glass down, shoved my cup aside and said, "I've got a plan."

"What?"

"Join my church."

She let me take her hand and hold it across the table, as she explored my meaning.

"You mean that way we could 'meet' and be like thrown together and —"

"Of course. I'd put you on committees I'm on myself, begin to see you home, have eyes for you. I don't want to make a churchwoman out of you, but this way it would have the effect of happening under my congregation's eyes, and obviously they'd take it better if I found a wife from among them rather than sprang a total stranger on them. In fact I can see the parish ladies taking one look at you and planning the match themselves. After the well-known discreet interval, of course."

"Now *that's* the sixty-four-thousand-dollar question. What is the discreet interval?"

"A year is the customary idea," I said, "but this is a more sophisticated community and maybe we could knock a few months off that figure." I took a sip of my brandy, whose low quality seemed to galvanize me into swiftened calculations. "But the thing is, going together might be acceptable at six months, *if* you were a member of my congregation. Have you been baptized?"

"I'll ask Mother. She has an uncanny memory. Andy, whom do I see? About joining."

"Well, my housekeeper is clerk of the parish, as a matter of fact. Just phone her and say you want to join P.L."

"What's she like, this housekeeper of yours?"

"Miss Pedlock?"

"You called her Hester."

"Yes. She's all right. Very conscientious. Puritan conscience, I might add. She has this tremendous emotional involvement about Ida May. One of those sister crushes. That and an almost fanatical sense of duty made her rush in and fill the domestic vacuum left by Ida May's sudden passing. She's simply stayed on in the parsonage, cooking and mending, and so on."

"I see."

"Funny." I smiled. "People don't talk about a thing like *that*. I mean a man and woman living under the same roof together day and night. That's different. Of course Hester's a relative. All one big happy family."

"Is it?"

"I just thought of something else. We have what's generally taken to be a terrific little theater at P.L., and you might have fun there. Don't look down your nose at it. We've had Broadway people in our productions before. In fact the director is a professional theater man. Rather a character, but I think you'll like him. His name is Todarescu."

Molly's face lit up and she clapped her hands together with a loud exclamation. "Mike! You mean *Mike's* here? I *wondered* what became of him. I heard he'd taken on a little theater group but nobody knew exactly where. But this is wonderful!"

"You know Todarescu?"

"Know him! He's the one I went to Actor's Lab with. Tell me, does he still have that Jaguar?"

"He still has it," I said, signaling to the waiter for another brandy.

Molly Calico went on in the same vein of delight for several minutes, shaking her head with fresh bursts of surprise.

"So Mike's here," she said. "How wonderful! I'm *dying* to see him again. When did you say the group meets?"

Four

TODARESCU was a lean, mahogany man in his forties, who seemed always over- or underdressed. In summer he strode about in Basque shirts and Bermuda shorts, often being reported barefoot, and in colder weather was to be seen bundled into tweeds and frogged coats secured by wooden pegs and fitted with cowls, reminiscent at once of the merchant marine and monastic orders, and sporting a red or yellow scarf which, streaming behind him in his flying Jaguar, gave him an appearance of flaming and even violent nonchalance. Darting black eyes and glittering teeth conferred a certain crafty charm, Oriental in feeling and possibly partly of extraction, as of a rug merchant by whom one is sure to be bested. He had a curious method of laughing which arose from a habit of clenching his teeth when he did so, as though warring elements within him required that he strangle mirth aborning. The result was a kind of smothered bark or cry, "Hm plim-plam-plom! Oh, plim-plam!"

I often dropped in to hear him rehearse our players, out of whom he got surprising performances by simple threats and abuse, and none of the flamboyant *mystiques* that had supposedly ruined himself for the stage. He turned out to have gone south for a couple of weeks, between productions of the church players, and it wasn't till he got back from this holiday that Molly had a chance to see him. I was sitting slouched in one of the dark rear rows of the auditorium when she walked in that night, a Friday. Curiosity was too great for me to deny myself the sight of this reunion, and sight it was.

When they first saw one another, they were at opposite ends of the center aisle, Todarescu up front, Molly just inside the back door. They stood a moment with their arms outflung, and met halfway down the aisle with a series of outcries and embraces that I will make no effort to reproduce here, beyond saying that they abounded in terms like "Macushla," "Prettyhead" and "Mad Monk." Work on the stage — tryout readings for a production of Christopher Fry's *The Lady's Not for Burning* were being held — stopped while they chatted. There was the inevitable hysterically compressed gossip about what ever happened to so-and-so and have you heard anything about such-and-such. One acquaintance had suddenly turned up in a musical that had opened the night before in New Haven; another had married a very large baggage and vanished. And so on. When he was ready to resume, Todarescu said to Molly, "Doll, how about you in this? I'm needing a Jennet."

"Oh, I don't . . ."

"Can nonmembers of the church be in productions?" I had by this time emerged from the shadows to make myself known, and Todarescu addressed the question to me.

"They have up to now," I said, glancing at Molly, "but there may be a ruling any day . . ."

He coaxed her into reading a little of the part anyway, and, needless to say, I was all ears as I resumed my seat and watched her spring onto the stage to do so, assisted by Todarescu. Molly seemed competent and electric enough —

46

certainly by our poor parish standards! — but I thought her wholly unfit for the role of Jennet. I kept these doubts to myself, however, it being a firm principle at P.L. that Todarescu be left to run his own railroad. No casting was done tonight, and after an hour of very preliminary reading the rehearsal broke up. I walked out with Molly and Todarescu.

I had sensed some arrangements going forward between them, and as we reached the sidewalk and Todarescu stopped for a word with one of the players, Molly drew me aside.

"Look, Mike and I thought we'd run in to New Haven tomorrow to catch the matinee of this new musical. There are some kids we know in it. We'd love to have you join us."

"Oh, I've got something on tomorrow afternoon," I said. "Otherwise I'd love to."

"Anything you can't get out of?"

"Well, they're planting a tree in her memory," I said. "I think it's the Brownies, at the playground downtown. It's at three o'clock. You understand."

"Of course. But a tree at this time of year?"

"They want to get it in before the ground freezes. I believe there'll be some kind of plaque. I have to turn the first spade and all. Why, if you want to be in the play, perhaps you'd best join. I see you haven't yet, Molly."

Todarescu had by now finished his conversations and he came over shouting offers to drop Molly at her house. As she got into his car she expressed some laughing reservation about his driving, hoping he had got some sense since moving to the suburbs and slowed down.

"In the suburbs it's all I see, sports cars," Todarescu retorted, climbing in behind the wheel and organizing the skirt of his duffel coat. "Supposed to be the male's new sex symbol. Ask him." He jerked a thumb at me. "He knows all about those things. That right? Sex symbol?"

47

"I guess," I said, striving to insinuate my head into the tonneau. "Can't shoot jaguars any more so we drive 'em."

Todarescu threw his head back and roared. "Hm, plim-plam-plom. That's rich! Can't shoot plim-plom any more so we oh, plam-plom-plim. I must remember that."

"Well, you be careful," Molly said, looking hard at him. "There was another accident in one of these things last week on the Parkway. A man got killed."

"Blessed are the pacemakers, for they shall see God," I said.

"Mm, plim-plim-plim. Oh, that's really too . . . Hear the guy. Blessed are the oh, plam-plom-plim!" The roar of his motor drowned out his laughter and the rest of his remark. I watched at the curb as they shot away down the street and around the corner.

I stood a moment where I was, after they had gone, thinking about my housekeeper. Hester was leader of the Brownie troop, or chapter, that was planting the tree, and it was almost certainly her idea. I must get her out of this obsession about her late sister. It was unhealthy, and a stop ought to be put to it before it was too late. There was not a moment to lose. I would speak to her about it at breakfast.

I sat at breakfast in a coat, rather against my will. I regretted the domestic ease of shirtsleeves and wondered how long it would be before I recovered it. That familiarity wouldn't have done with a housekeeper, especially one who was herself a model of grooming, even at her chores. Why was the girl always dressed to the nines? There was nobody here but me. It was a puzzle.

I broke the tip from a warm brioche and popped it into my mouth. Then I broke the brioche in two, buttered it and sank my teeth into its steaming heart. I had eaten two or three and was licking jelly from my fingers when I became aware of Hester standing a little behind and to the right of me, watching me with pleasure.

"You certainly go for those brioches," she said. "You must like them."

I remained hunched over my food, wishing she wouldn't stand behind me, because it's my experience that from the back one always looks a little like a dog eating — something about the way the head moves up and down. At length she went to the stove for the percolator to refill my coffee cup. She was wearing a starched black piqué blouse with a scoop neck and a dark flannel skirt. Along one arm was a set of costume bracelets, of the kind that I remembered had annoyed Todarescu. A scent of perfume mingled headily with the more pedestrian odors of breakfast.

"That makes four you've gobbled already," she said, putting the percolator back, pleased.

"It does?"

She came back to the table and, smoothing her skirt under her, sat down across from me to eat her own breakfast. She took a brioche from under its white napkin in the bread-basket and broke it in two.

"I didn't realize you liked them this much. I'll make them often."

I chewed thoughtfully, mulling several gambits for the subject I must broach. If she gave me an opening herself, so much the better. I raised my eyes and, her own being now bent over her food, took Hester in.

Perspective at the moment exaggerated the geometric molding of her head with its wide brow, high cheekbones and severely parted hair. The hair was a rich auburn, drawn into a tight scroll at the back, giving her a kind of American Gothic look. It was drawn so tight that it gave the illusion of contributing to the slant of her eyes; which could hardly have been the case, as I had out of curiosity tried it in front of a mirror with such hair as there is of my own. She raised her eyes and I abruptly did mine, meeting myself in the mirror that hung, tilted slightly downward, in the wall directly behind her. Mackerel has a long, slender face, its rather peevish constituents relieved by red cheeks and blue eyes that have often been termed "boyish." Round and yearning, they stand out, among the drawn intellectual's lineaments, like eggs in the wrong nest. Such, at least, is the way my wife once described them.

"They've got a brand new shovel for you, Andrew," Hester said. "For this afternoon."

"They have?"

"Centapong's hardware store donated it special for the occasion. We'll pick it up on the way down."

"Will I have to dig the whole hole?"

"I don't think so. There'll be several selectmen there and maybe even the mayor. You can all pitch in."

I drank off my coffee, set my cup down and pushed my chair back an inch or two.

"Hester, I want to talk to you about all that. Not planting this tree in itself — that's a nice thing and very sweet of the Brownies — but the whole attitude of yours behind it. Frankly, it worries me."

"What do you mean by that, Andrew?"

"Isn't it your idea? To do this I mean?"

She nodded, a spoon with a stewed fig on it halfway to her mouth. "Yes. Different organizations are putting in new trees after that hurricane, and I thought it would be nice for the girls to give one this way. Why?"

I paused, wondering if I should have gotten into this. My relations with her were so complex, for one thing. It didn't seem right calling a housekeeper by her first name, yet it would have been idiotic, and in any case too late, to go back to calling her Miss Pedlock. I therefore did my best to imbue her first name with its equivalent in formality. I must keep my distance, especially if I nursed dreams of terminating her tenure and clearing the decks generally for a successor who was to be my wife. She had passionately declined wages, which I as angrily kept accumulating in escrow. Well, it was too late to retreat now . . .

"It isn't remembering your sister as such that I'm thinking of, but the other side of that coin — burying yourself alive in so doing. I know you loved her, as we all did, but in your case I'm afraid I'm beginning to see it isn't an altogether healthy affection, Hester."

"How can you say that, Andrew?" she said, lowering the fig back into its dish.

"With the greatest of difficulty, my dear, but also with the best heart. How else is your behavior since her death to be interpreted? You devote yourself day and night to her cause —"

"The clinic is important."

"You'll wind up well inside it if you don't watch out. You keep the house exactly as she did, follow her routines. It's as though you were trying to step into her shoes." I had risen to pour myself more coffee, and now returned the pot to the stove. "Her favorite flowers in their accustomed place!" I exclaimed with a gesture toward a vase of roses on the living room piano. As we looked, one or two petals fluttered to the keyboard, as if shaken by the force of my remonstrance. "If that isn't living with a ghost, what is?"

"Oh, we played duets together as girls." Hester dropped her gaze and twisted a ring on her finger.

"Well, you're not a girl now, you're a grown woman of

twenty-eight or so. You've got to come out of your shell and live your own life. 'Let the dead bury their dead.' Jesus tells us that. So not resuming our life where it was interrupted isn't just psychologically bad — *it's a sin*."

She continued silent a moment, her head hung. I sat down in my chair again, without immediately drinking my coffee.

"Don't you have any boy friends?" I asked at length.

The head shook.

Finding this point difficult to pursue with any intelligence, I dropped it and reverted to the enumeration of symptoms which I found alarming.

"You wear black."

"Maybe that's slenderizing."

"But you're thin as a rail as it is, girl!" I picked my napkin up and slammed it down again. "My dear —" I was about to continue, but was cut off by the jangle of the telephone in the next room. "I'll get it," she said rising, and raced me for it with friendly hilarity.

I picked up another brioche, broke the nipple from it and sat munching it moodily. I could hear Hester but not distinguish what she was saying. It sounded businesslike and formal; not a personal call.

She returned presently and said, "Just a new member. Another transfer from poor M.E. A Molly Calico," she read from a slip, which she then set down on the table beside my elbow. "That's her address. Be sure and put her on your list to call on."

I picked up my cup and carried it to a bird cage in which two cut-throat finches pecked and fluttered and spat music at disorganized intervals. I stood tweezing my lips at them, whistling a few bars.

"Were there any other calls?" I said. "Like last night?"

"Oh, that's right. Mr. Turnbull called. He said it was very urgent. He seemed upset again."

"What did you tell him?"

"That you were out on Kingdom work."

I squeezed the ear of my cup hard in my fingers, and raised it to drink. The front doorbell rang. It was the mailman and, setting my cup down, I beat Hester to that.

I sat down in the living room to read my mail, breathing rather heavily from the exertions of the morning. I read two personal letters and glanced at some advertising matter.

When at last I looked up, it was to see Hester standing at the window looking out. She was shaking her head. This was so long after the last words between us that I thought she had stationed herself there to deplore the view.

"I just don't understand you," she said. "First you say you hate fat in any shape, manner or form. The next thing you want me to go putting on weight."

Despair turned my manner sluggish. "Well, you do as you think best about that, Hester," I said, and rose, pocketing such mail as was first class. I went to the vestibule and got my coat and hat.

"Where are you going?" she said.

"Out."

"Well, if that's where you're going, you'd better wear your muffler. It's cold."

"I don't need any muffler. I'm just going to make a few calls."

She followed me into the vestibule.

"Don't be late. We've got to be there at a quarter to three, so that means we ought to leave here no later than two-thirty. And what about dinner tonight? It should be something simple. Do you like codfish balls?"

"I don't know, I've never attended any," I said, recalling a

53

joke from an old college revue, and, laughing unco-opera-tively, hurried out the door and down the porch steps into the street.

Hester stood shaking her head and laughing too. Then, thrusting her head out the door, she called after me in friendly sport, "Anyhow, I'm glad you like my brioches!"

I had been inside Molly's house only twice, after dates, and had never picked her up there but always met her at our rendezvous. The two times she had asked me in there had been nobody home. The idea of her having parents had therefore never crossed my mind, and so, in the excitement of my approach to her door, I was surprised to find it opened by a plump, very nearly perfectly round little woman in a knit shawl, wearing gold-rimmed eyeglasses. "Yes?" she said.

"I'm Andrew Mackerel — of People's Liberal Church? To see Miss Calico?"

"Oh, yes. She's not home. But come in anyway."

"Not home?"

"She's out of town."

"But she called only this morning . . ."

"She went to New Haven. She'll be back. She has friends in the theater. That's one thing she likes about your church — such a wonderful theater. Do come in and we'll have a nice chat ourselves."

The parlor into which I was ushered was one about which I had twice had occasion to marvel, even from what I could see of it in the dark. In broad daylight I had all the more reason.

It was furnished on the requirement, dear to the New England mind, of everything's having once been some-thing else. A coffee table was a former cobbler's bench, a lamp an erstwhile coffee grinder, andirons were bronze cherubs that had in a previous existence supported coach lights. The room was fragrant with flowers and plants that ascended, in each case, from something other than a vase. There were spice jars from which sprouted tongues of green; a glazed porcupine bristled with kitchen matches. It amazed me that Molly Calico could come of stock exemplified by this taste, until I remembered with a jolt my own. Nothing is more natural, of course, than that extreme environments produce their opposites. The sovereign motif here was Coziness, to which Mrs. Calico herself in no small degree contributed. I was a few mesmerized minutes putting my finger on the exact bell she rang, but after watching her execute a few stitches of the knitting she busied herself with while we "sat," I had it. It was of the animal illustrations in bedtime stories that she reminded you.

She looked precisely like some clothed and bespectacled forest creature sniffing and philosophizing in its chimney corner. She was Mrs. Tiggy-winkle, who did the washing in the Beatrix Potter books. Or Tabitha Twitchet, who ran the grocery store and did not give credit; or Goody Tiptoes, or all these rolled into one: an anthropomorphic thing in a ruffed gown and, at night of course, a lace cap. Already I could see her pushing moss under the thatch with her nose to keep us snug all winter.

"Now then." She composed herself with a wriggle. "I like the church becoming again what it used to be — a social center," she said, hooking up a strand of yarn with her little finger. I saw her smile downward, and deduced that a cat was playing at her feet. It would explain the abundance of hairs that compromised an otherwise immaculate room.

"There's a going-back-to-old-ways feeling in the air," Mrs. Calico went on as her needles flew. "Even the winters we're getting are old-fashioned, if you know what I mean."

"I think I do," I said.

"Snow is what it was under McKinley." She put her knitting by and rose, not that it materially altered our eye levels. "Now then, what will it be — tea or coffee?"

"Either one," I said. "It makes no difference to me."

"Then a nice pot of tea it shall be on this cold, nasty day," she said, and disappeared in a manner that made her seem to have been drawn from the room on strings, like a toy. She was only five feet high and her skirt fell so nearly to the floor that her feet were unseen, as well as undoubtedly shod in felt. She flowed without apparent effort and certainly without sound from my presence, the cat capering in her wake.

She was gone a long time. A tall clock ticked in the hall. I stared at the starched lace curtains hanging stiff as iron down the clean windows. I had the illusion of being a visiting rabbit, whose own feet didn't quite touch the floor. Out of the tail of my eye I caught the gaze of a general in oils, a man who resembled the Kaiser, though dressed in American regalia. It was an archaic uniform, and the manner in which one gloved hand rested on a sheathed saber conveyed a sense of old turmoils and crowned accomplishments. What came into my mind was what William Jennings Bryan had exclaimed in a Chautauqua oration on the eve of our entrance into the First World War: "The quickest way out of this is straight through it!"

There was a rustle of beaded portieres and a teacart hove into view, laden with goodies.

"The important thing is roots," Mrs. Calico said, trundling the cart to her chair. I had the sense of being unable to rise, or if I did, that it would be to find myself on all fours and only eight inches high. "From the day I married poor Willard — that would be Molly's father, who ran away to sea

56

when he was forty-two and she was twelve — it was apparent. I try to tell Molly this. Restlessness is the curse of our time. Put down roots, *belong*. My husband had been a rover — he was a commercial traveler — but he thanked me for getting him settled, at least till he ran away for good. I did that for him. I gave him roots."

I was tempted to ask whether she cooked them any special way. Indeed, I wondered if I wasn't about to be served them myself. However, a slice of pound cake came my way, along with the tea. We stirred our cups and smiled.

"It was touch and go though, at first," Mrs. Calico mused. "He very nearly drew out the gypsy in me instead. The way he acted on me was amazing."

"Sort of a catalytic agent."

"Well, he was an agent for Standard Oil, was what he was, and that had pretty much taken him around the world. So he'd 'had it,' as you young people say today, and why shouldn't he now put down roots rather than pull mine up? At any rate, he came to thank me for it in later years," she concluded rather shrilly.

I took another cup of tea and another slice of pound cake, resisting the bread and jam offered as option. I tugged my vest down over my tummy, half expecting to find a gold chain there and a watch which I would pull out and exclaim, "Goodness, I must go. Mrs. Woodchuck will be furious." Instead I sat immobile, my will gone.

"*I'm* going to join your church, Reverend Pickerel."

"You are?"

She nodded brightly, smiling. "Our old Reverend Yarrow is gone and I have really no more feeling for M.E. I've heard so much about People's Liberal and everything they do and this wonderful clinic and all. It's what we need, it really is. Tell me, do you direct the dramas too?"

"No. We have a man named Todarescu for that. Don't you know him?"

"Todarescu . . ." She looked at the ceiling in the effort to recall. "Where have I heard that name?"

"He's a foreigner, Mrs. Calico. Not our sort really, but he does his job. I thought he might be the one who took Molly to New Haven this morning."

"It might very well be he. She's out so much. A fine, healthy, popular girl. Tell me, what play are you doing?"

"It's called *The Lady's Not for Frying* — I mean *The Lady's Not for Burning*," I said. "It's by Christopher Fry. Dear me, what am I saying, all sixes and sevens today. Anyhow, it's written in poetry. Or a kind of poetry."

Mrs. Calico wet a finger end and blotted up the last crumbs from her cake plate. "Poetry went to the dogs under the Taft administration," she stated. "Modern poets have nothing whatever to tell us."

"You're so right. I was saying only the other day to Mrs. Wilkins, they only write for each other. Well then, why publish it? Why not just send it to one another in letters?"

I should have liked nothing better than to sit in this room while the clock ticked on and the sun's angle steepened along the figured rug, discussing the Taft administration and the emergence of vers libre under the rotten mob, drawing Mrs. Calico out on this and many other subjects, while we sipped our tea and nibbled our cake. But after a few minutes I rose with the protest that I simply must go. Other forest folk expected me.

"Well, it's been *such* a nice visit," Mrs. Calico said. "And it won't be the last of our little chats either, never fear, because I'll tell you something. When I join something, I join."

She led the way into the vestibule, where I got into my

overcoat. She watched me put it on, her hands folded above her stomach, smiling.

"I'll tell Molly you called, but don't worry if that sluga-bed girl isn't up on time for service tomorrow. *I'll* be there. And I'm so glad you believe in being active in all of life, Brother Halibut. Because after all, that's what Jesus wants us to do, isn't it?"

Five

"THANK God you've come."

Turnbull took my hat off and unwound the muffler from around my neck. He drew off my overcoat and hung the wraps on a peg under the one-eyed elk. He seemed even more agitated than usual, but I was prepared for this by the breathless telephone summons I had received on my return home from the tree-planting ceremony. He failed to wrest from my grasp a pair of pigskin gloves, which I myself tucked into an overcoat pocket.

"Maybe now you'll admit there's a righteous God," he said as he led the way into the living room. "When you hear what I'm going to tell you."

I took my customary chair and prepared for another rehearsal of past rascalities, with details more graphic than most.

"Maybe now you'll believe in an Old Testament God who visits the sins of the fathers upon the children, unto the third and fourth generation."

This was a new note. I steeled myself now for a tale of adolescent misdeed. Turnbull had a boy of seventeen, Steve, in his last year at Andover. The youth must have gotten into a scrape of some sort, perhaps with a girl. Like father like son. Blood had told. That was it.

"Is it Stevie?" I said. "What's he done?"

Turnbull took something from a table beside his chair and tossed it into my lap. Picking it up, I saw it to be a small book bound in limp leather, privately printed. It was by Steven Turnbull. The title was *Some Notes Toward an Examination of Possible Elements of Unconscious Homosexuality in Mutt and Jeff*.

"It's my punishment," Turnbull said. "And I had such high hopes for the lad. He would continue his psychology studies, get involved with some nice girl and settle down and work here at the clinic maybe. But *this*."

"Now, now, calm yourself," I said. "It may not be as bad as you think." I knew the boy had been interested in the American comic strip, and bringing the analytic technique to its study would certainly be nothing new. I told Turnbull this and added, "Maybe he was assigned the subject."

"It's a term paper, yes, but they could pick their own subject. And why would anyone pick that unless they were personally — Then the term paper was rejected and he wanted to have it privately printed. I gave him the money, how did I know what it was? Look at the dedication," he finished bleakly.

I had been paging through the monograph, my eye caught by lines like, "Though Mutt is married, his wife rarely figures in the action. He appears generally to be living in shared quarters with Jeff . . ." I turned to the front and read the dedication. It said, "To Cyril Sharpe." "Who is that?" I asked.

"His roommate. Some character with a fear of italics or some damn thing. Oh, God, is this what I deserve?"

I thought it wise to pause and take up that question non-rhetorically.

"For one thing," I said, putting the booklet by, "boys going off in that direction are supposed to have lacked a strong father image to pattern themselves after. Have you offered him a stable masculine example?"

Turnbull met this with a smile of ironic tolerance, even pity.

"Stable masculine example. I was only always high-tailing it after everything in skirts, that's all. Rutting about the continent, chasing one woman after another. Stevie knew that. What more example do you want?"

I let that pass and pursued another aspect of the matter.

"How about his relations with his mother?" I asked.

"She died when he was five, of course. After that I was a single man, which was partly why I lived the life I did. He was raised by a succession of nurses." He heaved a great sigh and parted his hands in a gesture. "I don't know whether that's supposed to cut any ice in these cases."

"I'll try to find out, but let's not go calling it a case yet, Turnbull. Let's pull ourselves together till we see what we see . . . Would you like me to call on him? I'm going to Boston shortly, and I could stop around that way."

"I'd appreciate that. Or he may come home for the holidays."

I left presently, having other calls to make, and he saw me to the door.

"When you do see Stevie," he said, winding the scarf around my neck, "don't make it too obvious that you're spying. Be casual."

"Of course. And meanwhile don't you worry about those arty fancies. Boys will be boys."

"That's all I ask." Turnbull stepped back to see whether

he had my hat on straight, bending his knees to bring himself down to my level. Walking out to the porch, he apologized for not having reached a decision about the memorial. "I've been too upset," he said. "But I'll hit on something soon, and the minute I do I'll call you."

"Take your time. There's no rush."

"One idea I did have was signs, yes, but *clever*. Like 'Have you been living it up? Jesus will help you live it down.' What do you think of that?"

"Forget about Jesus, and about signs too. Try to get a whole new viewpoint," I said, and fled down the stairs.

I was back in the heart of my problem. Which was, in a nutshell, to take a second wife while the town was still so First-Mrs. Mackerel-conscious. Holding one's emotions poised to strike at the earliest possible moment consonant with propriety, this was wearing enough without its even more ticklish corollary, keeping Molly interested, willing to "wait" till that psychological moment was reached. Every time I saw her leave the Players with Todarescu it struck me the more acutely that time was running out. He had given her the lead in the Fry piece, for reasons perhaps not altogether based on suitability, but in doing so he had certainly got himself the inside track. I racked my brains for ways and means of recovering it. One evening as I was climbing out of the plastic bubble in front of the parsonage, I saw them emerge from the side door of the auditorium and walk toward the Jaguar, parked just behind me. There was no way of avoiding a meeting, and I went over to them. Todarescu had his usual dark vitality, with a bright neckerchief glimpsed under his coat and the sudden, spastic smile, with its reminder of barbaric pasts. He removed and explained for us a new foam rubber cap of the kind that can, in summer, be soaked in ice water and remain cool on your head indefinitely. It continued to be the theme of forced pleasantries long after he had put it on again, Molly and I regarding it with fixed smiles and protracted study, as though our attention were hopelessly imprisoned there, or would be so unless someone had the strength to change the subject. I asked how the production was coming, and Todarescu frowned. "It's not ready yet. I want to try it out in some of the smaller parishes out of town," he said. "Bridgeport and maybe Darien." We were drifting slowly toward the Jaguar. Todarescu revealed an interest in the classics. "I'd like to try something fresh and exciting with Shakespeare," he said as the two got into the car.

"Why don't you do him in Elizabethan dress?" I said, thrusting my head into the tonneau. "That would be a new slant these days."

"Plim-plam-plom," he said, switching on the motor and away they shot, their necks snapping. "Shakespeare in — oh, plim-plim-plam. Oh, that's rich!"

I knew that I had to do something fast. What? That night as I lay in bed I had a brainstorm.

Hire Molly in the parish office. Why not? We needed a full-time secretary there now, to supersede the part-time makeshifts with which we'd been worrying along. Molly had had some secretarial schooling (was it not a business college from which she'd run away to New York?) and she had professed boredom with her city hall job. I phoned her there the very next day and proposed my scheme. She thought it a wonderful idea. She quit the following week and went to work immediately in my office.

She broke into harness slowly, but I expected that. For a time, the arrangement entailed my retyping the bulk of the correspondence I had dictated; her stenography was a bit rusty and had to be brushed up on. Meanwhile she was perfectly adequate for typing out my sermons (which made accessible to her the contents of the many which only Tabitha Twitchet would otherwise have heard). The main thing was that we were now, at last, together. There was nobody else in the office. Inside track indeed! Todarescu had her one or two nights a week, I five days. Thus, too, was devised that conjunction which my parishioners might now in all good humor assess as "He married his secretary." With what joshing affection we would be talked about; how well we would be liked. To open the valves of this gossip there remained but the final step of getting Molly on some committee where she might show her interest in church affairs to be more than narrowly occupational and theatrical, and where I might be seen as having eyes for her in open society. By now I had been six months widowed, Turnbull had not been heard from, and neither had Hester been moved to any new commemoration of her sister. Things seemed to have quieted down on that front. The psychological moment — the moment for my first public date with Molly Calico — seemed at hand. All the signs indicated that I could take her to the annual parish Harvest Supper.

Fortunately it was late this year, having got shoved on from the Thanksgiving period into early December, and I prefaced my seizure of the moment by a period of walking around town with the lost air of a single man who really ought to find someone again. My chin sunk in a black overcoat, one blustery afternoon in late November, I was aware of three women of my congregation standing on a street corner, watching me. They were Mrs. Comstock, Mrs. Cool-Paintey and Mrs. Sponsible, all fresh from the Wednesday meeting of the Ladies Auxiliary, where they had no doubt been discussing plans for this very supper. Trudging by on the other side of the street with my head lowered, I could well imagine their conversation. "I hate to see a man all by himself like that." "So do I. He ought to remarry." "That's what I say. I was telling Gerald last night, Ida May wouldn't want to see him this way . . ."

Other groundwork was laid in the case of Tabitha Twitchet. Molly had me home to dinner, and I did my best to win her mother over, on the principle that, having her blessing, you couldn't possibly have any man's disapproval. She had not only joined the church but had quite blitzed the Ladies Aid, to which she had got herself elected treasurer in a vote to fill a vacancy. The Ladies Aid was dominated by the Old Yankee element with which Fairfield County is, for all its sophistication, still heavily seamed. My cause could have no finer emissary there. They cottoned to Mrs. Calico all right, and I was at conversational pains to have her do the same to me — with Molly as an eager interlocutor.

"Tell Mother about the boy who wanted to put a Santa Claus in the Christmas crèche," she said after dinner one evening.

"Do, do, *do*," Mrs. Calico said, wriggling with pleasure over her knitting.

"Well, that's all there's to it really," I said. "There was this boy who wanted to put a Santa Claus in among the Wise Men. I objected at first, but later relented."

"They can be so cute. When Molly was a little girl she used to think *Noel* was 'Oh well.' We'd go caroling and there'd be this one singing away at the top of her voice:

'Oh well, oh well,
Oh well, oh we-ell,
Born is the King of Israel.' "

66

I felt the conversation to be sliding rapidly downhill. However, I added to it, "When I was a boy, I used to pray, 'Hallowell be thy name.'"

We laughed at this a bit, and then Molly said, "I'll make us some coffee. You stay where you are, Mother, and get acquainted with Andrew."

" 'Andrew,' is it?" said Mrs. Calico, casting up her eyes and pursing her lips in a manner that, perhaps together with the bowl of nuts she kept urging about, revived for me more vividly than ever the impression that she was Goody Tiptoes the squirrel wife, who would keep us warm all winter. "How shall I entertain a man like him?"

"Tell him about your *faux pas* with the bridge game. This was in like 1925, before I was born even, but it's still good," said Molly from very nearly the kitchen. Then she disappeared into it, and Mrs. Calico and I were alone.

Mrs. Calico smiled in preparation for her story.

"It's just that people rather fancy me a matchmaker," she began. "Well, anyway, I had these two spotted as made for one another. She was a lovely young lady, tall and elegant in the old-fashioned manner, and dressed for it too. This was when women's styles still had grace and beauty, before they went to pot under Coolidge. Well, so I got them together for an evening of bridge here — I was a newlywed at the time myself — and when they were introduced they said, 'Oh, I'm sorry. We've already *been* married.' It turned out the beasts had been divorced a few years before." She straightened a row of stitches on her knitting needle. "Showing, you see, that I was right in my hunch about them. That they were meant for each other."

There was silence, broken only by the soft clatter of her needles and the crunch of an occasional nut in her teeth.

"Negro toe?" she said, thrusting at me a bowl dominated by salted Brazil nuts.

"No, thanks," I said.

"You like my Molly?"

"Very much indeed."

"She's a prince. A prince of a girl, and there aren't many of those around."

"No, that is certainly right."

"Balls." Mrs. Calico tugged crossly at her yarn, with which the cat was apparently again rollicking. "That's all she wants to play with all the livelong day is balls. Fatima, go away. Scratch the rug, claw Reverend Flounder to bits, but do leave my yarn alone."

She retrieved the ball of wool from the floor and set it on her lap. The cat wandered off, and as though acting on the second of the alternatives posed it, sprang into my lap and began to shred the knee of my trousers.

"Well, when she gets married again, I hope this one sticks," Mrs. Calico said. "Four is enough. I keep telling her, my dear girl, it's now time to settle down. Roots!"

Molly returned from the kitchen where she had set the coffee to brewing. We chatted till it was presumably ready, and then Mrs. Calico rose and went to fetch it. I had again the conviction, this time almost overpowering, that I was four-footed and would spring down from the chair and follow her into the kitchen. There we would sit and talk of Mrs. Raccoon, who took in washing, and what Freddy Frog had said and how the Otters had behaved at Mrs. Woodchuck's party. We would drink our tea while the sun came in the window or the rain pattered on the roof, and no harm would ever find us there.

I said to Molly, touching the tip of the cat's ear, "You were married all those times. You didn't tell me that."

68

"I thought you wouldn't like it." She took a small cushion onto her own lap and pressed the tassels down. "I thought you'd like it better if they were just passing fancies? Not so checkered? I tried, Andy, I really did. It wasn't my fault. Some people just have this fatal attraction to the wrong mates. I just want that to end. I want it to *stick*." There were tears in her eyes. "I do love you."

"Have you been seeing Todarescu?"

"Todarescu's awful. Still he's rather nice."

"You really thought I'd think you more, well, sullied that way than this? If they were actual marriages?"

She nodded.

"You're a bijou," I said.

"You're no bargain yourself."

The cat jumped out of my lap as I shifted toward her, and she dropped the pillow. We were on the sofa. She yielded her face up to be kissed. I felt her tears on my cheeks, and then the tip of her tongue like a delicate fang against mine.

"I'll take you to the Harvest Supper," I said, huskily.

"You don't think that's pushing it?"

"I've got to have you. We can't go on tearing one another to shreds." Her warmth and her scent sickened me. I pressed her back against the sofa, and she drew my head down till we were lying length to length. My hand reached to touch her and she drew back with a sound that was both like a sob and a gasp of laughter, as though a bubble of hysteria had burst within her.

"You won't think it's the other way around, will you? That I was lying to Mother that they were marriages?"

"I never thought of that," I said, ill. "So that's the way it was."

There was a tinkle of china as the wheels of the teacart bounced over the edge of the rug and into the room.

"The family is coming back," Mrs. Calico announced.

"You have relatives arriving?" I said, almost falling to the floor in the act of rolling back off the couch.

"No, as an institution. I just heard it on the radio. The divorce rate is going steadily down. The figures for this year are considerably below last."

"Statistics show a marked decline," I said, my voice hoarse with passion.

I tidied myself while Mrs. Calico stood pouring coffee with her back to us. There was a great shaggy coconut cake, which looked delicious. Molly sat with her legs tucked under her, screwing on an earring.

"Let's make one thing clear," Mrs. Calico said, her back turned to us as she sliced the cake. "When we speak of putting down roots we don't mean sticking in the mud. The home will never be the rigid thing it perhaps once was, but it *is* reviving, and I'm glad to see that because I witnessed its deterioration. I can tell you exactly when it started to go. It started to go under Woodrow Wilson, the so-called idealist. Well, a good deal of world vision there, to be sure, but a thoroughly miserable administration on domestic counts . . ."

Thus everything appeared to be shaping up. Everything seemed to be moving toward that psychological moment, for which I would time that quick dash to the altar for which I pined. And then the unforseen happened.

Cat hairs were seen on my coat.

Hester slipped across the arcade between the rectory and the church office, one bright, gusty morning, to consult with me about some household detail. We had to discuss the seating arrangement for a luncheon I was giving the supper committee ladies. When we had finished our talk, she jerked her head toward the closed door beyond which Molly's spasmodic typing could be heard in the outer office.

"Quite a looker," she said.

"The new member who called you that morning, I believe. Incidentally, now that we've got somebody full-time in the office I think it only fair that she relieve you of the clerk stuff," I said. "Why, yes, she is quite pretty. And so interested in the church, Hester. Probably be a ball of fire on the right committee. You might mention that to your ladies. Need help on the Harvest Supper arrangements, don't you?"

Hester's reply, though an affirmative "I will," was rather abstracted. She was coming around behind the desk, staring at my coatsleeve. "Don't tell me I haven't been brushing your clothes any better than *this*, Andrew."

She began to pluck strands of a light yellow color from it and to drop them to the floor with fluttering fingers.

"Hm," I observed, picking off a few myself. "Seem to be cat hairs."

"Not just ordinary cat hairs. More like Siamese or something. Who's got one of those?"

"Oh, I don't remember. I make so many calls. People have them. Ah, me," I said, emitting a harassed breath, and turned back to my loaded desk. "Do you know that I made sixteen calls last week? *Sixteen.* Well, I believe I told Mrs. Comstock and her ladies twelve-thirty."

Hester slipped out, closing the door quietly behind her. I drew a dictaphone toward me and resumed reading my next Sunday's sermon into its mouthpiece. I was delivering a series on historical American legends, in which I showed how in deifying national figures we often draw them out of their human focus, to our loss. The new one was on Betsy

71

Ross, whom I praised as possessing that large vision that enables man to rise above individual mischance.

"The seamstress lost her husband in the war of the Revolution, but she continued his upholstery business and married again in 1777 — the following year," I read into the dictaphone from notes. "Betsy's second husband, Joseph Ashbourn, died in 1783 in an English prison, but did she despair? No! Again she remarried, and that right quickly, that fine and noble woman. We could all learn a lesson from her . . ."

I paused, hearing women's voices raised in conversation in the outer office. I rolled the dictaphone away and stole over to the closed door. I put my ear to the crack and listened.

"It takes a while, but I'm getting onto the ropes," Molly was saying.

"Of course it takes a while," Hester chatted. "Beautiful skirt."

"Oh, do you like it? Thank you. I wasn't sure about the color."

"It's nice. I like that oatmeal weave."

I squatted down on my heels to peer through the keyhole. I got my eye to it in time to see Hester, who had been standing beside Molly's desk, come over and finger the material she was admiring.

"Tweed isn't the most flattering thing in the world, but it's practical," Molly said. "It doesn't show everything."

"Somebody's got a cat who's shedding."

"I'll say. All of my coats look like fur coats. You can't sit down anywhere in the house without picking it up."

"Siamese?"

"Mm," Molly nodded.

I rose and turned to my desk. I picked up my typewriter

hood from it and hurled it across the room with all my might.

I was not surprised to hear what I heard at breakfast three mornings later.

Hester gazed out the window as she ate. "The air is like wine," she said at last.

"How do you know?" I said.

"I've been out to burn that box of trash you've left on the porch since last Saturday. But it was too windy."

"I'm sorry. I'll get to it today sometime."

I got behind the Avalon *Globe*. Turnbull was in the news this morning. There was a series of articles running entitled "Topsy Town," which outlined the agonies of local merchants in finding sites on which to build the stores with which to reap the trade made possible by the city's swelling population. There was no hope of obtaining such acreage to "improve" in the heart of town unless Turnbull was willing to sell a large tract he owned along the river. He refused. I admired his stubborn protection of the land in question, but the businessmen were up in arms. The Chamber of Commerce was at its wits' end. Things were said to be in a state of crisis. "All the trade," the mayor wailed, "is going to Chickenfoot."

I set the paper aside and attacked my grapefruit with a will.

"I'm rather looking forward to the Harvest Supper," I said. "Talk of a dance along with it this year. Excellent idea."

"And so appropriate."

"How do you mean?"

"It's the way she'd have wanted it. Ida May."

I wedged a grapefruit pip from between my teeth and laid it on my dish.

"What's she got to do with it?" I asked.

"Oh, haven't you heard? This year's affair is to be in her honor."

I finished the grapefruit and picked up my coffee. I held it in my two hands, regarding Hester over its rim as I blew on it.

"Oh, Andrew, don't look at me like that. I know how you hate speeches but —"

"Speeches!"

"Yes. It's to be a testimonial banquet, is what we thought we'd have, but the tributes are being limited to five minutes, and when you're called on you don't have to say more than a few words. It's just five years since she began her fund-raising drive for the clinic, and this seemed like a natural way to commemorate it. And then off to the ball!"

My impulse when I had raised my napkin was to slam it down, but I checked myself with an effort, and made as if to be flicking crumbs energetically from my person.

"Ida May loved dancing, as you remember," Hester said. "We were always alike in that respect."

I was digesting the implication of this turn of events, particularly as to its bearing on my own plans for the evening in question. They would have to be canceled, of course. You couldn't take a prospective second wife to a do in honor of your first.

"Hester, are you behind this?" I demanded.

"Well, the women all thought —"

"Oh, the women! Do you have a date for it?"

"Not as yet," she said, lowering her eyes.

"Not as yet," I repeated, as though to emphasize both her sexual isolation and the conversational style to which it was leading. "Why haven't you, if you're so fond of dancing? Why haven't you ever, if it comes to that? Hester, you've got

74

to come out of your shell — be a woman. Live your own natural life."

"I intend to do that."

"When? When you wake up some morning and find you're like fifty-five, and it's too late? Why not start now? Why don't you go out with men? Do you know what I've heard said about you? I didn't intend to go this far but it's for your own good that I do. Remember that in these days gossip is often inverted, and people tend to suspect virtue as they once did its opposite. Especially in women," I added ominously.

"I'll take that risk," said Hester of the parted hair, not turning or raising her eyes. "What do they say about me?"

"That you're a prude. I actually heard someone say that, my dear."

"And what did you say?"

"I said: 'He that is without sin among you, let him cast the first stone.' "

"That was very nice of you, Andrew." Hester rose and walked with her characteristic prim grace to the stove for the coffee pot. "Thank you very much. I'm glad to know I have someone defending me. A little like having a knight, almost."

When I got to the office Molly greeted me with, "You're late. The printer phoned twice already this morning. He wants to know the text for Sunday's sermon. The bulletin's all ready except for that. What's the matter with you?"

"Molly, I'm afraid the date's off," I said. I explained what was afoot.

She reached for a cigarette she had smoking in an ashtray on her desk, drew on it and twisted it out.

"So it's Chickenfoot for us again."

"We still have this office," I said grimly.

"I was hoping I could quit work and get married."

"Oh, my dearest."

She rose and walked slowly to the window. She stood looking out, nursing her elbows. The spirals of gold at the back of her neck made me ill, and I went over and wrapped my arms around her from behind. I cupped her breasts in my hands, the breasts I had never felt naked. I stroked their full tops with my two thumbs. I smothered her shoulders in kisses till I had to gasp for breath.

"Here comes the paper towel man," she said, drawing away.

It was about ten minutes later that the phone rang and she answered it.

"It's the printer again," she said, holding her hand over the transmitter. "Have you got your text yet?"

"Yes."

"What is it?"

" 'How long, O Lord, how long?' "

Six

"DEARLY beloved," I said, my lips close to the mouth of the dictaphone and speaking eagerly, as I would when actually delivering my message at morning worship, "the Bible is at worst a hodgepodge of myths, superstitions and theologies so repugnant to a man of taste and sensibility, let alone a true Christian, that its culmination in the latter ethic is perhaps the greatest miracle we know."

I continued for some minutes, and then paused to play back what I had done. From beyond the closed door could be heard the soft, steady clatter of Mrs. Calico running off something for the Ladies Auxiliary on the mimeograph machine. When she finished with that, perhaps she would help out with a little of the office work. Molly had a cold and was staying in bed. It was highly doubtful that she would be in today, or the next day, or even perhaps the next. She would go see Doc Chaucer at the clinic, free, as all church employees might, and he would tell her (and let him) that her cold was psychosomatic. He was one of those doctors who run their practice on the firm theory that ninety-nine per cent of their patients are quacks. It was also highly doubtful, meanwhile, that Mrs. Calico could help out much in the way of actual stenography, which meant that I would now

77

be retyping the *sermons* that I dictated too. I didn't mind in this case. This was one of those sermons of which a good chunk could go into a book I was slowly and surely, over the years, getting together. *Maturity Comes of Age* was a study of the myths in which all human systems are steeped, and a plea for their adult recognition as such, a recognition which need in no wise diminish their psychological value for the individual or their potency as a source of order for society. Indeed, the more void the universe may be of meaning, the more precious the lanterns by which man picks his little way through it. As to the book itself, the more work I had to do on it the better; let it ripen slowly, with its author. I was personally quite excited about it. Knopf had expressed interest, without even having seen any of the manuscript.

I rose after an hour's work and knocked off for a breather. I walked around my office, rubbing my fists into my back, which was sore and stiff from sitting in one position. I drifted to the window, where I stood a moment gazing out.

The Jesus Saves sign was gone. My own part in the protests had been unnecessary. The Episcopalians, who had shuddered, and the more influential Presbyterians — the more desirable element generally in Mobile Bay — had between them pulled enough weight to have the eyesore removed. Now, looking through the gap left among the trees where it had stood, I felt a pang of regret for old Turnbull. I liked him more than I'd known. I liked him better the more he got in my hair, it seemed. But it was no use trying to explain to him that this sort of thing gave the church a bad name. What about Stevie?

It was one of those instances of mental telepathy. As I turned back, the phone rang, and it was Turnbull. His voice sounded pleased. In fact, ecstatic.

"Guess what," he said. "Stevie's coming home for the holidays, and guess what. He's bringing a girl."

"Oh, how wonderful."

"He seems anxious to have me meet her right away, so I don't know. He may even have her in trouble."

"I'm so happy for you."

"Yes . . . Well, with that off my mind I've been able to think about the memorial, and I think I've come up with something. I don't want to tell you over the phone, but I have a hunch you'll like it. Of course the problem has been to hit on something appropriate."

"Always remembering her dislike of monuments as such. For her, life was the thing, and must go on. 'Forget me,' she often said. 'I don't count.'"

"Right. So something big, that will take the public's fancy and keep her alive among us for a long time to come. I'd like to talk this over with you privately. Can you have lunch with me tomorrow at my club?"

"I think so."

"Swell. How's twelve-thirty then, at the Stilton?"

"Twelve-thirty will be fine. And as you say, don't breathe a word of this till you've talked to me," I said. "Mrs. Mackerel was a woman of very strong opinions, and who is in a better position to know that than I?"

The Stilton's being one of the few clubs in the suburbs does not mean it was suburban. It was metropolitan in the old-fashioned sense, with mostly old men comprising its roster. Such an air of antiquity pervaded the club, which was housed in a pleasantly decaying graystone, that even its younger members, partly in the general wish to belong, partly in an unwitting adoption of its mood, affected the

79

stance and gait of senility and scuffled about as though they were old men too. Chaps of thirty-five and forty, wearing Ivy League suits and button-down shirts, were seen pottering from chair to chair with newspapers in their hands or shuffling into the dining room beside their sponsors. The quality reached out even to its visitors. I myself, after yielding my wraps to a mummy at the door named Luke, availed myself of a copy of the *New York Times* from an assortment on the lobby table and made in a bent fashion for one of the chairs, where, instead of reading it, I sat awaiting my host.

Everything was dead as a doornail. Several relics occupied mates to the leather chair into which I had sunk. Most of them dozed, but one or two slumped behind open periodicals. Occasionally a withered hand crept from behind a newspaper to reach for a glass of sherry. From behind one paper issued a continuous throat-clearing which identified Joseph Meesum, dean of the club, a man of epic riches obtained by selling parcel by parcel a thousand acres of inherited land. Rival genealogical societies, independently retained for speed and certainty, had traced his ancestry to conflicting sources — Geoffrey of Anjou and feudal Holland — and he had never been the same since. His sixty-two-year-old son Arthur was mayor of Avalon, and part of the club's new blood. I spotted a pair of Argyll socks under one outspread newspaper and wondered who belonged to them.

I noticed on the table copies of the *Manchester Guardian, New Statesman,* and *Punch,* and missed the pair of members for whom these were regularly taken. They were the Arbuckle cousins, two Anglophiles who read only British periodicals, ate only British sherry biscuits, and concerned themselves solely with British politics. No American political campaign ever drew more than moderate interest from them, but they argued heatedly over forthcoming British elections. My last visit here had been at the time of the crisis resulting from Eden's resignation as prime minister, and I remembered the intensity with which they had sat in their corner debating the relative merits of his possible successors. Needless to say the Arbuckle cousins came of the best old New England family stock hereabouts and were regarded with special awe as an exclusive little group of their own at the Stilton, whose members would never dream of addressing either of them unless first spoken to.

I rarely drank in those days, but I signaled to a waiter wearing carpet slippers, who limped over to take my order. "I'm waiting for Mr. Turnbull," I said. "Could you bring me a Manhattan, please? Dry."

The paper above the Argyll socks came down and a grinning face appeared.

"Andrew Mackerel!"

"Charlie Comstock," I said, recognizing one of my parishioners. His greeting had made a sleeper sit bolt upright and comment angrily on the disturbance. Another head came into view from behind the wings of a chair, and its owner glared at us with a Harvard accent. "Come on over," I said, patting a chair near mine. "I don't see you except in church."

"You see me there all right." Comstock came over, carrying a glass of tomato juice. "But I miss you at the mid-week Bible study group. Why haven't I seen you there lately, Andrew?"

I murmured some apology about being busy, and promised to try to be more faithful in attendance in future. I was fond of Charlie, but he had the one characteristic I always find it hard to cope with, piety. I tried to understand the experience that had laid its hand on Charlie, and to bear with him in that light.

Charlie Comstock was a reformed alcoholic. While not having touched a drop in eight years, he nevertheless retained the manner and attitude of the drunk. In fact, a casual observer not familiar with him would have thought he was stewed to the gills as he rose and wobbled over to join me. He slung his arm around me as though we were tavern cronies, and spoke in the slurred accents which his speech had never lost. He habitually ran his tongue from one corner of his mouth to the other, and his eyelids hung in a perpetual smiling good will. In the mounting excitement of parties, his foot always kept feeling for something, and eventually would come to rest on a chair rung. Holding a Coke, he made any group of men appear to be about to burst into the strains of "Sweet Adeline." The marks of past indulgence on his face increased the illusion that he was three sheets to the wind, an illusion no doubt valuable to Comstock. In his drinking days he had been literally picked up out of the gutter, and there were those who thought he might very well be again out of sheer autosuggestion. From behind, he seemed to walk down the street with an unsteady, even staggering gait. Religion had straightened him out, as it has many another drinker, but more than merely salvation-tipsy, he was a practical egg whose business head was an asset to any church or community project. He was co-publisher of the local *Globe*, for which he also wrote. Needless to say he struck a divergent note in the Stilton.

"Been enjoying your articles on the state of our fair city," I said.

"Oh, thanks. State is right. Hope Meesum doesn't get ap'-plexy when he shees old Turnbull walk in here. Turnbull's villain piece. Downtown boys certainly making it hot for him. Ah, speak of the devil." Comstock rose, tomato juice in hand, and threw an arm around the newcomer. "Glad see you, you old coot."

Comstock remained for the exchange of greetings, then withdrew to buttonhole Meesum, with a view to picking his brains for an article about our "Topsy Town." I saw Meesum, whose paper had at last come down, shoot a glare at my host. Meesum was honorary chairman of the Chamber of Commerce.

Turnbull ordered a highball for himself and another Manhattan for me, though my first had no more than arrived. He set fire to a long cigar and settled back in his chair. I saw it would be a while before he came to the point for which we were supposedly meeting. Turnbull was quite himself again.

"I've been prey to such remorse I can hardly sleep," he said. "Oh, wicked man that I am, who shall deliver me from so great guilt? Have I ever told you about the dancer in Biarritz?"

"No, I don't believe I've heard that one," I said.

"I tossed and turned all night thinking of her."

"I know that feeling."

"It's something you can't escape from. You carry it inside of you — here. If I take the wings of the morning and fly to the uttermost parts of the earth, he is there and his eye shall find me. If I make my bed in Sheol, lo, he is there. What a worm am I."

"Doesn't it ever seem to you that you're rather giving yourself airs?" I said, as I had before.

It is a pet notion of mine that certain theological systems (like Calvinism) are inversions of the humility they profess, since they appeal to human vanity rather than deflate it. Poor man, that he needs the doctrine of the Fall to

83

invest him with a little glamour! Pitiful ego, that must sit in sackcloth and ashes and fancy itself the butt of Reproba- ion! Unvexed, however, by either my remark or its broader implications, Turnbull went on:

"We all have our shortcomings, but mine are so great that it would take another lifetime to expiate them. What haunts me is not the dancer as such, but the impact I made on her whole future. She had been engaged, you see," he continued after a swallow of his highball, "she had been engaged, as I understood it, to a Brussels businessman. Security he could give her, yes, but not, I'm afraid, some- thing else demanded by her *Lebenslust*. You understand German?"

"Enough to get the point. Go on."

"Well, I was sitting on the beach at Biarritz one after- noon," he related, settling fluently into the raconteur, "when out of the water rose this . . ." He expounded in de- tail the scraping up of acquaintance and the episodes to which it led, listing among his "shortcomings" the number of times he had satisfied his companion in one night.

Here I felt a twist of irritation, enforced no doubt by the months of abstention to which I was myself condemned, and which were beginning to tell on my nerves.

"Are you quite sure of your figures?" I asked tartly. "It's a sin to tell a lie, you know."

Turnbull assured me of the accuracy of his audit, and hit his narrative stride with brightening eye. The details of this "confession," more lurid than any before, drew only rudi- mentary attention from me, who had become fascinated with the rather interesting problem in casuistry it posed: that of a penitent asking to be shriven of transgressions he had not committed, at least not in the degree claimed. Per- haps I was myself in error in giving the man his head? But I had decided it would be pointless to commence to Turnbull exhaustive analysis of what lay behind his bouts of contrition. That I knew very little of his complexities was suddenly driven home to me with a remark for which I was totally unprepared.

"What I owe womankind in general is nothing compared to what I owe your wife, of course," he said.

I had not the slightest notion what he was talking about. "What do you mean?" I asked.

"You know what I mean." He looked away to pick up his glass. "What happened that day at the cove."

I still hadn't the foggiest idea what he was referring to, though the day of which he was speaking was clear enough, being the one on which my wife had met with her fatal mishap.

The scene had been the annual parish picnic at Diamond Cove, on the nearby sound. It had been a warm summer day and both bathers and boaters had been disporting themselves in large numbers when a fluke occurrence had thrown the entire seaside into a hilarious uproar. A man in a motorboat had been towing his girl on a surfboard some distance out. She had toppled off and the man had stopped the boat and dived in after her — not because there was an emergency, since she could swim, but more or less in the spirit of fun. The push of his feet leaving the gunwale had somehow jiggled the gearshift, which he had left in neutral with the engine running, back into gear. Without a driver the speedboat had gone winding crazily about the harbor, sending bathers screaming with laughter in every direction. Not all were aware of what was loose in the cove, however, and one of these was Turnbull, afloat on an inner tube with a cigar in his mouth. He reported later that he had dozed off in the summer sun, and that in any case his ears had not caught any sound above the shrill cries that are a common part of bathing beach life. The speedboat seemed finally to be spinning straight for him, but, the warning shouts unheard, he bobbed along oblivious to what was in store for him. Or, rather, for Mrs. Mackerel.

We had been out in a canoe among the boaters, nibbling sandwiches from a hamper and playing records as best we could on a portable gramophone. Seeing what was amiss, my wife had instinctively stood up and begun to shout and gesticulate with the rest, capsizing the canoe. She sank to the bottom and was not seen alive again. Overturning paraphernalia, undoubtedly the gramophone, had dealt the fatal blow to which death was traced as much as to drowning. No one noticed that mishap until it was too late, indeed, until it was all over — not even I who jumped into the water as the boat tipped, or a split instant before, to help catch the speedboat. In the excitement I was not even aware that the canoe had tipped. A lifeguard and I stopped the motorboat, by managing to catch hold of her gunwales and turning off the ignition.

It was this accident the old fool was now bent on rehashing. I racked my brains for some clue as to why. Suddenly he was explicit.

"She was trying to go to my rescue, wasn't she?" he said.

I looked at him blankly — unwilling as well as unable to believe my senses.

"What?" I said.

"It's no use. You're just denying it to spare my feelings. That's why nobody else ever mentioned it either. A conspiracy of silence. It's so kind of you. But it all came to me in a flash last night as I was lying in bed. She jumped."

"She fell," I said firmly.

86

"She jumped."

"She fell."

"She jumped."

"Fell."

"Jumped."

The absurd crescendo of this argument brought looks from others in the lobby, and even from the adjacent dining room where members had begun eating, and we lowered our voices.

"But, my dear Turnbull," I resumed none the less earnestly, "this is the most — You mustn't punish yourself with such a thing . . ."

It was no use — that much of what he said was right. All my attempts to dissuade him from this mad construction of events were futile. My sensation was like that of careening wildly down a twisting road in a car that has gone out of control. Reminders that it was rather I who had gone into the water to help did not figure largely in my expostulations, may I say in my favor, but I did my best to show why my wife could not have, all to no avail. Just what form such aid could have taken in the case of so negligible a swimmer as Ida May did not long detain Turnbull, who could adduce too many instances of the instinctive heroism of women in emergencies, and had apparently no trouble seeing himself as the object of this supreme concern. That was the point — he wanted to believe this. I sensed the pattern in all of it: wallowing in claims of women ruined had the same narcissistic root as the delusion that one could give her life for him.

"That woman will have a memorial the like of which this town has never seen," he promised, bringing us back, at last, to the reason why we had supposedly come here.

"Now, then," I said, "what *did* you decide on?"

Turnbull dropped his half-smoked cigar in an ashtray and drank up. "The whole picture's changed, actually," he said. "What I thought of was a fund in her name to train missionaries for service in heathen lands, but that would involve too many problems of what kind of training they would have and so on. It's got to be more interdenominational." He glanced into the dining room. "It's filling up and you must be starved. I'll tell you in there."

Club protocol required that each newcomer take the chair beside the last man seated at the long communal table that ran the length of the dining room. This landed me between old Meesum and Turnbull. On Meesum's other side, his left, was Charlie Comstock, scribbling madly on a notepad as Meesum held forth on the subject of the local Crisis. It is to this chance juxtaposition that I owe the whole course of my present life. Here were the seeds of that calamity that was so soon and so speedily to engulf me, whose origins and development were obscure to me at the time, but which, from the vantage point of ruin, I could look back and assess in all clarity.

"Why, I was thinking of a fountain," Turnbull said as we drew out chairs. "The idea is that her spirit flows on among us." I murmured some acknowledgment that this was certainly nonsectarian, but before I could say more, Meesum pricked up his ears, paused in his diatribe, looked over at its subject and growled, "Hello, Turnbull. What's that about a fountain?"

"Nothing."

"Where, a fountain? Where would you find the ground for such a thing?" Meesum went on with needling irony.

"None of your beeswax," Turnbull said, and bowed his head in prayer.

I joined him in grace, rather against my will, and aware

that all sounds of conversation and even eating had ceased. Turnbull seemed an unconscionable time at his devotions, but when he did raise his head the pent-up curiosity broke out in an excited buzz.

"What kind of a fountain? When? Where?" Henry Meesum the mayor, who was still known as Junior, inquired eagerly across the table and two places down from me. When Turnbull answered reluctantly, "Memorial," Junior asked, "Who for?"

Turnbull jerked his head in my direction. "His wife."

In the respectful pause which followed that, and which was marked by a solemn regard of myself, he added, "She lost her life because of me, and I've always wanted to give something to perpetuate her name."

Here the city fathers raised their ears as one. " 'Give'?" said the mayor as their spokesman. "Why, that's wonderful. And you know we'll co-operate to the full. But where would you put it? As Dad here says, where's there room for the setting such a treasure deserves?"

Turnbull straightened in his chair. "You know damn well I've got all the land I need for it myself, Junior."

During this silence the elder Meesum elected to drink his soup which had been growing cold in front of him. The hydraulic problem of its transfer to his mouth grated on some of his listeners. He put his spoon down and looked past me straight at Turnbull.

"Frank, I've been saying a lot of things about you. I've called you a string saver and a skinflint and I don't know what all. Such names I now find it hard to forgive you for inciting me to. Why didn't you *tell* me you were O.K.? If I've been abusive it's because I thought you lacked the civic spirit that's the only thing that'll keep this city from withering into a ghost town, which it will do if we don't do something fast to keep the trade from going to Gilead and Chickenfoot. In short, I thought you were an obstructionist." As he spoke he made faces that had no bearing on what he was saying but that were technically exciting in themselves. "Now it turns out that you wouldn't sell your land because all the while you were planning to *give it away*, with the aim of *opening up that whole waterfront in a dazzling and daring new conception of Avalon*."

"I don't believe I —"

"Forgive me. I thought it was just that you were holding out for a price. But I guess you can read the papers as well as any of us. You know juvenile delinquency is spreading because children have no room to play. That congestion is the great evil of our time and the crying need. So you come along with this breathtaking vision for our town: twenty acres from your land augmented maybe by filling in the river there some, and presto — overnight elbow room! Congestion relieved! Children playing in the sun! Shoppers pouring into the twenty, make it thirty, new stores springing up there, with a theme uniting them all architecturally." He paused to wipe the corners of his mouth with his napkin, as though in his ecstasy he had begun to salivate. An architect at the end of the table began to writhe erotically in his chair, ogling a contractor there. "Make that a hundred new stores, with ample parking space. The greatest modern shopping center in the state. Not just one street front exposure but a double avenue — I know you're way ahead of me — along the river front there, with a green esplanade between. And that fountain sparkling in it day and night."

If this was sly — and it could hardly have been sincere because Meesum was a skinflint himself — it had its effect. Turnbull stopped protesting the assumption of limitless donation and became infected with the vision. Someone whispered "Turnbull Avenue," but he shook his head. He sat transfixed, looking over the assembled heads. He was witnessing an apocalypse. Someone said later that a tear coursed down his cheek. As if out of a trance he whispered, "The Mackerel Plaza."

They gazed at one another with a wild surmise. Then a hubbub broke out such as had not been heard in the Stilton since its founder had died in his sleep in a sitting position and that swelled in volume as the vision vouchsafed the philanthropist became the emotional property of each in turn. The fountain sprang into play for Chisholm, the architect dying to do a civic center. For Kerfoot, an electrical engineer, the lights bloomed each evening like voluminous pearls along the esplanade. The mayor was already cutting tape and leading motorcades on special days. Miles of feature copy unreeled for Comstock, writing feverishly on a fresh pad. Cars were parked in neat herringbones for a bald man named Scanlon, who was seated at the head of the table and ran a paving concern. Old Meesum was floating loans for the bank with whose board of directors he could still sit up straight.

"How soon can we get the property deeded over?" the mayor asked.

"I'll search the title this afternoon," said Sprackling, an up-and-coming partner in the oldest law firm in town. "What Frank will want to decide is what land he wants to give to the city for the esplanade and fountain, and what he'll sell to those who want in on the shopping center. Those, I take it, are the two parts of which the Plaza will consist."

After ten minutes more of this, somebody broke in with a thought.

"We haven't heard from Mr. Mackerel about this. Does

he have anything to say? Perhaps we could call on him for a few words at this time."

The hum of conversation died. All eyes were turned on Mackerel. He was drawing deep grooves on the tablecloth with the tines of his fork.

"Well, my wife was a simple woman," he reminded them. He smiled reminiscently. "Her favorite expression was, 'No fuss, please.'"

"We'll put it on the fountain," the mayor said. "It ought to have an inscription. Now, what else should we bear in mind, thematically speaking? Some little touch, an angle that might be stressed and that we ought to include in our thinking before we get rolling, which will be right now and full speed ahead, of course. Dad, did you have a thought on that?"

"Well, she was crazy about mental health."

"And that is of course already her enduring monument — the clinic." This from Mackerel in a loud voice.

"Right. That's why I was thinking some other inscription than the one proposed might be better, with all due respects to the Reverend," Sprackling put in. "What about '*Sans mens sans corpora.*'?"

"That's all Greek to me." Old Meesum had lit a cigar the length of a scepter, which he tended to flourish as such. "I'm a practical man and I say let's ring in the Chamber of Commerce *this afternoon*. With them in the picture we can coordinate and move intelligently on all fronts. If we haven't gotten much out of our friend Mackerel here, let's remember he's in mourning and will probably be for some time to come. The loss of Ida May is ours as well as his, and that no woman can ever, ever take her place is something we join him in taking for granted. Our job is to enshrine in tangible form what is enshrined in his heart. So let's buckle down and, forgetting everything but the proper celebration of this woman, all projects that would interfere with its proper and respectful pursuit, make this the fairest jewel in the diadem of our city." There was a round of applause, and he glanced to the left to make sure Comstock was getting it all down. "Now if we get rolling right away, how long should it take?"

"I see Junior cutting that tape nine months from now," said Kerfoot, a lickspittle in whose eyes slumbered a soft dream of contracts.

"Well, give it a year. A year from now, the Ida May Mackerel Plaza will be a reality."

Mackerel was deep in lightning calculations. He saw a quarterly period of obsession at either end of the inevitable Ida May Day — when the Plaza would be dedicated, et cetera — but if that weren't till a year from now, he and Molly had a good six months clear of canonization in which they could with grace wed (this lull to be reckoned as beginning, of course, after the Testimonial Dinner now in the works was over and that hoopla had subsided in the public mind). He was glad now the dinner was imminent, as it would get the cooling-off period started that much sooner. He was entertaining the image of himself darting to the altar through this chink in time, so to speak, when the mayor dashed cold water on *that*.

"Of course there'll be a ground breaking ceremony."

"To kick it off."

"When do you figure that?" Mackerel asked, raising his battered head.

"Oh, early spring."

(*Damn!*)

"Why not this winter?" said Mackerel, aiming at some overlapping in the encomiums.

93

"Ground's too cold."

Mackerel sat back with the expression natural to a man bereft. He said no more for the duration of that lunch, but kept his own counsel. He had said so little, all in all, that they took his silence for more than private feelings on the score of the project now so well launched, and for more than modesty in reflected glory; they took it as a sign of the greatest respect for the Stilton. And on their part they hinted that he might before long find himself enjoying the full member privileges of same. One or two murmured that they might personally put him up. Mackerel, who had till then patterned his bearing on that of his hosts by dragging his feet and walking with a stoop, threw his shoulders back and strode out of that club at a rate calculated to put an end to any *such* nonsense.

He sailed similarly through the door into Molly's house early the next evening, after phoning to say that he had something urgent to tell her.

Seven

MOLLY was home alone. After letting me in she ran back to the kitchen where she had some beef tea on the stove. She drank it as we sat in the living room together. She really did have a cold. She was curled up on the couch in a quilted bathrobe, belted tight and drawn up around her breasts. Thus did the fruit sway out of reach of Tantalus, his head bobbing on the stream 'neath the cruel branch withheld.

"You say you had lunch at the *Stilton* Club?" she asked in surprise.

"You don't think I should eat with Republicans and sinners?"

"Darling, what's the matter? You don't act right."

"How's Todarescu these days?" I said.

"Oh, all right I guess. He has this terrible *Weltschmerz*."

"Is he taking anything for it?"

"Look, what's it all about? You intimated you had something to tell me, and I gathered it wasn't too good. What is it?"

I blurted out my news, giving a full account of every development at lunch.

She finished sipping her beef tea in silence. When she had

tipped the last of it back, she set the cup and saucer aside and rose. She walked across the room, picking a cigarette from a box on a table in passing.

"Well," she said, "I must say, your wife casts a long shadow."

"Steady."

"How long will we have to lay low now?"

"I warned you about that from the start, darling. Of course I wasn't prepared for anything on this scale. What we must do is develop a certain detachment within our ring of secrecy — loving, offhand, yet antiseptic withal. A kind of *dolce far niente* behind drawn blinds. That appeal to you, sweetheart?"

"There's a kind of mockery in it," she went on. "As though someone's having a laugh on us. As though she's reaching out from the —"

"Whoa, there. I must insist you stop this, Molly," I replied. "You said yourself she'd be the first to understand."

"I didn't know her then. Now I feel I'm beginning to. My problem is how long can I live with the ghost of another woman."

I hoisted myself to my feet, bringing my hands down on my knees.

"I must say, what cheesy, wheezy neo-Noel Coward did you get *that* line from? Pray favor me with the rest of the speech in that play that folded after three performances. Go on, I'm waiting."

"A living rival you can fight. But this." She nursed her elbows, shivering a little. "I seem to feel a draft . . ."

I sprang into action.

"Watch," I said. I drew an appointment booklet from my pocket, shuffled its pages and ringed a date with a pencil. "I told you we were going to set a date, and, by God, I meant it.

Come here," I said, sitting down on the couch. She came over and stood behind me. "If the ground-breaking ceremony is then" — I poked the month of April with the butt of the pencil — "or about then, and the Big Day isn't till fall, that gives us a good four or five months when the coast will be clear to announce our engagement. And set the wedding date for — *then*." I vigorously darkened the circle I had made on the calendar. It was in the very month of June.

She nodded, not as though acquiescing but as though revolving my logic in her mind. She asked at last:

"Did you figure on a church wedding?"

"No, I thought a quiet ceremony would be better. Steal away somewhere. I know a minister in Chickenfoot I went to seminary with. There's no problem there."

She scratched an eyebrow, looking down at the memo book open on my knee. "Since we can't date openly till the ball is well over with, we're going to have to crowd a lot of courtship in a short time, bud. They'll no more than see us going together than we'll have to spring the engagement on them."

"Call it a whirlwind romance."

The phrase seemed to satisfy her, as though a tribal shibboleth had worked its potent spell. Then I did something that actually did sweep her off her feet. Putting the memo book away I drew from another pocket a small black jeweler's box, and released the catch. A diamond ring sprang into view.

"Andy," she said.

She came quickly round the sofa and kissed me. I slipped the ring on her finger and her arms went round my shoulders and she melted into my embrace. Then she lay back with her head on my breast, gazing at the stone on her extended hand.

"I don't suppose I can wear it?" she sighed regretfully.

"The time will come."

Molly remembered a bottle of champagne someone had given her last Christmas and we chilled it. We kissed again, laughing about her cold which I would surely get, and sipped the wine and were happy for an hour. "We'll bring it off," I said, "when the time comes. Don't worry." Then the phone rang and she went into the next room to answer it, carrying her glass and drawing away from one of my kisses with a giggle of pleasure.

I turned the bottle in its ice during her absence, rolling the neck between my palms as they do in the movies; I don't know why this is done and perhaps the actors don't either, but I did it, smiling to myself. I could hear Molly in the next room but couldn't make out what she was saying.

She came back without her glass.

"Well, I'm on a committee."

"Ah! That ought to blitzkrieg them. What sort of committee, sweets?"

"Your wife. The Ida May Mackerel Memorial Committee, Women's Church Auxiliary branch. We're having our first meeting Tuesday."

I raised the wet champagne napkin, which I'd been rearranging around the neck of the bottle, and smacked it down on the table. "That's the last straw."

"Is it?"

"Who called?"

"A Mrs. Comstock. She's heading it."

"That downtown bunch certainly don't let any grass grow under their feet! So they've asked the parish ladies to form a group to work along with the Chamber of Commerce. Well, we're in it up to our ears now."

She plopped down on the sofa with her elbow on her knee

and her chin in her hand, in the classic female attitude of disgust.

"This was your bright idea. Me working on a committee."

"Not this committee!"

"I told you there was a hand reaching out from the Great Bey —"

"Couldn't you have said no?"

"After that build-up you've been giving me? I'm the greatest little old fireball church worker ever seen in these parts, to hear you tell it."

"It was part of the plan."

She raised her head and seemed to look thoughtfully out. "Your plan," she remarked slowly, "but maybe not the divine one."

"Oh, rubbish!"

"Maybe it's a warning that we're not compatible. I seem to be more religious than you."

"As evidenced by the frequency with which you attend church."

"Well, there are places that I do go." She averted her gaze and said, "I've been to Mrs. Balsam. Do you know her?"

I was genuinely aghast at this. "The theosophist!" I said. "This is the limit. I know you theater people are superstitious and go to clairvoyants and all, but I thought it was no more than that. A medium! This is really too much."

"I'm worried and confused, and, besides, what can you lose? Nothing, while you have everything to gain. You quote Pascal that way to me about Christianity. Why doesn't it apply to a séance?"

"Séance!"

"I thought if I could get in touch with her . . ."

She had risen and started to turn away. I seized her by the

shoulders and swung her around. "I'll thank you to leave my wife out of this," I said. "You give me the creeps."

"There *are* more things in heaven and earth than are dreamt of in our philosophies," she said gently.

"I know, Molly, I know." I dropped my hands and turned away myself. "Why is it people never believe in the hand of God till they get the back of it?"

There was a silence, and then I saw that she had begun to cry. Or at any rate to tweak her nose with a wadded handkerchief. "Our first quarrel," she said.

I went to her and put my arms around her. I gave her a clean handkerchief to complete freshening herself with.

"Now let's get back to where we were. Let's see, where were we? Man proposes, woman accepts, as the fella said. Right, sweetie? Now let's pin up our hair and try to get on top of this thing," I said. "It does occur to me to ask — I'm only thinking out loud, remember — couldn't you have said no?"

"Not gracefully. Andy, it would have left a bad taste in my mouth," she said. "You know what I mean. It would have been a — well, a fly in the ointment of, well, of 'us' forever after. I couldn't look myself in the face again."

"And I love you the more for it."

"Oh, don't start that again."

"But it just isn't fair to a man! It's like one long funeral service. No man should have that asked of him." I circled the room, fetching up behind the sofa, on which she was again sitting. "It's all such a senseless jumble."

"On the contrary I'm beginning to see a definite pattern in the whole thing. Don't worry, I don't mean a divine one. I'm talking about a human one now." She turned her head toward me but not enough to meet my eye, resting her arm along the back of the sofa. "Mrs. Comstock said she got my name from Hester Pedlock, who told her I was high up on the list of eager beavers. Was it you who told Hester that?"

I held both fists in the air like a conductor leading an orchestra in a prolonged discord, at the same time gnashing my teeth.

"We should have declared ourselves sooner, struck out boldly, let the chips fall where they may. Now it's too late. She's got us trapped. Boxed in. It's this fixation I explained she has about her sister. It's so deep she won't let me remarry. That's the whole thing in a nutshell."

"Is it?" Molly said, smoothing her bathrobe along her knee.

"I'll do something about her, but meanwhile here we are with the eyes of the world to worry about. Oh, why should an early remarriage have to be justified anyway?" I protested. "It may be a measure of the gulf that has to be filled. Of the very depth —"

"Yes, yes, I know. You've explained all that to me."

"In fact, I'll go farther. I'll say show me a man who doesn't marry again and you've given me a pretty good idea of what the first one was probably like."

"All *right*. Nobody's judging you. Don't let's start all that again either."

We lapsed into another silence. After a moment I said, "I'm thinking out loud again, but what about getting your mother to serve in your stead?"

"Don't you see that would go against my grain too? And besides, what good would it do? We can't get married anyway with all this going on in town, so I might as well *be* on the committee. I'm going to get all the paper work for it piled on my desk anyhow, as usual. My God, that's where I'm going to be busy!"

"Have some more champagne."

I went into the other room for her glass. When I returned, it was to find her drawing the ring from her finger. "Better not let Mother see this. I mean it's best not to take any chances with anybody." She put it back in the box and the box in the pocket of her robe. I stood over her with the empty glass; she stared at the floor. "Back to Chickenfoot," she said.

I set the glass on the table. I was myself as deliberate, as summarizingly direct, as she, but what I said transposed our relationship into a permanently new key. "But this time with a difference," I said.

"What do you mean?"

"Be lovers?"

She rose as if startled to her feet. I took her musingly by the shoulders and pursed my lips in the manner of Walter Pidgeon to rule out any implication of crassness. She turned her head away and said, "Golly . . ."

"It's not our fault. We haven't wanted it this way. They've driven us to it. They've won. Outward sanctions are apparently to be denied us for the time being; does that mean we should deny ourselves one another? 'Hope deferred maketh the heart sick.' "

"At last I've heard it. You're quoting the Bible."

"The demands of taste we should and will meet — gladly — but society has no right to ask a man to behave like a medieval monk! I love you, I yearn for you, I toss and turn for you," I went on, stumbling blindly into rhyme. "Adultery is just a word in a case like this. But if that's what it's called, let's commit it!"

"You needn't preach. I don't stand on ceremony any more than you. It's just that — well, I wanted it to be *right*, and beautiful," she said wistfully. "Besides, where would we go?"

"A hotel."

She gave a slight shudder, and the truth of the matter is I winced a little under the word myself.

"I can just see myself slinking up to the desk with a ten-cent wedding band on my finger and a suitcase with house-bricks in it."

"Housebricks?"

"Something I read in a novel once," she explained quickly. "The lovers bought a cardboard suitcase and a ring at Woolworth's, and on the way to the hotel passed a vacant lot where they stopped and put a few bricks in it."

"What happened then?"

"They were surprised in the room by the girl's husband, who whipped out a pistol and pumped them both full of lead. But the idea of the housebricks, Andy, is so when the bellboy picks it up it won't feel empty? Ugh! Could I bring it off? I shouldn't look right, Andy."

"Would you rather I rented a small flat? A little place to call our own," I said, warming to it. "We could fix it up, have meals there —"

"That scares me even more. A whole double life. Such a thing would kill Mother if it ever came to light. No, I suppose a hotel is the way. Maybe I could brazen it out."

"Of course you could. Too, there are hotels where that isn't necessary. They're that *type*."

I had turned away and now stood at a table not facing her, where fidgeting of their own accord in an open box my fingers brought up a cigarette. Momentarily forgetting that I didn't smoke, I lit it and took a few nervous puffs.

"Chickenfoot has them in quantities, in the very district

we've been meeting in," I said. "I mean we've half come to it already."

"Like what?"

I spread my hands philosophically. "The Coker —"

"The Coker! Why, it's notorious."

"That's just it. Nobody we know would ever see us there."

"But that's all it's ever *used* for. The Coker!"

"Would you rather a place where one of us might be recognized in the lobby? Don't you see that's why it's right for us: the very fact that it's just not our sort."

"But why a *dive?*"

"You forget I'm a minister of the Gospel," I said quietly, turning to face her with perhaps some stiffness. "I have to keep up appearances." I went on with the air of one repeating something he had explained fully more than once before. "I told you from the start a minister's wife has certain obligations from which ordinary women are exempt. Certain standards to meet. She has a special place to fill in the community, and often a difficult one. No stain must touch her. I was fair about that all along, Molly, I was perfectly honest with you from the start. We can't afford to get off on the wrong foot now. Nor can I in all fairness guarantee that the situation won't arise again, in some form or other. So there's still time if you want to back out . . ."

She shook her head, which was lowered.

"No, it's all right. I'm game." She sighed after a moment. "But I must say, the strain of being a minister's wife is beginning to tell on me already. Give me another drink."

Eight

THE Coker is a nine-story building of no specifiable color but leaning more to gray than to brown, though the bricks beneath the film of soot that covers it are brown, and of no architectural interest save its inclination toward the building next to it at an angle seemingly in excess of the survivable degree. Three stone steps grayer than the building lead to a revolving door flanked by two swinging ones. On the day on which we availed ourselves of its facilities, a square of cardboard served to patch a broken pane in the former. "Snowdrift Cake Flour," I read as I bumped through a segment of it with the luggage.

The suitcase I carried was my own Gladstone bag and contained, rather than ballast garnered in vacant lots, the normal changes of clothing and grooming appurtenances a man would take on an overnight trip, which was what I had told Hester I was away on. I said I was running down to New York for a day or two to look up some source material for my book at the public library. In addition to this I carried Molly's cosmetics case, into which she had tucked a nightgown and a few other odds and ends. She had told her mother she was staying with a girl friend. She had taken a phenobarbital to relax her before setting forth, and had another in her handbag in case it was needed. It was dusk when we entered the hotel and the lights were on in the lobby. The time was also, I may add, a good month after the incident in which we had resolved on this course. The Testimonial Dinner had had the effect of sobering us to volunteered restraint, apart from its public extortion, and then the Christmas spirit had come along and thrown cold water on the project by prolonging the period in which it wouldn't have seemed "right" to go to the Coker, and all in all it wasn't till nearly February of the new year that we felt anything like physically and emotionally able to proceed with our plan.

I was exhausted when I reached the desk, where I dropped the two bags with a thud behind a couple who were ahead of us. It was at this juncture that I recalled that the Coker is banally known as the John Smith. I tried to study the couple's faces for signs of self-consciousness, furtiveness, excessive nonchalance or melancholy (the last being what I personally mainly exuded), but the man was writing in the register with his back to me and the girl drifted over to the magazine rack. At the man's feet was a suitcase that, whatever its contents, could itself have been found in a vacant lot. I peered over his shoulder and saw him sign "Mr. and Mrs. Harry McQuade." I suddenly realized that I had as yet neglected to choose a pseudonym for myself! I frantically put my mind to it, but panic froze it solid. Luckily there was some conversation between the guest and the desk clerk, and I had time to think of something suitable. That done, I felt a little more secure. I smiled at Molly, who stood a short distance off — the offhand inexpressive smile common to married couples. Her response was a tremulous twitching of the lips that made me look at the floor. She turned and walked to the water fountain beside the magazine rack, where the other girl was still browsing.

She dug something out of her handbag, put it in her mouth, and bent over to drink from the fountain.

I wrote "Mr. and Mrs. Nicholas Plantagenet" on the registration card in bold flourishes. My theory was that if I made it fantastic enough it would be convincing, because nobody would make *up* a name like that.

A bellboy appeared, rather to my surprise, and took us up to room 518. The elevator was piloted jerkily upward by a youth who read a comic magazine on the way and sniffed continually through one nostril. The bellboy held his head straight but rolled his eye at Molly once. She looked down and drew a glove on tighter.

The room managed to be cold and muggy at the same time. The bellhop made a great show of snapping on lights and feeling radiators by way of implying "appointments" which the room simply did not have, till I packed him off with a dollar bill.

Finally the door was closed. I squatted to peer through the keyhole, but there seemed no eye on the reverse side looking in. I locked the door softly and turned back into the room, and this was the moment round which all my ravenous daydreams had wound: the moment when Molly would cry "Alone at last" and fling herself into my arms. Instead she flung herself into the only chair in the room and burst into tears.

I stood watching her inactively. My mouth was dry and had a metallic taste.

"What."

"If you could see yourself in that derby," she said, in accents that seemed, apart from the content of the statement, shrieks of genuine grief.

"I'll get us a drink. Usual for you, dear?"

I hung up the derby which I'd been holding and sat down

on the bed to phone down. I imagined that we were on our honeymoon and that brides behaved in this way.

The switchboard operator seemed amused at the implication that they had room service, but gratefully so, as though that was the nicest thing anybody had said to them in a long time.

"This is a real dive," I said to Molly after I had hung up.

Molly was doubled over in the chair with her forehead touching her knees. Her bag lay on the floor, open. I had the sense of having stumbled into some strange rite rather far from the revels for which we had come and whose existence I had not suspected, but which was instructive and stimulating in itself and calculated greatly to widen my horizons. I felt a trickle of perspiration go down my torso. I picked up the fallen handbag and set it on the night table. I watched Molly a moment longer. Then I snapped my fingers, remembering something, and turned to the bed across the foot of which the bellboy had hurled the suitcase.

"I nearly forgot. My Bellows."

"You're going to start a fire?" she said, looking wildly around for a hearth.

"No, whiskey. I took a pint along just in case."

With that she burst into peals which were like nothing I had heard, or hope to hear again. I hurried with the whiskey, pouring her a copious drink into a glass which I got from the bathroom, first removing a mote of matter from its rim.

"Here. Take this." I shook her shoulder — or rather sharply stayed its own shaking — and put the glass to her lips. She drank it all, dried her eyes and took my hand. "I'm sorry."

"I know. This sort of thing isn't for us," I said, running a disdainful eye around the interior.

"Let's go."

"No. It would look funny if we left right away. Come lie down a while."

I took her coat and hat from her and settled her on the bed, which was hard as a rock. I drew the pillow out from under the spread and laid it under her head. Then I took control of the situation.

"Now then. You've taken the other sedative. That makes two. That ought to calm you down fairly soon, and you'll be all right. Just relax."

She ground out a hollow in the pillow with her head and smiled up at me. "Maybe I'll be O.K. pretty soon."

"Sure. Forget everything." She could not have known my relief at finding her otherwise than skilled at profane love. No one with a casual past could have exhibited such signs of nervousness. If the hour were completely botched, it could do no worse than change to soaring joy the one doubt I'd carried in my heart for months.

"I'll go out and get us some sandwiches, as long as there's no room service. We'll want something later, anyway. There's a famous delicatessen on this block — the neighborhood has some compensations — and we'll have a snack of supper. Pastrami O.K.?" She smiled wanly and nodded from the bed.

I felt more than ever like a newlywed foraging for his bride, as apprehension gave way to the proper emotion of tenderness, and I blew her a kiss from the door. "Be sure the door is locked behind me," I said softly, and, taking the second of two keys from the dresser, went out.

I removed the pastrami sandwiches from the sack in which the delicatessen man had put them and slipped one, wrapped in its own wax paper, into each of my overcoat

pockets. I didn't want the hotel personnel to see me carrying anything up to my room, for some reason. I hummed
as I mounted in the elevator, which was operated by the
same comic-reading youth. I went down the corridor to 518
with the key in my hand. I fitted it into the lock. The key
turned in it but the door wouldn't open. Molly had turned
the bolt, which was apart from the key, from the inside.

I rapped on the door. There was no stir in the room. I
knocked louder, then louder, till I was afraid of creating a
disturbance. Still no answer. The muted strains of Calypso
music came from a radio in a linen closet nearby. I leaned
toward the door and put my ear to the crack. All I felt was
a minute draft blow into it. The radio music momentarily stopped, and I caught the sound of Molly's breathing
—faint, easy, rhythmical. The sedatives had taken effect.

I stood a moment in the darkened corridor, debating
what to do. Two barbitals were quite a dose, and there was
little hope of awakening Molly without bringing heads from
every other door on the floor as well. I went back down to
the lobby to think things over.

I sat in a chair for some time without coming to any
conclusion except that Molly certainly needed the rest
and that I probably shouldn't awaken her too soon. I di-
verted myself by studying the faces of guests in other chairs.
They sat under potted palms reading or smoking or doing
nothing. I soon tired of this. A half-hour had passed, I saw by
a clock which said six-twenty. I tried to calculate the hours
Molly might remain oblivious under present sedation, but
my ignorance of the tablet strength vitiated any arithmetic.
In any case, two made a substantial dosage to have to take
into account in the night's adventure.

I was very hungry. Changing my chair to one behind a
pillar in a corner, I drew one of the sandwiches from my

pocket and unwrapped it on my knee. Making sure I was not seen, I bit into it. It was delicious, and accompanied by a spear of dill pickle that was also capital. I remembered that Molly didn't like pickles, and took the one from her sandwich and added it to my repast. I picked the last remaining crumbs from the wax paper with a moistened finger-end and dropped the wax paper into a large ashtray. It was one of those tall heavy-based ashtrays that right themselves no matter how far you tip them, and for a few minutes I amused myself by slapping this one down and watching it swing up again. I noticed that a girl attending the newsstand was looking, and stopped.

It was ten minutes to seven. I had sat there an hour already. How much longer? If Molly slept the clock around, as well she might, I would be here all night. The only alternative was to rent another room for myself for the night. That wouldn't look right here, so I would have to engage it in another hotel. There was one across the street.

Then I realized that I could telephone Molly. I got laughingly to my feet to do so. However, on the way to the phone booth I checked myself. Why not let the poor girl have an hour or two more in dreamland? She certainly needed it. It had all been a terrible strain. I would go out for a walk.

Strolling down the street, I found myself approaching the movie district. I recognized one of "our" theaters. Why not take in a film? It would help pass the time. I consulted a marquee or two and chose a picture that had Kim Novak in it. I paid my admission and darted hopefully inside.

Kim Novak was my favorite actress, and as I settled down in my seat I wondered why. I thought about it as I ate the second sandwich, and at length worked out a theory that seemed cogent.

I decided, watching her now, that her appeal lay in some

sheer incorporeality. She was impalpable. She was a soft gold cloud of a girl, who drifted through scene after scene of the utmost intimacy without being *there*. She had flung herself on Frank Sinatra's racked body without being there. She had died in Tyrone Power's arms without being there. She was flawlessly unpresent, weaving an abstraction called love. I ran into the lobby for a candy bar, still ravenous, and ate it in my seat with the wrapper peeled down. A scrap of foil got between my teeth as I nibbled in the dark, and I had a time fishing it out. I dropped the wadded-up wrapper under my chair, settled my coat on my knee, and slumped drowsily down. After a while I dozed off.

I awoke with a jerk in the middle of the co-feature. Pirates with drawn knives were pouring out of a hatch and yelling mutinously. I scrambled to my feet and made for the phone booth in the lounge downstairs, my overcoat flying behind me. What if Molly had awakened and found me gone! A clock said five minutes to ten. When the hotel switchboard operator answered, I couldn't remember my room number. "Just a minute," I said, fumbling for the key in my overcoat pocket. But I couldn't read the tag in the booth, where the light was broken. I'd had to dial the operator to get me the number.

"Are Mr. and Mrs. Plantagenet registered there?" I said.

"I'll give you room information."

They were registered there, and presently I heard the room phone ringing. Twice, three times . . . "Keep ringing," I told the operator. "I know they're there."

"Would you like us to page Mr. Plantagenet?"

"No, that won't be necessary. Just ring again please."

She did, and finally I heard Molly's sleepy voice say "Yes?"

"Darling, it's me. Look, you've got the door *latched*. That little round knob, you know? Turn it back. I'll be right up."

"So sorry," she mumbled. " 'Bye," and hung up.

I got into the room this time all right, but she was asleep again when I arrived there. She lay sprawled over in a pale nightgown, the covers kicked down in a jumble at her feet. She muttered apologies as I began to get ready for bed, lifting an arm and letting it flop again as if in some cryptic salute to my durability under the stern demands of the hour.

I soaked in the tub for half an hour and then brushed my teeth. I drew on fresh red silk pajamas and sat in the chair drinking — a habit I seemed to be acquiring. I had three or four whiskeys-and-water, raised the window an inch or two, turned out the light and went to bed, where I soon fell into a deep, if not exactly untroubled, sleep.

I awoke from a horrible nightmare. I dreamed that Mrs. Calico had put down roots at a garden party I was giving behind my house. She had been sitting on the grass with the other guests, and when it came time to go was found to be unable to rise, being affixed to the lawn. It took the combined efforts of two men pulling her by the arms to uproot her, and when she finally came free it was with a tearing sound, taking a great deal of sod with her. I came to to see Molly bending over me, shushing me and trying to quell my threshing arms.

"Wake up," she was whispering. "Sh! Wake up and be quiet."

"What sa mah?" I mumbled, sitting up frantically. "Where are we? Wha's 'is?"

"Sh! We're in a hotel room. We're at the Coker. Are you awake?" I now appeared to be, and she asked, "My God, what did you dream?"

It was broad daylight. The room swam into focus, without, however, remaining precisely fixed. I had a splitting headache, besides being slightly dizzy — the dizziness that comes from the so-called middle ear disturbance with which I am recurrently troubled. Under this arrangement, the room in which a patient is lying tends to rotate in a steady flow, like the picture in a television set that is in need of vertical tuning. It's something like the sensation that arises from a hangover. The difficulty seems to be caused by a circulatory distention affecting the balancing apparatus in the middle ear, and is said to be the result of emotional tension or stress. It is often accompanied by marked, though never conclusive, nausea.

"Do you have some aspirin?" I asked Molly. She was still bending over me. Her features were mangled with sleep, and one eye was glued shut. She looked strange and even a little sinister.

"I believe so," she said, and turned away to get them from her bag on the bedside table, where I had put it.

She started to leave the bed to get me a glass of water but I stayed her with a hand and said, "No. Let me." I faced the crucial discovery of learning just how dizzy I was. If it was bad, I would be bedridden for a day or two; if not, it would wear off as I went about my normal activities. I put a foot carefully on the floor and sat up. The room wavered violently and I thought I was for it; but then it settled, and when I rose and started for the bathroom it seemed a little better.

Downing the two aspirin she had laid in my palm, I caught a look at myself in the bathroom mirror. I put the water glass down and inspected myself stoically. My face was pinched and blurred, so that I resembled a wire photo of myself. I thrust out my tongue to find it thick and deplorable. I turned it over and moodily inspected its underside. My pajama coat was open and I observed a morning ritual

I have of punching my stomach to see if it is still satisfactorily hard. At the least sign of fat I immediately start walking great distances and dieting. It seemed all right now. To one side of it I have a reddish blue mark, like the government stamp on dressed beef.

I went back to bed. Molly lay on her side, away from me, the covers up to her ears.

"So sorry," she said, her voice muffled. "I didn't think two pills could do that to you. Just absolutely *doped*."

"Think nothing of it," I said.

She said, cozily, "What was your nightmare?"

"I don't remember. It was nothing."

"Of course you remember. What was it?"

I couldn't very well tell her it was about her mother, so I related a nightmare I'd had earlier in the week.

"I dreamed I was in this barn, a kind of livery stable, really, and that I wasn't an animal exactly, but not a human being either," I said. "Then I was forced, or at least I was supposed, to get down on all fours while a couple of characters who seemed to know what they were doing started to brush me down. Brushes and curry combs and one thing and another, just as though I were a horse. After a while somebody came in and asked what the big idea was. And one of the men with the brushes said, 'He's being groomed for an executive position.'"

She gave a single, indolent laugh, and then, turning over, slipped an arm around my waist. I snuggled over closer and put mine around her. My dizziness was going to be all right, thank God, but I was still dizzy, and the headache was as splitting as ever, so any ardors beyond an inert embrace was simply more than could be confidently undertaken at the moment.

"This is just plain not for us," I said, giving the room a

contemptuous glance as it went by. "We want it to be beautiful. We want it to be right."

We lay together, cherishing the carnal jewel of purity. "So *dopey*," she murmured, and dropped off again. After a half hour of listening to her quiet breathing, and of stroking her hair and inhaling her delicate scent, I climbed carefully out from under the covers to shave.

I was oddly exhilarated. I felt our failure to have sprung from elements that lay somewhere close to the heart of human worth. Think how we would have felt if we had done what we had come to this cheap hotel to do. Now the cheap hotel was part of our triumph, a pleasant memory to carry into married life instead of an embarrassment. Too, I derived from the whole experience that sense of widened horizons in sexual matters, of understanding women, and of the mastery over them.

As I was buttoning my shirt in the room, a few minutes later, something shot toward the bathroom on the edge of my vision. It was Molly, clutching a dress which she had snatched out of the closet on springing out of bed. "I've got to get to the *office*," she said. "It's half-past *ten*. I thought my watch was stopped from last night but it isn't. Mother's spelling me till I get there, but I don't want to arrive too late. What if she takes it into her head to phone this girl I'm supposed to be staying with?"

Most of this came from behind the slammed bathroom door. When she came out again, wriggling into her dress, I felt a lash of desire.

"Darling," I said, "let's wait till tonight. I can't wait to have you, and we may be in the mood then."

"I can't possibly stay out another night. Mother thinks there's something fishy already."

I sighed, and walked to the dresser to tie my tie. "I suppose. But I'll be lonely here tonight."

"Tonight?"

"I told Hester I was going to New York for a couple of days to do some research at the library. So I can't really go home till tomorrow."

In the mirror, I saw her walk over. She stood looking hard at my reflection.

"You mean you have to *account* to her? With *stories?* Like a *wife*, for heaven's sake?"

"What did you tell your mother?"

"That's different and you know it. But this woman — you might as well be *married* to her."

I went on lining up the ends of my tie in preparation for knotting it.

"Now look. You do something about her and do it right away. She's the roadblock and you know what I mean," Molly said.

"Right. So your rival turns out to be flesh and blood after all, and not a spiritual one," I said. "Don't you feel better already, sweets?"

"Ah! I'm glad to hear you use that word at last. It's been on the tip of my tongue for weeks, but I haven't said anything because — well, I wasn't sure. Now you've said it. It's out in the open. She's my rival, and I think now we understand each other." She tapped her palm with a hairbrush, fixing me in the mirror. "*Don't we?*"

"Of course. I know what you mean. And I'll do something about it right away. You watch."

"I don't care how you do it — tell her off, give her notice, throw her out of the house — but *get that woman off my neck*. This may sound tough, but everything's fair in love and war, as she herself seems to know! She's got you under her thumb like a husband, and we're going to fix that!"

I continued tying my tie, knotting it so as to conceal a small grease spot on one of the stripes, by way of outwitting my dry cleaner.

"I mean it, Andy. Make it plain who's going to be boss of that house. Show a little independence."

"Yes, dear," I said, with a sardonic smile that pretty much soured the remains of that hour together.

We finished dressing and went down for a bite of breakfast, and after breakfast Molly, who had taken her overnight bag with her, got into a cab and hurried to the office.

I had an extra cup of coffee, which I drank in pleasant leisure. With a decent breakfast under my belt I felt a lot better too. The dizziness was about gone and my headache was clearing up. After paying my check I went out for a walk. I was conscious of the stores I passed, looking for a place where I might pick up a little something for Hester, who probably expected a trinket of some sort from my trip to New York. Besides, it was important to keep her in a good frame of mind if I expected to throw her out of the house.

Nine

I GOT caught in a shower during the course of my stroll and took refuge under an awning in front of a shop. As I was waiting for the rain to let up, a car with a vision of a girl at the wheel glided to a stop. She was going to park at the curb there. A patrician head and a fine throat leading to some cleavage warned me what I was in for. I gritted my teeth and looked for defects.

There was no incompetence in the way she parked the car; it was whipped into place with shattering skill. She rolled the windows up tight and appraised the downpour, debating whether to wait in the car or make a dash for it. Her hair fell in one angelic torrent to her shoulders, and was blond. Didn't it seem, though, to come rather far down on her forehead? It would prevent needless suffering if so, for a low brow would definitely undo that face.

She leaned to crank the window on the curb side down and looked up at the sky, her teeth flashing in a grimace. A gust of wet made her withdraw, but not too soon to show me that my first impression had been wrong: the brow was clear and symmetrical after all, and a ripe red mouth added to what must be borne.

Two alternatives are always posed me at this stage of the

game, which is crucial, and they are precisely those of gambling. I can quit while I'm losing but still have a few coins of doubt to jingle in my pockets, or I can stay and play the possibility of thick ankles or a bad gait's canceling out my turmoil against, of course, that of a voluptuous figure's intensifying it. In other words, double or nothing.

I stood irresolutely under the dripping awning. The girl looked out again, keys in hand. Suddenly she jerked the door handle down and sprang out.

Getting out of the car exposed a span of thigh that stung my vitals. The ankles were finely hewn and swelled into shapely calves. She slammed the door shut and scurried under the awning. She was standing beside me.

I looked the other way to generate nonchalance. After some moments I stole a glance. Ah, her chin was imperfect, and thank God there were blemishes on her skin. I developed this. The skin was quite rough, was it not? She would be like that all over: heavy and coarse and reddish along the neck on down to the shoulders, and from there to the breasts, the hips, the thighs turned in voluptuous languor — Hey, how about the rough complexion? — I pasted my mouth to hers and we were rocking through the American night in a Pullman berth, then drifting aboard ship through delinquent seas, and each morning at breakfast — Breakfast, that was it — the way off the hook. Every time she opened that stupid mouth you would shudder and curse the day you laid eyes on her.

I must make her say something — anything — to confirm this. A phrase, even the inflection of a laugh could betray the entire mental level.

"I'm waiting for the weather report to take hold," I said. "Intermittent showers."

I grinned encouragingly, but she did not respond, save to

cast me a sidelong look. I tried again. Her manner itself did suggest a lack of style, a certain want of *esprit*. I hurried hopefully on with the business of flunking her out. A word would do it, but I must actually hear her speak.

"Do you have far to go?"

Her manner now had *esprit*. The look she gave me was crisp and not tentative, and ended in visual reference to a policeman reporting at a call box across the street. I excused myself and ducked into the shop.

Taking stock, I found myself in a book and greeting card store. A salesman was advancing with a smile, with a pantomime of soaping his hands.

"Yes?"

"Just browsing," I said, "if I may."

"Certainly."

I might have done worse. As I was looking, it struck me that a book might be a good solution for Hester. I went to the fiction table, but found nothing that seemed right. My eye was caught by a corner shelf of art books. Among them was an album of Rousseau prints. I remembered hearing her say she liked Rousseau and I bought it. I asked the man to gift-wrap it, which he did, using, I was glad to notice, paper without the name of the store on it. By the time he had finished tying the ribbon around it the girl was gone. The rain had stopped too, and I stepped briskly along the street with my purchase under my arm, consoling myself with the knowledge that the girl was a goose and certainly deserving of the zero I gave her on the score of intellect.

I watched Hester unwrap the package and exclaim with delight when she saw what it was.

"Something for the house," she said. "Why, how nice."

"No, no, it's for you. I thought you said once you

liked Rousseau. He's not a particular passion of mine, but anyhoo . . ."

"It's awfully sweet of you, Andrew," she said. She came over to the kitchen sink where I was standing to give me a kiss. Then she sat down again in her chair at the breakfast table and took a closer look at the individual prints in the album. "I'll have them framed," she said at last.

"*All* of them?"

"It'd be a pity to break them up. They go together so beautifully, as a set."

"Where would you put them?"

She considered the question, mentally scanning all of the house she could not see from there.

"I'd run them up the wall along the hall steps," she said at last. "That gray wallpaper always looks bare to me, and these would brighten it up a lot."

"Look," I said, "I don't want eight Rousseau prints marching up the stairs with me every time I go up, and down every time I go down. I don't want them there. Now there's an end of it."

"You don't?" she said in surprise. "Well, there's no rush. We'll figure out a place. But they are just lovely, Andrew. Thanks so much."

I remained leaning against the sink long enough to watch her put the album aside in the wrapping paper. Then I walked over and stood behind my own customary kitchen chair. I faced her, gripping its back.

"Hester," I said, "I would like to get married again."

"Oh?"

"But there are obstacles."

"What do you mean, Andrew? Like what?"

In keeping with my injunction to dress more casually around the house she had appeared in a loose-fitting negligee that seemed to consist of a silk morning wrap over her nightgown. She poured me a cup of coffee and depressed the latch of the toaster in which two slices of bread stood ready.

"Like this endless memorial," I said. I drew my chair out and sat down. "Do I detect your fine Italian hand in all this?"

"But why— ?"

"To keep me prisoner in the same emotion in which you choose to incarcerate yourself. What you want to do with your own life is your business, but what if I refuse to spend the rest of mine dissipating my normal energies into a succession of respectable intervals!"

"Really, Andrew," she said gently.

"I can't help it. All I want to do is live happily again with another woman. It's as simple as that, damn it! I'm sorry I can't share your well-intentioned but believe me unrealistically narrow plan for perpetual mourning."

"Not mourning — celebration!"

"It comes to the same thing. A situation where it would be gauche to marry. You can't ring wedding bells while that other bell keeps tolling. Can you now?" I demanded.

She shrugged, not to express indifference but a kind of earnest deference. "Why, I think you should get married again, Andrew. I see marriage very much in your future," she said, passing me the cream. "Whom did you have in mind?"

"Miss Calico."

"Molly!"

"I knew you'd approve." I poured some cream into my coffee. "But how can I with all this going on? Now the last straw, they've put Molly on the Ida May Committee. Did you give her name to Mrs. Comstock as a Willing Woman?"

"But you —"

"Yes, I know. But the way it turned out, as well as the speed, makes it seem a little fishy, if I may say so. You threw up quite a roadblock, girlie."

"But why should I want to do such a thing? You've only told me now what's between you. How could I have known that then?"

My charge was a difficult one to support short of admitting that I went around peering through keyholes. I now felt an irritation with Molly for having pushed me into this trap. Women were always spurring men on to hit the boss for a raise or to speak to so and so about this or that — generally to wage aggressions they themselves harbored. I suddenly remembered that from my own eight years of marriage. However, there was nothing to do now but accelerate the offensive in the hope of inciting evidence of its justice.

"You don't want me to get married again," I said. "That's clear."

"Why don't I?"

"Because of this hero worship of your sister. That unhealthy emotion I was telling you about."

She lowered her eyes. I plowed ahead with renewed confidence.

"Why don't you go out with boy friends?" I said. "I don't think this sheltered life is good for you. Purity carried to an extreme becomes its own opposite. Rémy de Gourmont classifies chastity as a form of sexual perversion."

"Well, every man to his own taste."

I twisted my napkin under the table as though it were sopping wet and I were wringing water out of it. "Rejecting all men is a species of promiscuity." The neglected toast sent up a black billow of smoke. Hester took the ruined slices away and opened the door to clear the kitchen. I watched her dig fresh slices out of their wax wrapper and slip them into the toaster slots.

"So forget me. It's you we're worrying about," I went on. "You're a girl in danger of more serious psychological consequences than you may realize. You'll go from Dr. Chaucer to von Pantz, now I warn you. You're tense, pale, and the victim of what I know to be an uncommonly strait-laced family. Oh, I know your family, my dear, and I'm not surprised at the end product I see: that sick orchid of Puritanism, a hysterical woman!"

Intoxicated by my own words, I saw all the elements in the situation rush into place about a dramatic cliché like filings around a magnet. "A warped New England house" was the term that came vividly to mind.

Hester scraped her chair back and crossed her legs away from the table. I was aware of folds of silk falling about her legs, and of bare thighs beneath the silk nestling warmly against one another. What other garments?

"We must put an end to these morbid thoughts! There's not a moment to lose!" I exclaimed, rising. "The mind is like a balloon that'll stretch just so far, and then — bang."

Hester pressed the tablecloth flat with her fingertips and stared thoughtfully while the second pair of bread slices went on to incineration.

"Mother always used to say you can't run away from something that's inside of you," she said.

"She has gone to her reward."

"Just what do you expect of me? Just what did you want me to do?"

"Give me a break. You're close to the central commissariat of women," I said, a humorous name by which we sometimes called them, "your word will swing a great deal of weight. I need an ally in the parish before I come out in the open about this. You got me into this spot so it's only fair that you get me out. I just want to get out from under long enough to get married. So take up my cause, around town and all. Give this your blessing. Would you do that, and thereby be a pal? Otherwise the situation between us must be considered insupportable, and I shall expect your notice in the morning."

"Will she keep her job? It's hard for a woman to mix marriage and a career."

"It's sometimes no cinch for a man either! So take up my cause, say this is O.K. and all, around town. Be a matchmaker even. And stop all these confounded commemorations!"

She rose to dispose of the new batch of burnt toast. "Well, I don't agree with you there. Mother had her quirks, it's true. She wore her wedding ring on her right hand because she herself was left-handed. And other things. But she did say this one thing about family loyalties. That if ever — Andrew, what is the matter with you?"

I was sitting with my head bowed in my hands, shaking it. "So it's Mother we're bucking. The inextirpable and quenchless Mama again. Mama who would want this, Mama we're obeying across the years as well as Sis we're still playing those duets with. You must go to von Pantz. There's not a moment to lose."

"Listen to me, Andrew. Listen. Mother always said that if anything should stick together it's families —"

"That all-devouring and agglutinate mass. I'll make an appointment."

"Families are the links in the chain that gives man the only immortality he has. Human continuity was always sacred in our family. We almost made a kind of ancestor worship of it."

"Fine, but don't bury yourself with them! The Bible tells us —"

"It's too late. You told me to read Korzybski instead of the Bible, and I have, and Korzybski speaks of 'time binding,' the ability to pass on from generation to generation that gives man his distinction above other forms of life. If survival isn't true, then let's make our own! Let's all pitch in and keep those we love alive."

"With adequate parking facilities!"

"Why not? And I like the idea of a fountain. There was one in our garden when we were little girls in Belle Isle."

I raised my head.

"Ah, then it was you who put that bug in Turnbull's bonnet too," I said. "You're at the bottom of *everything*."

She smiled a little. Her face shone now with a pleased radiance, as if she were the little girl again, watching the fountain plashing in the garden at Belle Isle, in that far-off time. She spoke with a gentle but firm resolve.

"We will keep her memory green."

My shoulders drooped, the muscles of my face sagged into repose. "I see."

I rose and went to the office, where I took off my overcoat and slammed it down on top of my desk. It fell with its sleeve in the Out basket. I walked to the window shaking a cigarette from a pack, for I smoked habitually now too. I was halfway through it when I heard the front door open and my help arrive for work. Tabitha Twitchet or Molly Calico?

I remained at the window, not turning around. I heard whoever it was hang up her duds in the outer office and come to my open doorway, where she stood evaluating the set of my back, no doubt.

"Good morning," Molly said.

I greeted her and without delay related the events of breakfast.

"So it's worse than I thought," I concluded. "We must get her to von Pantz. He isn't much, and God knows what he'll do with a case of necromancy, but he's all we've got, and he may be able to hack his way through this and give her some insight. It's ironic though, winding up in the place founded by the person she's mixed up about."

Molly was sitting in a chair, where she had been giving the impression of brushing cobwebs wearily from the surface of her face. Now she rose and looked at me open-mouthed, with the expression but not the sound of laughter.

"Mixed *up!* Is that what you think this is all about? Do you really for a minute believe that's behind her shenanigans?"

"I've seen some queer things in my line of duty as pastor," I told her in calm tones. "This is New England, you know."

"Oh, you fool! How dense can you get? She wants *you.*"

I trundled my dictaphone toward the desk.

"I'm really terribly busy this morning. I'll have another chapter of *Maturity Comes of Age* in an hour or so. That'll be enough to shoot to Knopf."

"Maybe that's why you couldn't see it — because it *was* under your nose. But it's perfectly obvious to another woman. She'll keep this up till she's got you married to her, and then this necromancy, as you call it, will vanish like a fog. You mark my words." Molly followed me around the desk, and now stood pretty much over me, pointing toward the parsonage. "Now you go back there and do the whole thing over right."

"Just what do you call right?" I said. "And how do you propose I go about announcing myself as not eligible?"

"That's your problem. But put your cards on the table

and make her do the same with hers. Smoke her out somehow, bring it all out in the open, and for the love of God, put an end to this mare's nest!"

She turned away. She looked nowhere, and sliced the air with a sigh.

"I'm sorry, but you know how I feel," she said apologetically. "Oh, Andy, I want to get married."

It was a protest, not an amorous cry, and I wisely did not try to turn it to amorous account. I watched unhappily as she turned and went to her own desk and drew the hood from her typewriter. The war of nerves was on.

"Well, all right," I said, "I'll take another crack at it on that basis. But I'll say one thing. I hope you know what I'm doing."

Ten

MOLLY's theory could have been right or wrong, but right or wrong, there was nothing to lose by giving it a try. If her hunch was correct, then Hester's removal as an obstacle to our plans could be achieved in a much subtler fashion than "throwing her out of the house" or "making her lay her cards on the table": namely, by the elimination of myself as an object of desire. It suddenly came to me as being that simple. With that end in view, therefore, I set about the systematic depreciation of myself as a catch.

I addressed myself first to the important and most obvious sphere, the domestic, by lapsing in matters of tidiness. I left my clothes lying about; I put things where they didn't belong; I was unpunctual for meals and irregular in my habits generally. I did all this gradually but nonetheless firmly, with marked changes in that previously well-run household. There was always something for Hester to pick up or to straighten out or to overlook. I left the knots in my ties and hung them on doorknobs and drawer handles, and I set wet towels on chairs in rooms into which I wandered with them. Smoking gave me a chance to be slovenly where there had been no contrary precedent of neatness, since I had just acquired the habit, and I made the most of it. I spilled ashes on the rugs and on myself, and doused cigarette ends in my coffee dregs in the manner of a man who is no bargain. The same with drink, another indulgence into which the strain of accumulating events had driven me. I never became a heavy drinker, but I was by now a daily one; cocktails after a hard day at the office being a *sine qua non*. I would come home — at whatever hour caprice dictated and without reference to pre-arrangement — and immediately clatter up an Old-fashioned. I could overturn a kitchen foraging for incidentals, and moist paper napkins adhered like stamps to half the furniture when I was through. Dinner could wait even if it meant burnt dishes — for me to complain of when I finally did sit down.

While I thus added ill temper to bad habits in the all-out drive to lose ground with Hester, her own mood of undamaged good spirits in the early weeks of the experiment was a source of surprise, and made me wonder if it wasn't going to take longer than I had anticipated. She would pick up my shirts and remove the knots from my neckties with no expression but a smile of infinite understanding. Her table talk displayed no visible discouragement with my own.

"How do you like the spaghetti?" she asked at dinner one evening when we were having that.

"Stringy."

She held up a bottle of Chianti in pleasant inquiry whether I would like more. I grunted affirmatively and extended my glass. I would have to pull out another stop.

Feeding habits offered a particularly rich area in which to be deplorable, and I left no stone unturned there. I developed a disquieting procedure — at least to me. I would consume the contents of one plate at a time, shove it aside and attack the next, and so on, downing large quantities of wine or beer the while. Sometimes I carried whiskey to the table. When I had finished the spaghetti that evening, I broke off a crust of bread and swabbed my plate.

"I thought you didn't like it," Hester said, tossing a green salad.

"My parents always taught us to clean our plate, no matter what, and they were right." This was a point on which I did feel strongly, and so my rejoinder rang true. "The waste in this country is appalling. It's worse than the overeating."

"I agree with you. I never throw anything out if I can help it. To me the test of a good cook is what she can do with leftovers. Look, I know you prefer romaine, Andrew, but the only lettuce I could get today was the iceberg. I hope you don't mind?" She passed me a plate of greens. "And I hope the dressing is O.K."

I cleaned that dish as well, and praised the dessert, a fresh fruit cup doused with kirsch — a specialty of hers. I even took a small second helping.

"Fruit isn't fattening," she said, spooning it up. "This hatred of yours of·fat in any form," she went on after we had munched in unison a moment, "I wonder how many people realize that's behind the quality in your sermons. That lean, athletic style. Do you mind if I call you the Ernest Hemingway of the pulpit?"

"No, I don't care," I grumbled indifferently.

"I mean how many people realize you *slave* to keep them to ten minutes. I had to defend you to Mrs. Sponsible about that at the committee meeting last night. She said she didn't want to be bored by hour-long sermons either, but *ten minutes.*"

"What did you say?"

"I told her the story of the man who had to write a long speech because he didn't have time to write a short one."

"And what did she say?"

"She said that was a speech, not a sermon."

"And what did you say?" I fished a pip from between my teeth and laid it on my saucer.

"I reminded her of the Sermon on the Mount," said Hester, who, gazing between the candlesticks that bathed her cheeks in rose and gold, looked like the meek who shall inherit the earth. "What would you have said?"

I shoved my empty dish aside and tilted my chair back. I opened my mouth and prised a shred of pineapple from between my teeth with a finger. "That hit the spot," I said.

I was not losing ground, or not enough. I sensed that. I could see it. Each turn of the screw but gave her the more opportunity to show her own style. The only weapon in the war of nerves was calm. Still there was nothing for me to do but give the screw another turn. How? Having lapsed in matters physical, there was nothing left to lapse in but the mental. My conversation became untoward. I told off-color stories.

"It seems there was this parlormaid," I said, as we sat in the living room with our after-dinner coffee one evening, "this maid who kept bumping into everybody. Running upstairs with a stack of linen she collided with the husband. The next day she stumbled into the son who was coming out of the closet she was on her way into. Then into the grandfather going down cellar, and so on. So finally she said to the lady of the house, 'I'm afraid I'm going to have to leave, Mrs. Brompton.' The woman said, 'Why?' The maid said, 'Well, I seem to be in the family way.' 'Good heavens,' the woman said, 'the family way, what do you mean?' And the maid said, 'Well, first with your husband on the stairs, then with your son in the closet, and now with grandfather in the basement.' "

This disgusted nobody but myself. Hester was on her knees, poking the fire, and a small crash of settling logs made her recoil with a laugh and rub the smoke from her eyes. She set the poker on its stand and walked back to her chair.

"Why, I guess everybody wonders where all these stories come from that you hear," she observed, reverting to the thread from which we had digressed. "A lot of them originate in vaudeville and burlesque, and of course bawdy houses, but that can't account for all of them. Do you know an interesting explanation I've heard about who make a lot of the darn things up? Prisoners. They've got nothing to do all day and can't live a normal sex life so that energy gets turned inward. Does that make sense to you?"

"It certainly does," I said emphatically. I took a sip of coffee, then picked up a glass of brandy I had poured myself, which instead of drinking I swirled pensively in my hand. I was thinking of something. I remembered the story of the convicts who numbered their stories, and how I had failed to get much of a rise out of Molly with it. I remembered humor as the mind's magnetic needle, and its fame as a test of kinship.

Across the room, Hester's head was bowed as she stirred her coffee. I took a sip of brandy and set the glass aside.

"Have you ever heard the one about the convicts who were so used to one another's stories that they just gave them numbers?" I asked.

"No, I haven't," she said, detecting a subtle shift in mood. "Tell me." She smiled expectantly.

I told the story, drawing it out. I watched her as it neared its conclusion. " 'What's the matter, isn't that a funny story?' 'Oh, sure,' said the cellmate. 'But he don't tell it right.' "

Hester set her cup down on the end table beside her chair.

Then she laid her head back and laughed. She brought a hand down on her knee in delight. She was naked except for skirt, blouse, underthings, stockings and shoes.

"Well, I think it's funny too," I said, gazing into the flames. "I don't know whether it's that funny."

Hester smiled into the fire. After a moment she cleared her throat and said:

"Now tell me something. Is that a shaggy dog story, Andy? Maybe I'm dumb, but I can never get it straight. Can you explain to me about that?"

"I wouldn't say that's one, no. The basic thing shaggy dog stories have in common, I'd say, is the kind of logical let-down ending — the reverse of the explosion produced by the conventional story through surprise and so on. A sort of calculated deflation that sets you down in the middle of nowhere, and that may be related to *angst* in the distance you find yourself from home. I preached a sermon about it a while back."

"I guess I missed that. Could you dig it out for me?"

"I think so. But I wouldn't call that a true shaggy dog, no. That's just offbeat."

I felt that I had to get hold of myself. I was being bought off. I lit a cigarette and pitched the match in the direction of the hearth. A length of ash ripened and broke down the front of my vest.

"The rarer human sensibility becomes, the closer it gets to the logic of insanity," I observed after a silence. "That's why offbeat stories, to which intellectuals' tastes so often run, are in a sense quite literally 'crazy.' "

"This has nothing to do with wit though — right?"

"Oh, no. Humor has its marshy edges, but wit must be clear as a bell. Abraham Lincoln has been made by legend into a sweet old codger, but actually he was an intellectually

135

arrogant man. Jesus is presented by the evangelists as a bleeding heart, but he had a wit like a razor. Nine-tenths of what he said was repartee. Read the Gospels. You find him flashing ripostes at the Pharisees and dishing out aphorisms to his disciples one a minute. Of course he was an obvious neurotic."

"That's a very interesting slant. You ought to do a sermon on it sometime."

I slid up in my chair and took a firm grip on the conversation.

"We have insanity in our family," I told her, "speaking of that. I had an aunt who was quite wacky all her days, and an uncle who was actually put away. Our uncle twice removed we called him — once for good."

"Well, everybody has some of that."

"Not as much as we," I answered. "I mean really locked-up crazy. This uncle used to urinate in his shoe and pour it out of the second-floor window, and one day he went out and came home leading a donkey he'd bought, and they said, 'What did you buy a donkey for?' and he said, 'Because they're cheaper than cows.'"

"That offbeat logic again."

"That's not what I mean. I mean it's always been there as far as I can make out, going back a bit. Of course it sometimes skips a generation but then there it is again. Tainted stock. Anybody who doesn't like that had better look elsewhere." I tilted back my brandy and finished it off.

"I understand," Hester said, nodding and smiling at me with the same look of infinite comprehension.

I was now at my wits' end—no closer to knowing whether I was barking up the right tree than when I had started this. There was only one way to find out for certain, and I took it.

"Hester, have you got a date for the Kickoff Ball?" I asked.

The event in question was to mark the eve of actual ground-breaking for the Mackerel Plaza, early in March. So far municipal matters had come without my making an inch of private progress! I had been promised another fresh spade by Centapong's Hardware to turn over the first shovelful of earth.

Hester shook her head over the needle-point she had taken up in her favorite chair in the bay window that gave the living room its spacious charm. "No, I haven't. Too busy preparing for it to think about it, I guess," she answered with a laugh.

I stood at the piano ticking off a few bass notes with one finger. "Would you care to go with me?"

Hester looked up from her sampler, which was a representation of Rossetti's Blessed Damozel, shown leaning from the gold bar of Heaven with three lillies in her hand and seven stars in her hair.

"Aren't you going with Molly?"

"Oh, now, Hester, stop this foolishness. You know damn well I can't be seen in public with another woman until this blows over."

"What am I?"

"That's different. You're the housekeeper."

It may have been the wrong thing to say to make the test acid, or the right. I would know in a second. Hester bent over her hoop again and for a time there was no sound except that of punctured cloth and the dry rasp, curiously agreeable, of yarn being drawn through it.

"No, Andrew, I don't think so," she said at last.

"Why not?"

"The circumstances. It would be awkward, as you say.

Even this way. Thank you just the same though. It was sweet of you."

I was waiting for Molly when she arrived for work the next morning. I was sweeping paper clips from the front office desk into my palm, like bread crumbs, and dropping them into their proper tray.

"How's Todarescu's *Weltschmerz*?" I asked.

"All right I guess. I don't know."

"I've had it myself lately. All in through here."

"Well, what is it? I can always tell when you've got something to fire. You wait a minute before letting go — like hug it a minute. It's a female trait, so don't be proud of it," she said. "O.K., let's have it."

"*Well*," I said, wheeling around, "I took your advice, and I hope you enjoy hearing how far off the mark you were."

"What advice?"

"I acted on your theory. That Hester's got her cap set for me. I asked her for a date and she turned me down."

Molly turned from the rack on which she was hanging her hat. "Date for what?" she asked.

"The Kickoff Ball."

"Well, I like that," she said rather crisply.

"What difference would it have made? I'm not going with *you*," I answered in kind, nettled by the shift in grievance from myself to her. "Does that side of it mean more to you than the fact that I've made a horse's ass out of myself?"

In the strain and confusion of leading a double life I sometimes forgot where I was trying to tear myself down and where build myself up, and now I had blurted out in Molly's presence an expression I had been trying to get up the courage to use in Hester's.

138

"*Well!*" she said, shocked. "I must say that's a fine way to greet me."

"I'm sorry." I circled the room, grinding a fist into my palm. "She's winning. She's dividing and conquering. She's winning."

"Oh, stop chittering like a ninny and tell me what happened. I forgive you. But don't ever use that expression to me again. I hate it."

"So do I!" I said, spreading my hands at the wonder of it. "Happened? I've told you what happened. I asked to take her to the Plaza Ball and she turned me down. Cold. So much for your hypothesis."

Molly pondered intently the blotter pad on her desk.

"So she's trying to keep you guessing."

"You mean women are complicated? Yeah, splain dat to me, Kingfish, splain dat to me."

"You needn't get sarcastic. What's more natural, after she's been wearing her heart on her sleeve, than quickly to cover it up?"

"*Nolo contendere,*" I said, throwing up my hands, and walked into my office. "I do not contend." I had my hand on the doorknob when she said:

"Wait. There's something a lot more serious than this."

"What?"

She seemed suddenly to change her mind with a vague sign of dread. "Not now. I'm hoping it's a false alarm. I won't burden you with it till I'm sure it isn't."

I went to work, or tried to. I was doing a series of sermons based on the seven letters which the Voice instructed the author of Revelation to write to the seven churches in Asia Minor, each dealing with one of the faults or virtues common to human nature, then as now. I had preached four and just finished the one on Sardis, with Philadelphia and

Laodicea still to come. "And unto the angel of the church in Sardis write . . . I know thy works, that thou hast a name that thou livest, and art dead." Sardis represented defection from an ideal, wilted spirit. I was reading over what I had written when I was struck by something peculiar in the spelling of Sardis. I went up to Molly's desk.

"I notice you keep spelling this 'Sardi's,'" I said, showing her a passage where she had written, "'Thou hast a few names even in Sardi's which have not defiled their garments; and they shall walk with me in white.' I don't care so much about the sermon script, but I hope you didn't give the text to the printer that way? You might as well say Toots Shor's."

"I'll phone him and catch it," she said.

I smiled. "It's not hard to see where your mind is. Do you wish you were back there now, in all that? We'll go to Sardi's, you and I, the minute all this is cleared up, and we're squared away, the two of us. I can see us there now. Hot *cannelloni*, steak with sauce béarnaise, tossed salad and cherries jubilee. That about do it, sweets?"

"Well, we'll see."

"What are you typing?"

"Eulogies of your wife," she said. "For the souvenir booklet. Was she really so patient and understanding?"

"We could all learn a lesson from her."

Molly turned on the swivel chair to face me.

"There's gossip going around about you. In fact, scandal."

I stooped to pick up a match from the floor and drop it into a wastebasket. I hooked a rumpled rug to rights with my heel.

"Oh? Of what nature?" I asked. "What do they say about me?"

140

"That you were seen going into the Coker with a woman."

"Who told you this?" I demanded.

"They didn't tell me — they told Mother. One of those well-meaning friends who just hate to do this but feel it their Duty, you know? And Mother thought I should know."

I crossed to the front window, out of which I stood gazing into the street.

"Did she say who the woman was that I was seen with? Do they tell that part of it?"

"Evidently not. Whoever it was saw you go in apparently knew you but not me."

I asked the question that seemed to me logically next in line, at least from my point of view, and I made no effort to repress the rather sardonic smile that twisted across my lips as I did so. "And you, what are you saying in reply? Will you stick by me? Tell them you refuse to believe such a thing about me?"

"I told Mother that I was not interested in the talk of idle gossips."

"Idle! They seem to be working twenty-four hours a day at it."

Neither of us spoke for a few moments. Then I heaved a great sigh.

"Oh, if Ida May were only alive! *She'd* straighten this mess out in short order, believe you me."

Molly nodded, glancing at her day's chore, the mound of encomium still to be transcribed. "I can well believe it," she said dryly. Then: "If she were alive there'd be nothing *to* straighten out. Maybe you wish that too."

"What puzzles me is, how do they know about 'us,' that they feel there's any occasion to protect you about me? I thought we've been doing a pretty good job of keeping it under the bush." Something in the way she averted her eyes made me ask: "Is it your mother maybe who's talked? And the people she's told have blabbed it around?"

"Oh, Andrew," Molly answered restively, "what if she did? Isn't Mother entitled to bosom friends just like the rest of us?"

It was soon enough that Tabitha Twitchet descended in person about this matter. She had often promised to call at the parsonage to pay her respects, and she called that very evening, if not especially to pay her respects. When she did, it was to find me — in words I would not have chosen to describe the circumstances under which I was next fated to be discovered, or dreamed would be applicable — "shaking a leg with a hot patootie."

Eleven

AFTER dinner Hester pushed aside a few living-room chairs and rolled back the rug.

"Well, if you're game to help me brush up, maybe I'll reconsider about the date. What I was really afraid of was how I'd look out there on the floor after so long. Maybe we could both do with a little polishing up. What do you think?"

Mackerel did not know what to think. "You mean dance?"

"Yes. You'll find me rusty, but if you insist . . ."

Mackerel's own dancing could not be described as rusty so much as nonexistent. He watched Hester select and launch a phonograph record, and presently he was waltzing her around the room to the strains of "Jealousy," which will be remembered as a well-known tango of its era. She had on a white polka dot blouse with a starched bow, whose corners scratched the base of his neck agreeably. Instead of wearing her hair in one knot in back, she wore it in two at the sides, like earphones, with bangs in front. She had a perfume rather subtler than the nasal flavors that had visited Mackerel hitherto, but which in the exertions of dancing soon suffused his brain in a delicate mist. When a tangle in their maneuvers sent them against a table edge they both laughed, and insisted on the blame. "My two left feet," he said. "Think I'd better keep off the dance floor."

Neither of us heard the doorbell. The first notice I had of a caller was a sharp rapping on the window, and when I disengaged Hester and parted the curtain, the shadowy figure of a woman on the porch, bent to the pane.

When I opened the door a familiar face appraised me between a fur cap and a muff held at chest level. It was Mrs. Tittlemouse come to tea — or Tabitha Twitchet, or whatever. The apparitions shifted and changed according to how the nose twitched or the mouth pursed at the moment, while also blending into one. I very nearly greeted her as Mrs. Tittlemouse before I caught myself and said, "Ah, Mrs. Calico! Do come in."

She was already in. "Good evening, Mr. Mackerel," she said. "What I have to say won't take long."

Her tone dispelled the image of any cozy tea, fostering instead that of a woolly one going about the business of maintaining standards among the forest people. I felt like a rabbit again, with the advance in illusion, this time, of having to reach up for the doorknob as I showed her into a small side room, where I received visitors come for religious instruction or to have their lives straightened out. She glanced back at Hester, who had shut off the phonograph and was replacing the record in its album sheath.

"I shall come straight to the point," she said when we were settled behind closed doors. She occupied a tall wingback from which her toes barely grazed the rug. She declined the offer to remove her coat, as though fearing its theft, contenting herself with loosening its top button and laying her muff aside. "Mr. Mackerel, it has come to my attention that you are leading a double life. While courting my daughter you've been carrying on with another woman

144

at a place which, out of delicacy, I shall simply call place X."

"Oh, I wouldn't say that," I answered.

"There's no use denying it. You have definitely been seen going into hotels with other women."

"Women?" I said, dismayed by the plural.

"Well, woman. The nature and number of your misdeeds are immaterial. One is as bad as a thousand. The fact that you could be guilty of such a thing puts you forever beyond the range of my hospitality. The point of my call is to say that you are no longer welcome at *Toits Rouges*, and to advise you never to try to set foot inside it again unless you are prepared to deal with the police."

This was the first inkling I had of her house's having a name, and the fact of a city street residence of normal size and circumstances possessing one was too much for me not to linger over.

"*Toits Rouges?*"

"My nest in Timble Street that you've abused, so named because of its red roofs. My second demand is the obvious one that you cease and desist from seeing my daughter, under pain of legal measures."

"What hotel did you hear it's rumored I'm alleged to have been seen going into?" I asked, piling on as many subjunctives as the sentence could hold without shattering its syntax. "Would you mind telling me that?"

Mrs. Calico shut her eyes and gripped the arm of a chair other than her own, as though she were careening steeply down a roller coaster and had become intoxicated with peril. "The Coker. I can scarcely say it." She caught her breath, and then gave way to a curiosity she could not repress. "Do you care to tell me who the woman is?"

May I never be one to slight the ideal of gallantry, but

145

I hoped this brought to an end the number of women on whose behalf I would be called upon to exercise it. Still, I found the moment too tantalizing not to explore a speculation or two.

"What if it were someone you knew?" I put to her. "Knew very well."

"What is the use of frittering our time over manifest folderol?"

"But what if you *did*? I mean the woman in a case like this is always the girl next door to somebody? What if it were the girl next door to you? To *Toits Rouges*?"

"I should move."

"What if it were Molly?"

Mrs. Calico gave a cluck of impatience and tilted up her palms in a manner that would have enabled me to play pat-a-cake with her if I were so minded. "Mr. Mackerel, let's not sit here bandying absurdities."

"What *if* it were, though? I'm only trying to get your psychology."

"It would kill me," she answered primly, as though the fact were a basis for pride, which perhaps it was.

"Well, I can't divulge who the woman is," I responded at last. "You understand that."

"Yes. You have at least that shred of decency. I suppose I wouldn't want to know anyway."

"No, you wouldn't want to know." I then asked, "Now, will you tell *me* something. Who is your informant?"

"I can't divulge that. So we're even," she answered, a little illogically I felt.

I nodded on receipt of this thought, rolling my underlip between thumb and forefinger. I took a turn about the room. We were silent, not because neither of us knew the point the discussion could be taken to have reached, but because we both knew very well.

"Suppose I don't do as you demand?" I asked. "I mean apart from all this business about calling the police. Suppose I refuse to stop seeing your daughter but assume that she's old enough to make up her own mind about this matter?"

"I have a lever." Mrs. Calico raised her hand in a gesture as if implying a literal implement which she was prepared to bring down on my head. "Molly defends you now but that's natural. She's partial and run down. Mr. Todarescu defends you too, to his credit."

"That type would. He's Bohemian, Mrs. Calico. I suppose you knew that."

"People can't help their nationality."

"That is true, but we must draw the line somewhere. Condoning hotel assignations indeed! It's part of the whole decay of moral standards that goes back to—Teddy Roosevelt would you say? We must have tea and chat of all these things. I didn't do it, so that's that, and now we must talk of what concerns us so much more deeply. Countenancing assignations, dear me, what are we coming to. Cream or lemon?"

"Neither, for I do not wish tea, nor, Mr. Mackerel, do I intend to be led astray by such hanky-panky."

"But if he justifies my conduct then I am shocked. It was Todarescu who told tales, I'll bet that's it! Ah, I can put it all together now. He saw me at the Coker—or saw somebody he mistook for me, rather—which isn't surprising because that is a natural kind of environment for him, since he's Bohemian, as I say. Or maybe one of his friends saw this person who looked like me. Then he reports it *but only as a humorous story.* He doesn't condemn it in the least! Will *we* talk about *him!*"

"Forget about Todarescu, and please stop trying to confuse me with this fiddle-faddle, now there's an end of it!" Mrs. Calico said. "Where were we? I was saying Molly defends you, as a woman would, for her taste is on trial. But I shan't sit idly by and see her ruin her life by an alliance with a — socialist! Scandal doesn't blow over like a storm, it blows up like a fire. And, sir, if necessary, I shall be among those passing it on."

For the moment I was flabbergasted. Then I understood. "Is that your lever?" I asked, genuinely aghast.

"She'll give up when it gets bad enough. If the only way I can save my daughter is to hurry matters along to that point, then so be it. I am fighting for my girl's life."

The woman's logic induced in me a feeling of nausea. At the same time I couldn't help admiring her strategy, and ironically appreciating her position. She could queer me in my own Ladies Aid. There was a petard on which I could be hoisted sky-high in my own congregation. Events made me remember Molly's visits to Mrs. Balsam and the premise that an astral hand was presiding over their crystallization. I shook off this tenth-rate speculation with a violent snort and returned to the main track of the discussion.

"But don't you see, Mrs. Calico, that adding to the scandal about me will only tar her with the same brush," I said.

Here Mrs. Calico paused and seemed to assess her man with a canny little smile that was not unkindly. "Well, you won't sit idly by and watch that happen. Not if I know you. You'll give her up yourself first. That shred of decency I mentioned a moment ago. Libertines are often not without it."

"Can I get you a drink?" I asked, dabbing my brow with a handkerchief and casting a wistful eye at the door beyond which my bottled supplies lay, and beyond which I could also hear a telephone dimly jangling and Hester's footsteps going to answer it.

"Drink, that's another habit you managed to keep from me. I'm sure you have pleasures enough to console you for the loss of my daughter." Mrs. Calico glanced meaningly at the door. "I didn't realize you danced. You like to shake a leg with a hot patootie now and then, do you?"

"Well, not very good at it, actually," I answered idiotically.

"No, thank you, no drink." That arrested my passage to the door. When I turned back, it was to discern in Mrs. Calico's mien a sudden radical change. She sat with head bowed, as under the weight of turpitudes now revealed. She shook her head and moaned softly. "Oh, what a blow," she said, weeping into a square of cambric. "What a blow I have received to my pride, my vanity, my very self-respect. To think my Molly could become a victim of a thing like this."

I recalled that one of the Beatrix Potter illustrations had been of Tabitha Twitchet, the cat, lamenting to Cousin Ribby the disappearance of her son Thomas. He had been missing for some hours. Cousin Ribby was trying to comfort her. I began a consolatory gesture here, but it was not one I could bring to intelligent fruition and it died in mid-air as I heard a rap on the door.

"It's Mrs. Comstock calling for a committee of church women," Hester said. "She says they want to see you as a delegation on something urgent. They'd like to come immediately if it's convenient. How's nine o'clock?"

I would throw them out on their ears on what Yeats has called "the pavements gray," following which there would be an impossible situation ending in a period of total amnesia, after which I would be found in like Nashville or Albuquerque, cadging nickels to put into the slot machine. I would be penniless, underweight, and suffering from consumption. It would serve them right.

"Tell them to come ahead," I said. "That will be all right."

I wound up my interview with Mrs. Calico, who rose, tucked her able hands into her muff and, her ultimatum quite deposited, took her leave with great dignity. Fifteen minutes later the other women arrived.

I fully expected to be cooked in more of the same and I was not disappointed, but I was not prepared for the direction from which the women who came at nine approached the matter. They were supposedly just members of People's Liberal, but I noticed that they were all also members of the Women's Plaza Committee, and they lost no time in saying they had come to speak frankly of something that was embarrassing both to them and to the men who had their shoulders to the wheel on the riverfront project, namely the fact that I had, among a few chosen intimates and then more publicly, been "running down" the Mackerel Plaza. This was about to become a critical bone of contention, but Mackerel would not be less than honest. He told them candidly that his objections were not to the memorial as such but to the commercial hay being made of it. "It's no longer a monument, it's a lot of contracts!" I cried. "Fat ones!"

This was hardly the tone to take to the delegation's spokeswoman, Mrs. Sponsible. She was normally a nice enough sort, but she was also wife of the owner of the excavating firm whose bulldozers stood ready to carry on from Mackerel's inaugural ceremonial shovelful. Neither was it the thing to say to Mrs. Cool-Paintey, the mayor's sister. (Here I saw that the callers were all also the wives of interested businessmen.) She had means, of course, being old Meesum's daughter. She had been educated in the best schools and as a result now said "Chewsday" for Tuesday and "jew" for due. Mrs. Sponsible had for years tried to copy her but it was no use; she still said "Tuesday" and "due" hopelessly clearly.

"If your husbands have a bone to pick with me, why don't they call on me in person?" I said. "Or do they feel they can catch more flies with honey? I must say I've seldom seen a better turned out group of ladies. Heh-heh-heh."

"We're here for other reasons than your knocking the Plaza," said a woman named Mrs. Comstock, Charlie Comstock's wife.

"Now, now, Lily," said a woman named Mrs. Krakauer.

"Yes, let's get the first point cleared up first — his criticisms of the Plaza," said Mrs. Sponsible with flustered haste. There was a sense of something they dreaded getting to in the same degree that they itched to do so.

"All right." Mrs. Cool-Paintey screwed about in her chair the more directly to face me. "We feel an explanation is jew us."

"It is jew you and it has been given you, in a nutshell," I replied. "What began as a well-meaning gesture on Mr. Turnbull's part has been parlayed into a gravy train of the most blatant sort by a pack of businessmen."

"Are you against business then, Mr. Mackerel?"

"Oh, my dear Mrs. Cool-Paintey."

Mrs. Sponsible entered the discussion.

"The thing we feel," she said, pondering the toe of a waggled foot with that studious attention women can give their shoes under apparently any circumstances, "is that you might desist, if only for your wife's sake."

"She would have gone into the city hall and turned out the money changers long ago," I said, and she would. I know that woman.

Watch it, Hester's warning glance told me from the corner chair. The women had asked her to stay and sit in as an advisory member of the Plaza Committee, and I had certainly not demurred. Something warned me from another quarter too. I had recently written in a chapter of *Maturity Comes of Age*, "He who flies in the face of a myth does so at his peril. The tribe will give him short shrift, especially after the myth has got its roots deep in the cash fabric of society." And sure enough, Mrs. Comstock was saying, "Well, *somebody* has to get the contracts to build the monuments. And anyhow, Ida May deserves a whole big civic thing like this. I don't care. She was a saint."

"She was not," I said, sick of this fudge.

"She was too."

"She was not."

"Perhaps," interpolated Mrs. Krakauer, a peacemaker, "the truth lies somewhere in between."

"I knew her," said Mrs. Comstock, ignoring this. "Most of us did. And most of us feel that her death was a fitting end to her life. A heroic sacrifice."

This was the specific myth. Was this the moment to spike that old windbag Turnbull's legend? To rise and say, "Ladies and gentlemen, she did not jump — she fell in." I had confided the facts to Hester and to no other; it was the secret we shared. If she had known what was brewing in all this she had certainly given no sign. Turnbull was an old fool, but it nonetheless brought to three the number of persons on whose behalf I was being called upon to exercise grace.

"I know what you mean, Mrs. Comstock," I said, prudently taking in a little sail, "but I lived with her, and if I told you as her husband that she was a saint you'd probably smile. I don't want her canonized! I don't want her dehumanized — oh, yes, that's what's happening — I want to remember her as she *was*. I can't even recall what her voice sounded like for all this yacketing oratory. Let's have some honesty, please! Ida May was a brilliant woman, but she had her emotional limitations."

Mrs. Comstock rose stiffly. "Mr. Mackerel, I'll thank you to respect the honored dead of this city!" she said.

"And I'll thank you to use a little intelligence, if I am not asking the impossible," I said, getting to my own feet. "Ida May was a creative person and they are at the farthest possible remove from saints — as I was at pains to explain in last Sunday's sermon, and as you would remember if you hadn't been asleep."

"I was awake."

"You were asleep."

There was another nervous stir from Mrs. Krakauer who appeared about to repeat that the truth probably lay somewhere in between. But Mrs. Cool-Paintey spoke first. She had majored in psychology, and it was out of her wide knowledge in that subject that she was constrained to say:

"I wonder if I may go so far as to detect a note of professional jealousy in Mr. Mackerel's protests. He's a creative person himself, and the one thing they cannot stand is living under the shadow of another, more famous . . ."

This brought an audible laugh from Hester's corner.

"I think you're wide of the mark there, Mrs. Cool-Paintey.

If I may be permitted to say a word here." Smiling nods told her to go right ahead. "Andrew was always the soul of kindness toward my sister. I never heard him raise his voice to her the way he is to you tonight. They never quarreled."

"That's not a good sign to me," said Mrs. Sponsible, in about the voice level of soliloquy.

"Oh, but we did," I differed. "We did quarrel, often very bitterly. Mrs. Sponsible is quite right there. People must agree, to quarrel, as the Frenchman said."

Hester now got to her own feet. "Why don't I make us some tea?" she said.

An excellent idea. Tea had the effect of loosening everyone's tongue, but on a more convivial level, and for a moment it seemed as if the danger of serious eruption had passed. The day might very well have been saved had not an incident occurred in connection with it that angered the women conclusively and drew the fire they had been holding back. What happened was this.

I had braced myself for their arrival with a stiff drink, and now felt the need for another. Hester's return with the tea gave me an idea. As she poured it, I was struck with its resemblance in color to bourbon; in cups, the two fluids would be indistinguishable. If I could manage to fill one with whiskey I could sit there and sip it while the ladies did their tea and no one would be the wiser.

I drifted to the sideboard just inside the adjacent dining room where she was pouring and offered to finish that while she went back to the kitchen for some Vienna fingers she announced having discovered. Before going, she threw me a last cautionary whisper about my remarks. "Don't be an imbecile, you idiot!" she said.

"*Don't nag*," I whispered as she made off.

Turning my back as completely as possible to the

living room, I stooped and conjured a bottle of Old Fitzgerald from behind a door of the sideboard cabinet and filled one of the cups with it. I whipped the bottle back out of sight and set the cup on a saucer — or rather on one of the plates Hester had got out to accommodate the cookies we were going to have. So far so good. But here a crimp developed. Just then Hester returned from the kitchen bearing a tray on which were sugar and cream and the promised Vienna fingers, and as one the women rose with a babel of protest about being able to fend for themselves and of not having meant anybody to go to all that trouble. In a twinkling they were all elbowing about the sideboard, and in the ensuing confusion I lost complete track of the cup with the bourbon in it.

In another trice they were all seated in the living room chatting again. To this extent the tea had been a happy idea. I picked up the last remaining cup and carried it to my chair, not daring to look and see what it was, much less taste it. I preferred to be in doubt. They were talking about a man in an upstate city who had murdered his wife, three children, and mother-in-law. "When a thing like that happens," Mrs. Cool-Paintey explained, "it shows that subconsciously that was what they wanted to do." I held the ear of my cup firmly in my fingers, without touching the cup proper for fear of finding it hot. My eye met Mrs. Sponsible's across the room and I thrust out my pinkie, smiling innocently. She lifted her cup, drank, and went on in a normal way. So it wasn't she who had drawn the whiskey. That was one accounted for. My gaze went down and in that second I detected a pale smudge on the side of my cup, which could only be the cream filling of the Vienna finger melting against it. I raised the cup to my lips, shutting my eyes. The beverage in it was tea

I ran my eye in panic around the jabbering circle. Who had the whiskey? It was like Russian roulette. Six cups like six chambers in a pistol, one with the bullet. Mrs. Sponsible and I were ruled out. That left Mrs. Comstock, Mrs. Cool-Paintey, Mrs. Krakauer and, of course, Hester. Maybe Hester had drawn it. Dear God, let her be the one. Then she drank and took a nibble of her cookie — dashing that possibility.

I now pinned my hopes on Mrs. Krakauer. She was a slight, gentle woman with a sadly tolerant nature. By all means it must be she . . . I wiped my brow. Russian roulette with teacups. Add to which the grim detail that the whiskey might now have cream and sugar in it. I closed my eyes and waited.

"Perhaps some arrangement can be worked out satisfactory to both Mr. Mackerel and the business element," Mrs. Comstock was saying. "I mean get the fountain and the Plaza *dissociated* from the shopping center. See to it that it doesn't get to have her name, even unofficially. What would Mr. Mackerel think of that?"

I nodded, my eyes closed. "Fine."

"I mean if we all try to be reasonable, one give a little here, the other give a little there, why, I'm sure the differences can be ironed out. So I move a meeting with the Chamber of Commerce, say, which Mr. Mackerel will attend and air his views."

There was a violent spluttering followed by severe and prolonged coughing. It was Mrs. Cool-Paintey. She had taken a gulp large enough to have choked her, with enough left over to be liberally spraying the woman seated next to her, which happened to be Mrs. Comstock. "*What* in the *world?*" When Mackerel could bring himself to look it was to find the two women sitting face to face wiping one another's dress fronts with their handkerchiefs. The scene had the exotic gravity of some obscure rite from the comprehension of which all those not directly engaged in it were barred, even those witnessing it at first hand.

"That's not *tea*," Mrs. Cool-Paintey wheezed, when she could speak at all.

"I'll say it isn't!" said Mrs. Comstock, sniffing. This was the woman whose husband was the reformed alcoholic, and whose horror of the very word was sufficient to make her turn and regard Mackerel with speculative interest; with new eyes, as the phrase goes. Mackerel did something he knew he shouldn't have but which he was powerless to restrain. He smiled. He lowered his head and shook it, setting his plate and cup down. "I'm sorry," he said, laughing now. "I'm terribly sorry."

"Maybe someone can tell me what this is all about," Mrs. Cool-Paintey gasped in a piping whisper. Evidently some of it had gone down her Sunday throat.

Mrs. Comstock could tell her. Half a lifetime of drinks sneaked behind her back and of bottles routed from extraordinary hiding places equipped her to recognize the true boozer at a glance.

"It's whiskey," she said. "The very idea. Sneaking it into teacups yet, so we wouldn't know. He just had to have one. He couldn't wait. Well, the Lord took care of that little trick, didn't he, *Reverend* Mackerel? I'd never have believed it, but now I've seen it. The thing is, secret drinkers can sometimes go on for years unsuspected. Now it's out. We've seen it with our own eyes. And having seen that, maybe we can believe all the other we've been hearing too."

"What other?" Hester demanded.

"Women."

"In hotel rooms," Mrs. Cool-Paintey wheezed, and began

157

to cough again. She and Mrs. Comstock were still wiping away at one another's fronts. They looked very sisterly. The scene was too grotesque for me to feel it could possibly be the setting for anything sinister, or to pose any serious threat, and so when Hester pressed on with "What hotel?" I replied with ironic flippancy, "The Coker."

"Ah, so you admit it's true," said Mrs. Sponsible.

"It's what I've heard said," I answered listlessly.

"I don't believe it," Hester said, her eyes flashing. She was on her feet. "I will not have such things being said in my house! You ought to be ashamed. Idle gossips!"

"Idle, they work at it twenty-four hours a day," said I, who felt the witticism worth a second use.

Mrs. Comstock rose and pushed Hester. "Don't you call me that. I never speak without reason. We haven't passed a word of this on — we've only *heard* it. I've had an open mind — up to now."

"Just because you can believe he drinks, you believe it all? But he doesn't. Oh, one or two now and then, sure, but not on the scale you think. Could I live with him day in and day out and not know it?"

"Yes," Mrs. Comstock answered with simple authority. She turned with a kind of ambiguous outrage to the circle as Hester stamped her foot, burst into tears and went upstairs. "Send them away and come to bed," Hester said as she hurried off, completing the sense, which I had been increasingly experiencing, that I was in a madhouse.

"You see what you've done?" I said to the women.

Mrs. Cool-Paintey rose. Her voice was still a little rickety. "Shall we go? I think we've heard enough. Enough for our visit to have served its purpose, albeit a sad one."

There was a sorrowful sigh from Mrs. Krakauer. She was inclined by nature to charity, but she was far too buffaloed by words like "albeit" to press for it now. She followed the rest into the vestibule, where they crowded into the closet for their coats like sheep without a shepherd. I went to help them.

It was then, as I approached the group, that I heard Mrs. Sponsible say something *sotto voce* that I couldn't catch clearly but that sounded like, "What makes me feel a fool is all the matchmaking we've been doing."

"Matchmaking?" I said, wedging my way through them into the closet.

They looked embarrassed, and glared at one another. "Oh, well, let's not go into that," said Mrs. Krakauer, dropping her eyes.

My curiosity was too keen to stem at this point. Ducking in among the coats, I said, "Am I to understand that you feel the parsonage should have a mistress? Shall we put it that way?"

Mrs. Krakauer murmured another demurrer and was agreed with by one or two others. "All right," I said, "I won't give you these coats till you tell me." I had them all over my arms, four of them, worth thousands of dollars, if one included Mrs. Sponsible's and Mrs. Cool-Paintey's furs. "Just try to get them."

"We can get a writ," Mrs. Sponsible said. "We'll get them back."

"If you insist on acting like children," I said.

Mrs. Cool-Paintey relented — if it was relenting and not turning the subject to punitive account. She was the injured one, after all, and I could see her making it as part of my chastisement that I would know in full the womanly solicitudes from which I was to be exiled.

"Naturally we feel a parsonage should have a mistress —" she began.

"But not that a parson should. Heh-heh-heh," I put in. "But go on."

"— and a man a wife. We've taken a kind of, well, interest in you, yes. Up to now."

"But wouldn't you feel that — I mean under the circumstances — ?" I began haltingly.

"It's been a year now, or soon will be," one of the others said, "and that's enough."

I picked the coats from my arms and helped them into them one by one.

"Whom did you have in mind, if I may ask. I gather from all this huggermugger that you've had specific ideas?" I said.

"Oh, well, now I think this is really . . ." Mrs. Krakauer murmured.

"There's no point in being coy about it at this stage," I said. "A minister is public property, I suppose, so you need have no feeling about making his business yours. Go on, tell me. I'm curious."

They looked at one another, each declining the role of ultimate spokesman, but itching to hear another undertake it. Mrs. Comstock spoke up.

"He's right. It can't do any harm now — now that it can't do any good either," she said. They raised their eyes to the ceiling, where Hester's footsteps could be heard going from one room to another upstairs. Mrs. Comstock lowered her voice. "We all like that secretary of yours. She's a new member, but she's fit in so beautifully in both the Players and on committee — and incidentally she regretted she couldn't make it tonight. We think she's a jewel." Mrs. Comstock hunched her shoulders and exhaled sharply. "But what's the use talking about it? The Coker! She couldn't possibly have anything to do with you now."

Twelve

I SAT on the floor with my eye to the keyhole, looking into the vestibule where Hester was admitting Molly. I was secreted in the room in which I had received Mrs. Calico, the door of which (closed now, of course) commanded a view across the entrance hall into the living room. Molly had done her "work" at home that day and was delivering the "finished" typescripts to the rectory. Both women thought I was out, a belief of which I was taking advantage by doing a little much-needed eavesdropping. Rather at sea as to both women, I thought that if I could overhear them talking about me, aspects of my worth, or whatever, I might obtain some clue as to how I stood and how I might best act in the widening crisis. So I sat squinting through the keyhole with a hardboiled egg in one hand and a glass of beer in the other, which was proof enough of herd tyrannies.

Hester went by my line of vision to answer the door, humming "The Spanish Cavalier." I took a quick pull on the cold beer and a bite of the egg, snapping my teeth around it and emitting a low growl. The women greeted one another by first names.

"He's at that meeting in the city hall," Hester explained. "With the Chamber of Commerce."

"Oh, yes. Quite a mess all around."

"House is a mess too." Hester laughed apologetically. "I haven't had a minute all day. Hope you won't think I'm a sloppy housekeeper."

Molly started into the living room, but in the doorway to it she froze in her tracks. And my heart froze at the realization of what lay in her path.

Articles of my clothing were strewn everywhere. My coat lay on a chair, vest on another. My tie was on the piano, an end of it dangling into the works. My hat was hung on an ornamental metal spear on which the window drapes were hooked back. There would be cigarette dung on the carpets and a shoe, as I remembered it, kicked into a corner. A sticky Old-fashioned glass stood on a stack of sheet music, leaving its rings as planned.

Molly let out such a gasp she could only go on and say, "My God! Is he always like this?"

Hester laughed charitably. "Men are all alike. Each with his own individual quirks and crotchets to be put up with. Place does look like a cyclone struck it though, doesn't it?" She plucked a copy of *Time* hospitably from under Molly as Molly sat down.

"There isn't much to discuss in these." Molly flourished some manuscript and set it on a table. "A couple of spots where I couldn't make out changes he penciled in. One place I don't know whether he means the American Army is woefully uninformed or woefully uniformed. You don't know when he'll be back?"

"He's not the soul of punctuality." Hester was down on one knee digging the other shoe out from under an ottoman with patient grunts. She heaved a sigh as she rose and drew a hand across her brow. Really! I thought, setting my repast aside. It was Molly I moved to keep in view through

162

the keyhole, getting on all fours to do so. Molly watched Hester gather up the sea-wrack mentioned, plus a pair of socks I had discarded in an ashtray. I had gone too far. My one chance now was that, like the Russian people for whose benefit political confessions are exaggerated in hopes that they will recognize the burlesque, Molly would see this was not like me, and smile.

"He throws his coat on the office desk now and again," Molly observed to herself. "It's a good thing he doesn't undress there."

"Yes, it is." Hester stood picking the knot out of the tie. She paused to wipe a stain from the piano top with the hem of her apron. She started out of the room with her arms full and my hat on her head.

"Wait." Molly turned in her chair. "The drinking. Had you no inkling of that?"

I withdrew my eye from the keyhole and put my ear to it.

"It's not up to us to judge," Hester said. "So you've heard about that too? Well, don't believe all you hear, and remember that alcohol is a refuge which people like that seek from their problems, which God knows Andrew has plenty of."

"Yes. And now Knopf rejecting his book."

"He did? Oh, dear." Hester appraised the sea-wrack with new eyes; almost with Molly's. I wagged my hind-end to point up the infamy of events, the whole human betrayal, and howled like the dog I was reduced to, mentally. "What did Knopf say?"

"Knopf seems to think it's a collection of sermons, or rather Andrew seems to forget that it is. Knopf wrote a very cute letter saying it's the same with every kind of collection, even short stories — you're better off taking one up than getting one out. Unless you're Norman Vincent Peale."

I finished the egg and beer and left. I slid open a window

and backed out onto the porch, seething. This was no condition in which to go to the meeting, but there was no time to cool off; I was due there at eight and it was twenty to now. Nor was my frame of mind improved by the notice I read on the bulletin board in front of the city hall. It was typewritten on official mayoralty stationery and read, more or less in the form of a proclamation:

Effective tomorrow, there will be a tradition of dropping a penny into the wishing well on the common across the street and making a wish in memory of Ida May Mackerel, this wish to be in keeping with her known ideals. This charming custom will itself be in accord with an observation once made by Mrs. Mackerel herself, who according to legend observed on that very spot that if there were more well wishers (that is, people wishing others well) the world would be more well and less sick than it is now. The old wishing well will be regularly cleaned out and the proceeds to go for maintenance of the fountain in her name to be erected soon.

My teeth aching, I went on in.

The meeting was to be held in the council room on the third floor, and on the way to it I passed the office on the second where I had met Molly. I paused in the corridor and looked into the darkened room through the glass-topped door. I stood there letting melancholy roll over me like a breaker. I tried the knob, expecting to find the door closed, but it was open. There being nobody in sight I slipped in and shut the door behind me.

In the faint light falling in from the end of the corridor I could see the desk where I had caught sight of the Parrington book, her old chair, the bench on which I had first awaited her. Being a few minutes early, I stretched out on it, with my feet on the wooden arm. It was a deacon's bench, of course, a period piece. There'll always be a New England!

Distantly I could hear arriving footsteps, a muffled laugh; overhead, vague voices. It was peaceful in here. I closed my eyes. I fished two pennies out of my pocket and laid one on each eye. Now it was over. Now I was dead and done with it. The farce was played out.

I thought of Knopf, not without a certain compassion. He was apparently no longer to be taken seriously as a publisher. They would soon be taking up a collection for him at this rate.

I appreciate your emphasis on the role of the myth in society, he had further written, *but cannot feel it is the all-devouring Moloch you make it out, nor that martyrs must still be regularly popped into its mouth to keep it happy. Perhaps you have some private, emotional reason for your stress of this point? I guess what I am trying to say is that you have overstated the case. You have driven the nail clear through the plank and out the other side . . .*

Can't feel it, Knopf? Can't feel the myth is society's universal dragon-pet who must be fed its regular diet of victims? Well, the footsteps are gathering overhead this minute, for the sacrifice, Knopf. It is the cabal convening, the conservative interests in full cry for the blood of one who dared to make a stand against them. Come along, Knopf, and we will see how the tribe operates in this supposedly sophisticated community along the eastern seaboard in the second half of the so-called twentieth century (as the old lady said). The ram about to be led to the slaughter is known to you slightly; you have had correspondence with him. He has kicked against the pricks, and now it is turnabout: they will kick against him. Arise, Knopf, let us go hence.

The council chamber is a room forty feet wide, in which

the mayor and ten selectmen hold their official sessions. Mayor Junior was to have charge of proceedings tonight and already sat at the head of the long conference table in one of those black, high-backed leather swivel chairs, studded with buttons like navels, nursing a gavel. Strewn at his feet were members of the Chamber of Commerce and the businessmen interested in the Plaza, categories which greatly blended. Along one end of the room is a visitors' gallery with about forty or fifty seats. A handful of them were occupied by slouching spectators, who twitched tentatively when I strode in. Turnbull was among them, and likewise Comstock, covering the meeting for the *Globe*.

"Oh, Andy," said Mayor Junior, rising to shake my hand. "I guess you know everybody." I nodded crisply, declining his outslung arm, determined to have no soft soap but a clean fight. They would not embrace me in order to crush me. I sat down at the table behind a name plate which read "Melvin Pryzalski."

"I think we can make this brief and friendly," the mayor began. "My friend Andy here has taken exception — perfectly within his democratic right — to some aspects of the Plaza thing. We know what some of them are, but in case he has others, let's hear him out so we can whomp out a little agreement among us that will be satisfactory to all and leave no hard feelings with anybody. The main thing will be to separate the esplanade from the shopping center, to which I think we can all agree. However, if Andy — I'm sure he's that to all of us — has something further, why we can add that to the little agreement I've drawn up, sign it and get home in time to hear Ed Murrow, eh, fellows? He's got Gina Lollobrigida on tonight."

I saw what I was up against. The mayor was a numskull apparently without any sense of his role as a diehard reactionary. The smiles of the rest indicated a conciliatory attitude that also augured poorly for an open conflict, with battle lines clearly drawn and blood spilt where it must. "We'll do anything you want," Sponsible was saying, "within reason." Good Lord! Evidently I must instruct them in the rudiments of their own skulduggery if this thing was to be guided on classic lines, or anything like them. Very well, I would needle them into a proper assumption of their parts.

"Not so fast, boys," I said, rising. "Let's not muddle the issues with pretended sweetness and light. Society as it is constituted leaves no room for compromise with those playing the power game and those daring to say them nay. The struggle between them is total, and admits of only one result — a fight to the finish."

They exchanged baffled looks and bewildered shrugs. Their comprehension of the factors involved was more elementary than I had imagined. I must begin with the simplest fundamentals.

"Social elements thus in opposition," I continued, "enact dramatico-metaphoric embodiments of tribal drives which are at the same time religious in nature. When the economic interests of those in power — now get this — when they congeal with their emotional ones, we have the complete myth in a given culture. This myth operates on all levels and against all opposition, because that opposition challenges both the pocketbook and the prejudice. The Mackerel Plaza is an example of such a myth in our time and in our place because it satisfies all those requirements. It unites your material with your instinctual interests, and having embraced it as sacrosanct, you will defend it with every resource at your command."

"We will?" the mayor said, screwing his face up.

I nodded. "You will stop at nothing. It is an inevitable

167

part of the power pattern." I paused. "Are there any more questions?"

The mayor looked around at his colleagues again for help. He was clearly out of his depth. A man on his right spoke up.

"But we just said we're perfectly willing to sit down with you and —"

"Ah, ah. Cards on the table, gentlemen, please. We dispense with token displays of amity and strike straight for the essentials. No mealy-mouthed equivocation and transparent subterfuge."

A man whom I recognized as Scanlon the paving contractor scratched his head.

"But, gee, we think you're a nice guy and . . ."

"It's no use. Compromise is impossible. It's you against me. One of us must go down in defeat. Already the fire crackles and the idol yawns, but I warn you, gentlemen. Truth crushed to earth will rise again, and the blood of the martyrs is the seed of the church!"

The mayor crooked his finger at his neighbor and bent his head toward him. Others did the same, frowning in frank perplexity and whispering together. A thin man sitting all alone at the end of the table turned a pair of sad, chocolate eyes on me and said, "You don't have to bully us. We're only doing our best."

"I'm not trying to bully you," I said. "I'm only trying to bring to a head the inevitable. There's no point in wasting time in amenities that are doomed to failure. Let's have done with the politics and declare the war!"

He lowered his eyes meekly and resumed picking at a crack in the veneer of the table top. It was Kerfoot, the electrical engineer and lickspittle, who had been present at the luncheon where all this had been hatched. Others seemed equally cowed. Presently he turned to old Meesum on his right and

168

some distance down the table. Meesum had been making circles on a pad with the expression of a man who resents being smoked out. Finally he dropped his pencil and leaned toward a group which included his mayor son. The buzz of voices rose till it was like a beehive.

Are you watching, Knopf? Are you getting all this? They have their heads together, and their voices as they speak are as the sound of knives being whetted, and as wind in savage grass.

"Are there any other questions?" I asked. "Before we get on with it?"

A stocky man in a gray suit got up. It was Sponsible, the head of the excavating firm. He was a self-made man in the sense that he had himself once driven the bulldozers now operated for him by others. He had just returned from a sunny two weeks in Florida, and his face looked like a burnt pan. There are people whose very appearance bespeaks their line of work, and there was about Hugh Sponsible's knobbed hands and his figure and even his voice a loose, hard, easy-rattling something that seemed to say we are not dust but gravel.

"You say we're supposed to railroad you on all them levels."

"That is correct."

"Just how do we go about doing this? Could you give us a few pointers?"

"Certainly. You will do it first through your ownership of the mass media: the press, radio and television, the mouths of old women. You will engage in attacks both on my intellectual position and my character. The latter has already begun. All this will be aimed toward your final coup — the attempted removal of my means of livelihood."

Sponsible nodded, stroking his nose, in perfect willingness

to accept instruction in his role as oppressor but still retaining certain doubts to be aired.

"Can't we live and let live?"

"No. That is against your nature. Individually, yes; collectively, no. There your instinct is to protect the cash nexus of society, as Karl Marx has called it."

Sponsible sat down and a hand went up at the other end of the table.

"Yes?" I said. It was Scanlon again.

"I'm a simple man without much knowledge of these things, so I'll have to follow the leadership of others," he said. "But about this myth business. I don't quite get that. How we use that to make a buck and so on. Could you explain that a little more?"

"I'm glad you asked that question," I said. Now we were coming to grips. "I'll give you an example of how you're working it. The first thing you, the reigning oligarchy, do is popularize a utilizable figure, but in order to elevate it for the greatest number you vulgarize it. Just before coming here I read the announcement on the bulletin board about this wishing well twaddle." The mayor stirred in his chair and a small fidget ran along other parts of the table. "This is *real* mythology, boys."

"Why?" said the mayor.

"Why? Because Mrs. Mackerel had a mind like a steel trap, an antiseptic, sardonic, modern mind. One of often surgically cruel precision. She could never in all her born days have said a sappy, pappy, preposterous thing like that."

Wounded anger replaced the mayor's air of simple confusion.

"I don't understand what you mean," he said. "What's sappy about that story? I think it's nice."

"If you don't know, I can't explain it to you. Where did you hear such a thing?"

"Why, I found it in a publicity release. I . . . don't see our press agent here . . ."

"You see?" I shot at Sponsible. "Press agents making up little legends fit for mass consumption. And that 'effective tomorrow' bit. Who's gem was that?"

"Mine," said the mayor resentfully. "What's wrong with that? Doesn't every tradition have to get started *some*time?"

"That's right," I said with a smile. "Ida May used to say, 'One dreams of the goddess Fame and winds up with the bitch Publicity.' "

A red-faced man I didn't know shook his finger across the table at me. "I don't think she used language like that and I don't think you ought to use it here!" he said.

"And calling her cruel," Scanlon said to him.

"That story illustrates a fine little sentiment and I think it's true."

The hubbub grew in volume, supported by exchanged nods. The gallery loungers were now galvanized into quite erect positions. Charlie Comstock's pencil galloped. Turnbull kneaded his mustache excitedly. As Junior banged his gavel I surveyed the scene with an inward smile. The caldron was boiling briskly. Who could doubt my thesis now?

Junior was rapping for silence for his old pa, who had signaled for the floor. They were all glad to see the old fox rise and take it: he would represent them well.

"This memorial is close to the heart of all of us," he began, laying his hand on his heart, where his wallet palpably bulged, "and I am so glad to hear Mr. Mackerel speak of putting the cards on the table. But let's do one more thing. *Let's turn them face up.*" He paused to let this sink in, greeting it himself with a burst of unrequited laughter.

"Let's ask for his motives in all this. Let's ask whether he's opposed to just this bandwagon, this trough in which he says we've all got our snouts, or to *private profit as such*."

Swell.

"I'm opposed to cracking open to commercial exploitation the last smidgen of scenic beauty left in this damned town. You got your way by befuddling a philanthropist into parting with more then he intended."

"Where shall we expand then, man!"

"What do I care?"

"Do you realize how dense the population of this town is?"

"I have inklings," I said, looking him steadily in the eye.

"You quoted Karl Marx. Are you a Communist?"

All gall is divided into three parts, I have thought since. First there is the basic glandular structure from which the trait derives its name; second, the nervous make-up and shadings of temperament which result in the gift of aggression; and lastly a certain density of mind which blinds the character to the resentment he inspires in others. Meesum had all these requirements in an unabridged degree, and that was why he struck everybody, and not just me, as the brassiest man they ever met. One or two, including Sprackling the young lawyer who had slipped in late, laughed. Most of them, even those whom I had goaded into a sense of their function as oppressors, looked to me to answer this absurd question with a loud negative.

I was not going to let them off so easy. I must lure them on to a full measure of accusation, to drive home to them the depth of their complicity in this enterprise. Guilt by association turned around. They must see that they were equally yoked with their spokesman in a cabal against me.

172

"Well, the early Christians were Communists, weren't they?" I answered evasively. (They didn't have anything to share, but I must give Meesum enough rope.)

Meesum grasped his lapels firmly in both hands, and I remembered its having been said that he had once had ecclesiastical ambitions.

"Do you know how many sheep Abraham had?"

"Abraham who?"

"Abraham of old. How many cattle? How many acres of land? He was a very rich man."

"Not as a result of private initiative. I understood he got it all from God."

This was a barb that really went home. Nothing could more have incited Meesum, who had inherited everything he himself owned.

"I'm glad to hear you mention God," he said. "You do it little enough in church. You said once in a sermon that the common people must have loved gods, they made so many of them. Do you think that was respectful?"

"Of whom, Lincoln or God?"

Meesum raised and tightened his grip on his lapels, as though in his rage he had only himself to cling to for support. I suspected what was eating him especially these days. He had tried to settle the division, created in his mind by the conflicting genealogical societies as to his ancestry, by retaining a third, which claimed to have uncovered Moorish origins totally absent from the reports of the other two. This had unnerved him further and shortened his temper acutely.

"It is rumored that on Saturday nights you go about heckling street corner evangelists," he said. "Is that true?"

"I have often heckled them, yes."

"Is that conduct befitting a minister of the Gospel?"

"I feel it my duty to oppose vulgarity in any form. Such men are to religion what jingoism is to patriotism."

"Hear! hear!" shouted a voice in the gallery. It was a bull-necked man in a red mackinaw. "National sovereignty must go! Only world government will save us!"

Junior rapped him out of order, not, however, till he had let him finish his piece, to point up the type who might be expected to rally to my banner. Old Meesum improved the occasion by consulting some notes he had taken from his pocket. Evidently he had come prepared for this cross-questioning.

"You also once said — correct me if I misquote you — 'It is the final proof of God's omnipotence that he need not exist in order to save us.'" I acknowledged the accuracy of the quotation with a nod. "Doesn't that sound a lot like Voltaire?"

"Voltaire said something quite different. You're probably thinking of his aphorism, 'If there were no God, it would be necessary to invent him.' I go beyond that. I take the final step whereby theology, annihilating itself, sets religion free."

"Oh, you think you're smarter than Voltaire."

"Why, are you a fan of his?"

Meesum raised his cards above his head and slammed them down on the table. "I will not stand here and argue with a man who won't stick to the point!" he said, and sat down with almost as violent a contact with his chair as the cards had had with the table.

There was another silence. Mayor Junior looked miserably around. They looked at me with reproving, hangdog glances. The meeting seemed to have foundered. "Why didn't you bring all this up at the luncheon at the Stilton that time?" the mayor asked. "You were there."

"I didn't know at the time that it would take on this mythos-ethos opposition," I said. "How could I know that then?"

Sponsible raised his hand again and said a few words.

"Well, I just want to say that I appreciate Reverend Mackerel's objections. About the Plaza, the way it was gone at," he remarked. "But that's natural in a big enterprise. Mistakes will be made, excesses be guilty of. Sure it's a splash. Sure its ballyhoo. But why shouldn't we remember on as big a scale as possible somebody who gave herself on as big a scale as possible? After all, didn't she make the supreme sacrifice?"

He sat down to a round of applause and pats on the back. This was the moment, for me. He had stated the specific myth. It was up to me whether I was going to let it pass, or challenge it. Speak now or forever hold your peace. Are you ready, Prometheus?

I had an idea. Maybe I could get across by indirection what I had never been able to blurt out directly. Didn't I owe to Turnbull, even more than to them, this deliverance from the marshes of myth to the dry land of reality? I could put them one step from the truth, and let them take the last one by inference.

"Yes, I have always thought her deed a noble one," I said. "All the more so because she couldn't swim a stroke."

This was followed by a complete and absolute silence. In it, you could sense speculation like a soundless seething going on all around you. They seemed suspended in a vacuum for a moment. Then one of the heads turned slowly to Sprackling. Then another, then a third. They were making inferences all right.

Sprackling rose. He had come really only to relinquish his legal duties for the Plaza, having just been appointed an assistant prosecuting attorney, and had not expected to participate on these lines.

"If the late Mrs. Mackerel couldn't swim," he said, "how was it you could run the risk of taking her out in a canoe?"

I followed the trajectory of this notion with a kind of dreamy detachment, turning my head in a looping glance to the left, as if in pursuit of an object describing an arc.

"Risk?" I said, driving the word through a bung in my throat.

"Yes. I should consider it so. Canoes tip over."

"Now you're doing it!" I told them. "Oppressing me. Now you're getting the hang of it. This is what I meant. Well might you ask, 'To what green altar, O mysterious priest, lead'st thou that heifer lowing at the skies?' Might it not be, my lord, the altar of Mammon himself?"

"I should like to remind you that this is a serious hearing, despite its apparent informality, and not an exercise in this Machiavellian mumbo jumbo you seem to have on the brain," Sprackling said. "Now, I was asking you if it wasn't dangerous to go out in a canoe under the circumstances. They tip over."

"It never would have if she hadn't stood up and rocked it, which in turn wouldn't have happened if the crisis hadn't arisen that did. So from that point of view she did give her life for another, and the monument is in perfect order," I said. "Well then. Does that bring the questions to an end? If so, I think we can call it an evening and get on to Ed Murrow —"

"Not so fast," Sprackling said. "Aspects of this thing do arouse one's curiosity, which I hope you don't mind satisfying. Whose idea was it to go out in a canoe — rather than rent one of the numerous rowboats available?"

176

"Oh, hers. I was against it at first, my lord, but she won me over. We had quite an argument about it, but she won me over. She always won the arguments. Everything in order there, eh, my lord?"

I spoke, despite the witticism, with my head somewhat atilt and with that high assurance that distinguishes the true martyr from the sullen scapegoat. The vocative was a kind of arm offered to help them up a step onto this higher plane, too, while also supplying a dash of irony we all needed, a bit of the garlic of parody rubbed on the strong meat of these proceedings.

"Did you and Mrs. Mackerel argue often? Quarrel bitterly, perhaps?"

I executed a series of gestures in the air in front of me, as though directing traffic of great size and complexity. "Happiness is no laughing matter, as the Irishman said."

At this point a minor disturbance broke out in the gallery. Some, including the internationalist who had been furtively distributing pamphlets on behalf of his own cause, began debating the propriety of this line of questioning, and their words became a free-for-all which also divided the committee around the table. "You have no right to ask him things like that here," one of my defenders called out. "Wait till you get him in court." The commotion subsided when Turnbull's tall figure rose in the front of the gallery. He asked for the floor and got it.

"I think it's time I spoke up here," he said. "Andy Mackerel is my friend and so was Ida May. I'm not as embarrassed by this as you might think. She deserves this memorial because of her life anyway, so the way she died doesn't make that much difference. But it does for Andrew's peace of mind and future welfare in this community. So we ought to go into the facts of that accident a little more fully for his sake, and settle them if we can. Now can anybody shed any light on it?"

In the silence their expressions asked him what he meant.

"I mean there must have been eye witnesses to the event. On that crowded beach. You were all *there*," he said, spreading his rangy arms. "You were all eye witnesses to the scene in general. But did anybody see that particular *part* of what happened in the cove?"

Another silence followed this query. It lasted fifteen seconds, half a minute. No one volunteered.

"I guess that's that then," Turnbull said. "Obviously *I* can't settle it. I was bobbing around on an inner tube."

A small figure rose behind him and spoke up in a high-pitched voice. It was young Shively, the druggist's son.

"I don't know if this'll be any help," he said, "but there was somebody there who was taking pictures from the dock at the time. Movies, I mean. It was Waldo Hale. He had that movie camera of his along and started shooting when the motor launch got loose. That was all fun, of course, and he got some footage of it, but then the other happened. That was probably in it, so his mother said he hadn't oughta have the reel developed. In fact she wanted him to burn it, I remember. Whether he did or not, or ever got it developed, I can't say. I don't know."

Sprackling, who had momentarily sat down, rose again, fingering his Phi Beta Kappa key. "Is Waldo Hale here?" he asked.

"No," said the Shively youth, "and he ain't in town either. He's in the Army. Fort Bliss, down in Texas."

"Mrs. Hale?"

"His mother passed away last fall, sir. Neither of his parents is alive and the house is shut up. Waldo and I exchange letters once in a while, so maybe I could write to him and ask him about the film. I mean if I could be of any . . ."

"That won't be necessary," said Sprackling, hurriedly gathering up some papers and thrusting them into his brief-case. "We'll telephone Fort Bliss tonight."

Thirteen

WELL, they think I killed her."

Hester had been waiting up for me in the living room, to hear how the meeting had gone. I set aside the dregs of the drink whose consumption had attended my narrative of the events of the night. I spoke as one relishing a hard-earned vindication while giving another his just desserts.

"They think I took advantage of the confusion to tip the canoe over, see. Something along that line. They'll never find the pictures and I'll live out the rest of my life under suspicion, here or in like Escanaba, Michigan, or in Athens, either Georgia or Greece, it makes no difference which, because everywhere I go the story'll catch up with me — or they'll find the pictures and there'll be some fluke in the photography that looks funny and I'll end up with a rope around my neck. I hope you're satisfied now. You've had this coming to you for some time."

Hester was doing her needle point. She drew a thread through and reached for a highball she had asked me to fix her. She drank half of it like one quenching a literal thirst rather than imbibing liquor. "You romanticize things," she declared.

"I warn you not to nag. Persecutions, slander, character

assassination, and, finally, death by execution I don't mind — they're part of the game. I expect them. But henpecking I will not have."

She set her glass down after looking in surprise at its contents, as though sobered by the realization of the effect alcohol had on you. "Have you phoned von Pantz yet?"

"Then you're willing? Good, I'll make a date for you."

"Not me, Andrew — you." She drew a deep breath and held it for a prolonged interval in her lungs, as though she had momentarily forgotten what to do with air. She let it out with the same careful study of me with which she had taken it in. "The way you think people are after you and all, it alarms me. I don't mean you should go off to him in a panic and settle down to a long siege of treatments — I don't mean that. I only say this to show you that I'm worried."

"I wish I was dead and out of it," I said listlessly, to the wall. "I want to lie beside the ever-murmuring sea, on the hot sand, till all the flesh is bleached from my bones, and I can rest in peace. Or maybe I'll just stick my head in the oven."

"What good will that do? The stove is electric."

I must pull myself together, I thought, pouring myself a stiffer drink than usual. I padded back to the chair in stocking feet, for I had removed my shoes, which were tight. After sitting down, I tapped the arm of the chair with a forefinger. "I've spent a lifetime hacking out a coherent position, and I say they're out to get me. I'll stake my professional reputation on that."

She coughed into her fist and asked, "As an anthropologist, Andrew?"

"It can't be anything else. It fits. It's got to. It's just the way things are."

"You've got a theory and you'll prove it if it kills you. Is that it?"

I wedged my feet back into my shoes and rose without lacing them. I was going to bed. The metallic tips of the laces tinkled as I gained bare floor between parlor and vestibule, carrying my drink. "I'll tell you this, young lady. You read the papers tomorrow, and I'll bet my bottom dollar the whole story will be slanted their way. The hunt is on!"

"Andrew, do you ever have feelings that people are following you?"

"I'm not going to stay here and listen to crazy talk." I started on up.

"Wait." I paused halfway up the stairs. Her tone was an argumentative version of serenity. "When I was a little girl, we had a wonderful aunt. She lived in Seekonk, did this aunt," she went on, plying her needle and thread, "and we loved to visit her because she had nine children of her own. Well, she had a sound word for every occasion. Nothing threw her. One time when somebody was worried about something, anxious, she said, 'I've had lots of troubles in my life, but most of 'em never happened.'"

"A philosopher."

"She was a woman of breeding."

"Breeding! With nine children? No woman of breeding has nine children. It's a contradiction in terms."

"About this film. When will they get it?" We were shouting at one another now.

"As soon as possible. You'll read all about it in the paper tomorrow. Read all about it heah, wuxtry, read all about it! Lady killer nabbed for questioning . . ."

I settled down in bed with a book. I read a page and let it drop. Knopf had been asked to resign by his board of directors, who, as individuals, however, got together a small purse to help set him up in a book*store*, to see if maybe he couldn't do a little better on that end of the production of literature. But the same lack of judgment that had vitiated his choice of unpublished manuscripts vexed his selection of published, and that venture failed too. He was last known trying to get a job as a clerk, in a store that also sold greeting cards and small gifts along with books . . .

I reached for my bedside phone and called Molly. The third ring was answered by Tabitha Twitchet, past whom I got by asking for her precious daughter in a voice imitating Robert Morley. Twitching my mouth and sniffing, I said, "Is Molly theah-ahm?" Through Molly's own dramatically hissed protests, when I identified myself, I said, "I thought you might care to know how the meeting turned out."

"Yes, I've been meaning to call you. How did it?"

"Why, they're circling for the kill," I said, picking up the phone from the table and setting it on my stomach. "All according to pattern. Look, can you meet me in Chickenfoot tomorrow night? I've got to talk to you." The next day would be Saturday, so we wouldn't meet at the office.

"Yes. As a matter of fact that's what I was going to call you about too. I've got something to tell you."

"That you love me?"

"Fine, Hilary. I'll meet you there then."

"Good. Shall we say eightish, at that place next to the tannery that says 'Eats'?"

My fork struck an object in the hash which seemed immune to penetration. This left only the alternatives of circumvention or removal. I poured large gouts of ketchup on the hash, muddled the result together and shoved the plate to one side. Molly did the same with her hamburger, remarking, "I've always been a good judge of horseflesh and this is horseflesh." I ordered ice cream for both of us, and coffee. A sign on the wall advertised their "bottomless cup," which meant you could ask for all the refills you wanted; a managerial risk which became clear the instant you tasted the stuff. The ice cream was full of rock salt.

"Andy?" said Molly, stirring her coffee and addressing a point in space just above my head. "There's really too much secretarial stuff for one girl to handle. And now with these long letters you're writing to Knopf. I mean it's too much."

"Of course. I'll look for an extra girl the first thing next week. P.L. is growing, isn't it?"

She sucked thoughtfully on a spoonful of ice cream.

"So we lose our little haven," she said. "Somebody else in the office there with us."

"Yes."

"That being the case, there's no point in my staying on. So you might as well get two new girls right away."

I saw the whole farce being dismantled and reconstructed in reverse: Molly would quit. Then she would quit being seen with me. Then she would quit going to P.L. and go back to M.E. — or become one of those millions of unfortunate Americans with no spiritual affiliations.

"What a time we do have of it," I said, "but of course it'll all seem that much sweeter to look back on. Chickenfoot, places like this, the night we spent at the Coker." I reached for her hand. "Oh, my dearest, we didn't spend that night — *we put it in the bank.*"

She had both her hands in her lap, where her bag was. She reached into it and I caught a wink of something glittering.

"In the bank of our love, our future, our faith in one an-

184

other . . . Molly, what is this you seem to be giving me?"

"I can't wear it anyway, so you'd better keep it till — and — well, I might lose it."

I put the ring in my pocket. I took a suck of my own ice cream, and a sip of my coffee.

"We must meet again sometime," she said.

"Fine. Shall we say lunch a year from Tuesday?"

She sat stiffly with bowed head, about to burst into something, whether tears or words being still the question. I imagined that I was a dog and that my ears hung in my food, as an alternative to throwing back my head and baying like one. Lifting my cup to drink my coffee I noticed what I seemed to have the previous time, a hot trickle of sorts onto the knee of my trousers. It was the beverage all right, dribbling through a leak in the vessel.

"Is this your bottomless cup then, woman?" I said to the waitress. "Is that what the term means?"

"Please don't be angry with me," Molly said. "You — I — it's all so impossible. Not just the original situation but what's arising out of it. No, not what's arising out of it so much as what you're determined shall arise out of it. It's going to fit your theories or bust."

"Will you please explain what you're talking about?"

"This hearing and all — I heard about it today from somebody who knows Scanlon. You set their backs up so they'd act the way they were supposed to. Now there's nothing about it in the Bridgeport papers today and you're sore about that. So you'll pull out another stop."

"Putting the squeeze on the editorial department through the advertising takes time, as you may know."

"Oh, nuts! I know what's happening. This book and all that's at stake in it is now the main thing — not our love affair. It's your male type all over."

185

I broke in two a cookie that accompanied the ice cream, and poked a piece of it into my mouth.

"You might say you're egging them on just to show Knopf up. It's as bad as that. You've really forgotten me — or it's taken second place. Knopf is now your number one target. You'll prove he's wrong and your damn book is right if it kills you. There was nothing in any of the papers this afternoon and that's got you sorer. Now you're fighting mad."

I drew a careful breath to avoid inhaling any of the cookie I had suspended chewing, and turned and shook my head like a man who has only himself to consult with.

"It's true," she said, lowering her voice but speaking with increasing fire. "Oh, Jesus, you intellectuals," she said, clenching a fist and rolling the expletive toward the ceiling. "It's the story of my life."

"Perhaps you have a thesis of your own to prove?" I answered quietly.

"You're damned right I have," she said across the table, in a compressed whisper that made her words reach me like a kind of lethal gas. "All this maturity stuff is fine, but there are two kinds, mental and emotional, and you rarely get the two in one guy. In fact the more you get of the one the less you get of the other. Maybe nature just hasn't got enough to go around, specialization, the one at the expense of the other, et cetera. Anyhow, so we get the adult books and the adult paintings and the adult movies all turned out by spoiled children. 'Look, Ma, I wrote an adult book.' 'Hey, kids, look at the adult drama I wrote.' Oh, brother, can I pick 'em!" she went on through clenched teeth, her two bunched fists in the air before her as though she were leading the rooting section in a much-needed cheer. "The first one paints unicorns with adult flies on them. The second's occupation is eating strawberries with 'Harold in Italy' going, while secreting three sentences a day on a biography of Berlioz. Then another long-hair who's bald-headed on top of it, and then came Analysis with his trench coat, and then, oh, what's the use. And now the prize of the lot — he wants to put his neck in a noose to spite Knopf."

"How about Todarescu?" I said, swallowing the last of the cookie.

"You with your Baudelaires, all of you, and your infinite weariness, and your cultural patterns and your Voltaires and your Rimbauds and recurring symbols in Faulkner and now it's Dylan Thomas. Oh you intellectuals," she cried again, "smoking your literary cornsilk behind the barn of — of — I don't know what," she said, letting the metaphor collapse. "Todarescu? He's got something lined up for the summer, a directing job in Florida, working tents and one-night stands and so on with a variety show. They're trying to get *New Faces* material, but anyhow it'll be a variety bill. Sort of a revue. He can get me lined up for a part in it."

"So it's Todarescu who picks up the marbles. Is that it?"

"This will be strictly professional."

"Mm, plim-plam-plom," I laughed, imitating Todarescu. "That's rich. You and him in Florida on a strictly plam-plom-plim. In tents. Oh, plim-plom."

Molly closed her bag and collected her gloves.

"I don't want to get into a fight about this, Andy. The theater's in my blood, and it's none too early to think about the summer road. You don't seem to want to part friends, so maybe I'll just leave you here — rise quietly and go. No, Andy. No fuss, no tears, no regrets. You're really very sweet, but I just can't take any more. It's best this way. Good-by and good luck."

"Wait." I stayed her at the table, standing. "Would it

make any difference if we left Avalon and made a fresh start somewhere else? Because I have an offer from a church in Bridgeport. They'll give me five thousand a year, the house, of course, free light and heat, and a scooter . . . Well, think it over. *Don't give me your answer now.*"

One of the troubles with this middle ear business is that the nausea accompanying it is sometimes, after a while at least, indistinguishable from hunger pangs. The only way to find out which it is is to eat something, and then it's too late. After walking around alone a bit, I made for a place that was a combination bar and grill, a mile or so from where Molly and I had so sketchily dined. I walked at the edge of the sidewalk, finally with one foot in the gutter and the other on the curb, like a cripple with one leg longer than the other. How much more evidence was needed that elements in question were driving me out of my mind? I hobbled along experimentally for a block or two in this fashion, thinking about the scene with Molly and what things were coming to. Todarescu had a way of scratching his head gingerly so as not to disturb the part in his hair. Had she noticed that? This Bridgeport parish, would they have a theatrical director there? No, I would be expected to handle the dramatics myself, but they would consist in little more than sewing members of the congregation up in sheets and shoving them out onstage to yell, "Barabbas! Barabbas! Release unto us Barabbas!"

The bar and grill was on the other side of the street and I crossed over. There were four or five tables, two of them occupied. I went to the counter. It was littered with crumbs of food. A waitress with a cloth came over and flicked them onto the stools. I brushed one clean and sat down. The waitress, a plump, pleasant-looking girl in a starched green uniform, drew me a glass of water. "What'll you have?" she asked, and left.

I caught a glance at myself in a mirror behind the coffee urn and dishes. Just over a stack of reflected plates, I saw my face. My upper lip was drawn taut, exposing my teeth, and one nostril was curled in a snarl. My God, what were they doing to me! How much proof was needed? I turned away, but presently looked again for further signs. My ears twitched perceptibly and the snarl became audible, as I hunched safeguardingly over my water. What could more clearly indicate that they were unseating my reason?

I thought a moment, chin in hand and ticking my fingers along my brow, as though I might as well tap that as the counter — might as well drum that. The waitress returned with pad and pencil poised.

"Give me a piece of apple pie with cheese, and a glass of beer," I said.

"Beer with *pie*?" she said.

"No, with the cheese," I said. "What's wrong with that?"

She shrugged and made a record of my wishes, then hove off to fulfill them. She drew a wedge of pie from a glass case and flipped it onto the kitchen wicket for the cheese; then she went into the annex where the bar was, and I heard her say, ". . . he must be . . ."

And well she might. The more so, had she access to the inner man behind the one she saw, by whom she had, did she but know it, already been plucked and eaten. For here the pressures to which Mackerel was being so cruelly subjected were keenest, here was still the sorest crucible in which he was being tried. The stretch of continence to this length had grossly lowered his threshold, so that a not terribly attractive girl at a nearby table interfered with his enjoyment of what turned out to be a surprisingly good piece of restaurant pastry.

She was about twenty-five, and naked except for a green skirt and sweater, heavy brown tweed coat, shoes, stockings, and so forth, a scarf knotted at her throat and a brown beret. I regarded her breasts with melancholy, then my eyes began their ordained journey downward. A chink between the knees offered a gleam of white skin. "The secret where the stocking ends." Spender? Her companion, an older woman in a sweat shirt, was completely lackluster I noted with gratitude.

I returned to the other to ferret out a few flaws. She had a soft, pulpy pink mouth, which was parted in a rather moronic smile. She was saying to her friend, "Then he says to me, 'Get out. I never want to see you again.' I says, 'Don't be so possessive, telling me to get out, we're through. Who are you trying to get possessive with? It's your main trouble. You can't tell me what to do.' We had some more words, then he repeats, 'Get out. I never want to lay eyes on you again.' I says, 'Listen, who do you think you're taking for granted . . . ?'"

I gave a stir of delight. In thirty seconds the girl had drained herself of every charm. I could sit here and without ordeal contemplate the moist mouth, that heartbreaking prow, those hemispheres which, when she rose to walk would — Listen to her talk.

"So he says, 'We're through. You go your way and I'll go mine.' Just like that, imagine, out of a clear sky. He'll make the decisions. I says, 'Listen, buddy boy, I'll come and go as I please. You don't own me. I'm the master of my fate, you included . . .'"

I laughed to myself. I was off the hook. For this relief much thanks. I needed it. Because I didn't know how much longer I could go on like this. The obstacles in my way were unfair. I was human and I was normal. I must have a woman. A woman who would envelop my existence and befriend my spirit and leave her musk in my bed. The secret where the stocking ends. The flower where the fancy tends. The delta where the river wends. The garden where the hunger ends. Their thighs were like loaves of warm bread, their smell like that of warm bread . . .

My daydreams (which now went deep into the middle of the night) were no longer the cool, meandering reveries of contentment but the visual ravings of thirst. They ran to erotic etudes and chimerical methods of pairing based on hearsay and the most extreme data, sequences in which at last I saw myself locked in complex and carnivorous postures with women I had never seen before. I was in the country of those dark specialists in rumination who had left their phosphorescent print on a corner of nineteenth-century French literature; beyond it lay those visions, penultimate to madness itself, that turned the brains of the saints into nests of maggots. The fruit of chastity: the Temptations of Saint Anthony.

As I paid and rose to leave, I was put into a fresh lather, alas, by a black-haired belted figure leaving the restaurant ahead of me. She was a mare of a girl, her loins like a swaying bell. This was serious. I knew that I must evict this creature from my mind if I was to have a wink of sleep. As she left, she called a good-by to the waitress that showed an intelligent casual poise. Blazing with anger, I hurried to overtake her in the street, banking on some apparent plethora of chin to get me off the hook. Half a block down, as I was trying to scurry abreast of her to get a look, I bumped into another pedestrian. It was a woman carrying several bundles, which I knocked from her arms. I paused to help her retrieve them, and as I thrust them apologetically back into her hands I recognized Mrs. Sponsible. She gave a gasp of surprise, and I hurried on, excusing myself.

When I reached the corner of the street the girl was just boarding a bus. I stood there as the door closed behind her and it rumbled away through the Saturday night traffic. When I turned around, it was to see Mrs. Sponsible standing up the street where I had left her, watching me. Seeing me glance back, she turned and hurried off.

I went into a bar and had two whiskies. Shouldering myself in beside a stocky red-faced man in a leather jacket, I said in a low voice: "Say, Mac, what do you do for gash in this town?"

He lowered a stein of beer to the bar and shrugged. "Ask any cabbie. You new here?"

"More or less."

"Well, there's lots of places around here, though I personally wouldn't know any addresses. But any cabbie can tell you."

I gulped down my drink and hurried into the street, breathing heavily. Were they satisfied with what they were driving me to now? Was this the way I would end? Denial by no means always resulted in the sublimation credited to it then, did it? Often it worked the reverse. I thought of those animals that attack people and kick out the sides of their stalls until gelded. As I walked along, I encountered a pet peeve that drew from me more than its normal fire.

A street-corner evangelist was swinging a Bible and shouting, "Jesus is the powerhouse! Are you plugged in? Jesus is the transformer! Are you wired up? Jesus is the cable carrying that current from God Almighty! Is your trolley on? Oh, is your trolley on?"

My teeth grated, and my fists worked in my pockets. It was not merely the humiliation of this imbecile's being technically a colleague. It wasn't just the vulgarity of the scene, though that was of a shattering kind. It was the spectacle of a faith and a form in which I had some belief being debauched into a yapping ritual for boosting paltry souls into heaven. These men were worse than infidels, for at least many infidels were Christians.

The speaker must have detected the animation in my face, alone in the small group of sullen listeners who surrounded him, and mistaken it for approval. He therefore turned on the box on which he was standing and said to me:

"Brother, have you found Christ?"

"Is he lost again?" I said.

"Oh, brother, don't mock," he said, his face falling, but only for a moment, as he rallied to the attack. "Won't you take him tonight?"

"No, I will not," I said.

"Oh, brother, why not? Give me one good reason. Come on, I'm waiting. So is he." He pointed upward.

"Don't you see what nonsense all this is?" I hit out aggressively. "Don't you realize that the Gospels don't harmonize? That you can't use the Bible literally, that this railroad to heaven you think you're running makes a farce of a noble ethic?"

"Don't harmonize? Don't *har*monize! Oh, brother," he said, slapping his brow with a gesture that converted the word from a vocative to an expletive. "He says the Gospels don't harmonize."

"They don't. Even Martin Luther admitted that, and suggested we get on with it, on to more important matters. When I say I won't take him I mean I won't on your terms.

Where did Cain get his wife? Did you ever stop to think of that, if the Bible is literally true?"

There was no telling how the tide of battle might have gone between us, because I found myself involved with a new adversary. A drunk, or semi-drunk, from the other edge of the circle made his way around to me. He had been listening as phlegmatically as the rest to the evangelist, but took the opportunity to pick a fight with the heckler.

"Lis'n, bud," he said, swaying slightly, "do you know who you're talking to? Servant Lord."

"I'm not talking to you in any case," I said. "And now if you'll please clear out of the way."

"And if I don't, then what? I suppose you'll knock me?"

"I wouldn't be a bit surprised."

The drunk swung at me, missed and fell. That enraged him, and he got to his feet and came at me like a butting goat. I caught my heel against the curb, and down we both went in a heap. Before I knew what else was happening, I felt myself being collared and hauled to my feet by a burly cop.

"Now, what's this all about?" he demanded, holding the drunk and myself face to face.

A woman offered an analysis.

"Well, *he's* drunk and *he* was heckling the preacher, and *he* —"

There were too many he's. The cop couldn't tell smiter from smitten or drunk from sober. Off we were packed to the station in a cruising squad car, which he summoned from a call box and which appeared in an instant. The officers over to whom we were delivered told us that they were under orders to clamp down on the spreading rowdyism in that part of Chickenfoot. There had been complaints, from civic groups, from the pulpit, from parent organizations, and

194

the command was to run 'em in. Thus the original cop had much preferred chalking up an arrest to settling the disturbance on the scene. The drunk and I were charged with disorderly conduct and put in separate cells.

That done, however, the sergeant at the night desk relented. He had done his duty. He let me telephone home around one o'clock. I got Hester out of bed and she got Turnbull, and between the two of them they managed to bail me out in time to preach the next morning.

Fourteen

W uxtry! Wuxtry peebahs!" Knopf was shout-
ing on a midtown Manhattan street corner. "Read all about
it! Offbeat minister nabbed in slaying. Pleads innocence but
protests social guilt. Action corroborates prisoner's theory.
Read all about it! Get your late editions here!"

I was stretched out fully clothed on my bed, at fifteen
minutes till church. I hadn't gotten home till nearly four,
but not having slept, I was up and ready in time for divine
worship. With a quarter-hour to spare, I lay down to com-
pose my thoughts.

I lay very straight. Presently I reached into my pocket for
the two pennies and laid them on my eyes. I folded my hands
on my breast. What a shame, cut down in his prime. So
much yet to give, but done in by bungling hands, that flame
snuffed with the candle not yet half consumed. What they
did not understand was that he had no quarrel with the
myth per se but only with its inevitable misuse by brutish
men. They never understood his ministry, the meaning of
his life: that he had come to call, not sinners, but the righteous to repentance. Too late now. Those lips were cold, the
proud spirit flown. Now his house shall be removed from
him, and his bishopric shall another take.

There was a soft tread in the hall and a rap on the door and Hester said, "Andrew?"

"I'm dead."

"I know. You'll be able to rest after the service. I'll see that nobody disturbs you. I'm going along now and don't you be too long. It's only ten minutes."

I slipped my fingers under my shirt and massaged my heart back into vitality. I pocketed the pennies, and as I put my legs over the side of the bed a sob caught in my throat, torn free by the spectacle of heroism in our time. Seeming to be digging vainly in my clothes for a handkerchief, I reached to a nearby writing desk and dried my tears with a blotter.

So here was roughly how things stood with Mackerel in the public eye, I reviewed to myself as I walked over to the church building:

He was an alcoholic, a lecher and a Red. His drinking was in the main solitary and had therefore not come to light before, but it was now a known and openly discussed fact. He sought his women in the disreputable quarters of Chickenfoot, where, in addition to chasing anything in skirts, he also undoubtedly frequented vice and gambling dens. He was a brawler. While indulging these graphic and assorted passions along those and God knew what other fronts, he had been going steady with a nice girl. The nice girl had found him out just in time and broken off what some said was an engagement, hardly surprising under the circumstances. She was reportedly hysterical and being packed off out of the country, under a doctor's care.

Just how far back these habits of Mackerel's extended was hard to say, but it was known that he had been "keeping company" rather soon after his wife's death, and more than likely that he had been living this double life while she was still alive. A man who will cheat in the betrothed state will

197

obviously not hesitate to do so in the married! He had admitted that they had quarreled constantly, and the rumor was that he had beat her, no doubt on those roaring drunks — which no one now blamed her for having kept secret to her dying day. It was a natural thing for families to do — they had their pride. Poor woman, though, what she must have gone through. She had been more of a saint than they had dreamt! And now here he was trying to queer the memorial out of his rotten alien theories and sheer insane jealousy. No wonder it turns out there seems something fishy about that so-called accident at the beach. You mean — ? Yes. The police are on the trail of something. It's still hush-hush, but expected to break any hour.

The instant I entered the church I saw how far my reputation had fallen. The place was jammed. The worship area was not only full, it spilled over into the gymnasium-auditorium part from which it was divided by the accordion folding walls. P.L. had never packed in so many while I was a respected figure in the community and invited to dinner. Now that I was no longer received in proper society, they came from miles around to see and hear me.

We dedicated a new liberalized hymnal that morning, and as the congregation raised their voices in the strains of "Funiculi-funicula" and "Has anybody here seen Kelly, K-e-double l-y," I sat glancing through the text of my message. It was the last of the series on the Seven Churches in Asia, and luckily accommodated a few last-minute remarks on the events of the preceding night, the hasty incorporation of which a slight mouse on one eye and a few cuts and bruises called for.

"Our text for this morning," I began when the extended "sing" was over and I had taken my place at the pulpit, "our text for this morning, dearly beloved, is from Revelation three, verses fourteen to sixteen, where we read: 'And unto the angel of the church of the Laodiceans write . . . I know thy works, that thou art neither cold nor hot. I would thou wert cold or hot. So then because thou art lukewarm, and neither cold nor hot, I will spew thee out of my mouth.' "

The first stir that had gone among the audience on my rising to speak had subsided. They watched me in alert silence.

"Let us not congratulate ourselves," I commenced, "on the reasonable mind that sees both sides of every question. Civilized flexibility is a fine thing, and in a sense the aim of education, but there is a point here, as everywhere, where the law of diminishing returns sets in. Tepid liberalism that never lashes out at anything, intellects too stocked with information to draw a conclusion, educations scrimped and saved for, that one may dawdle in the green bowers of noncommitment — these lack something possessed by an honest bigot. That there is a time to throw stones is a principle I try to follow in my daily life, occasionally to my peril." I saw Meesum fidget and look down his pew at somebody. Mrs. Sponsible watched from under a dove-gray bonnet with tiny scarlet buds around its crown. I touched the mouse on my right eye and smiled.

"Last night I was strolling about the streets of Chickenfoot, as is my wont of a Saturday night" — there were several coughs into dainty gloved fists — "when I saw one of those open-air revivalists who always rub me the wrong way. Perhaps I was too anti-Laodicean here, forgetting that the poor man was only acting according to his lights, but I stopped to give him a piece of my mind. A not altogether sober bystander intervened, a fist fight followed, and then a policeman appeared who carted us both off to the local clink. You may imagine that your overheated Saul of Tarsus cooled off pretty fast at this point. In fact, it was worse than that. I felt a perfect ass."

Here Mackerel paused and gazed down at the floor below the pulpit, as though his thinking had stalled. Somewhere some mechanism seemed to have jammed. He smiled abstractedly and added: "Like the Englishman who reached down the lady's back for her pearls."

There was an absolute silence. Then the silence began to take on that faintly sizzling quality of a telephone connection. Heads turned and whispers became audible. Meesum's plucked-chicken neck twisted round to catch von Pantz's eye. Von Pantz caught the glance of another clinic staff member and the two rose and met at the back, where they were joined by Meesum and another trustee. The four of them went out, their heads together.

Are you satisfied now, my people? Is this the way you want it? If ye cannot shatter him one way ye will do it another, so that, caught in a vise of tribal manufacture and crazed by lust, he can be delivered over to whichever authority seems most in line to receive the pieces and seal his doom — that about it? Because the rest of the morning passed off without incident, no more ad libs, but ye have done your work well, O my townfolk. And you, Knopf, are you watching? "Maybe he's not responsible," they whisper in little groups as, forgoing the usual suburban handshake this time, he ducks out a side door and hurries along the arcade to the parsonage like one bucking a great wind.

Gaining which he sees Hester in the kitchen calmly assembling the noonday meal. "I'm baking the chicken in red wine," is all she says. "I hope you like it. And there's plenty of Heineken's in."

Nothing was said about the occurrence all that day and the next. On Tuesday morning I came down late for breakfast to find her reading the Avalon *Globe*. It was published twice weekly, and this would be the first issue in which it could have run a story about the city hall meeting.

"Any trumped-up charges?" I asked, taking the paper from her eagerly.

She rose and went to pour my coffee.

"There's nothing about the meeting at all except in general terms saying that differences were aired between you," she said. "Nothing about that other at all."

"Then it's to be a cat-and-mouse," I said, reading for myself the story, abounding in equivocation and tipping no hands, cunningly buried on page sixteen. "I suppose great secrecy would enshroud the recovery of the film."

"I think the paper's very nice to you," Hester said, filling my cup.

"It takes a while for a gang to seize the means of communication. Putting the screws on the editorial department through the advertising isn't accomplished overnight. You don't know anything about those things."

"You want them to do you wrong, don't you? You're itching to have them make a big thing of the film, only to find you innocent and have to be ashamed of themselves. But, Andrew, do be careful. This thing may backfire."

After breakfast I telephoned the *Globe* office and got Charlie Comstock himself on the wire. I thanked him for the kind write-up, then said, "How much heat are they actually putting on you, after seeing it? That started yet, Charlie?"

"Heat?"

"Yes. The well-known squeezeroo. Because you don't think they're going to let you get away with a soft policy on me, are you? They'll get to you, and you'll give me short shrift in the end. I just wanted you to know there's no personal hard feelings."

"But they actually have talked to me, only the other way around. They nailed me right after the meeting at the city hall and said to go easy on you. They knew they'd been a little highhanded and were sorry."

"Asses!" I said. "What about the movies?"

"Well, the detective bureau is running that down. George Chance, he's head of it you know, got in touch with Fort Bliss right away under Sprackling's orders, but Waldo's not there. He's been transferred to the White Sands proving ground in New Mexico, with a two-week transfer furlough, and nobody can locate him."

"I suppose they'll keep trying?"

"Oh, sure. But he isn't actually due at his new post till next week, you see, so there's nothing they can do till then. Meanwhile shurtainly hope everything works out for the besht," Comstock said in the quasi-tipsy voice which was especially noticeable in moments of strain. "Ashk Lord shtraighten you out, Andy. He'll help you. Look up to him."

I finished my call and carried a second cup of coffee into the living room. Hester was sitting there. After a moment of frowning silence, she said, "Andrew, about the film. I have a plan."

"That's what I was afraid of."

"No, really. What I'm really quite frightened of is that there won't *be* any picture to clear you, and all this will be left dangling. I have nightmares about it."

"I wish I had nightmares," I said. "It would imply that I was getting sleep. Never mind your plan. Are we making any strides getting a secretary?" Hester had undertaken to find me one, advertising in the surrounding help wanted columns and screening the applicants. Except that the applicants, however, were almost nonexistent.

"They've heard about you and, well, they're afraid to take a job in the same office with you," she said. "It's as simple as that. Only two answered the ad in the Bridgeport paper yesterday and neither was secretarial timber. I could tell that right away. One of them snickered when she asked what you were like. They imagine the main qualification is a well-turned ankle."

"They needn't worry about their ankles. I've got my mind on higher things."

"You going to talk like that in church again Sunday?" Hester said, lowering her eyes away.

"Well, we'll see." I backed against the mantel and stood there drinking coffee.

"Is it something you can't help?" she asked. "Something that comes over you?"

"Poor Yeats went out in a blaze of lust, and think of Dylan Thomas's last days. The same thing's happening to me. It's a malignant satyriasis, progressive and ingrown."

"Dearest Andrew, will it require surgery?"

"We'll see about that too. I can thank you for it all. I understand there's talk of cracking down on old Mackerel. The church board have something cooking, have they? Come on, girl, come clean. You know everything that's going on."

She broke her hands apart in an elusive gesture and dropped her eyes again. "I hear a Yale divinity student has been alerted to stand by, in case he's needed. That's all I know, honestly. If the board's doing anything more definite I'm sure they'll let you know."

They did. I was called on the next evening by a delegation who said they were anxious about certain rumors concerning my private life, which they wished ardently to doubt but which my behavior in the pulpit last Sunday forced them to give credence. They would like not to see it happen again. Profanity (used sparingly and to lend emphasis) they had no objection to, but smut was something else again.

"We know you're avant-garde and all that," said Freddy Residue, the junior member who acted as spokesman, "but you've got to understand other people's limitations." If there was a repetition of last week's occurrence, they would have to ask for my resignation, or at least that I take a rest of, say, three months till I was myself again. Perhaps I had been overworking, and strain had temporarily unstrung me. If so, the clinic was of course open to all members of the parish for whom any rest or observation was deemed advisable. I said I saw their point of view, and promised to desist from banking on greater resilience than could reasonably be asked of a folk still short of the desired urbanity, ideally speaking.

"I can't help feeling though," I said, "it's something of the old story. Break fresh ground and they'll bury you in it."

"Oh, I wouldn't say that, really," Freddy Residue replied in his eagerly amiable way. "It's just our old friend, enough-is-enough, if you know what I mean."

"So we have a hush-hush attitude toward sex here. Is that what we have in these parts then, Residue?"

"Oh, it's not that, Mackerel, fellow. Really, now, I don't consider myself a prig, but one does draw the line, you know."

"I suppose. Still I can't help feeling that the pressure is more than what's called for. That certain forces are leagued against me. I hope I'm man enough for the chopping block if it comes to that, but I must say, why can't we have progress without shedding all this bloody blood!"

They looked to von Pantz, also present, with an intimation of its perhaps having worked its way into his province. But he declined exercising a professional role except in private, and turned the conversation to other matters, the ultimatum having been presumably deposited. He made some vague rejoinder, and then inquired whether I had got another secretary for the office. They had some urgent extra mimeographing at the clinic and he wondered what the chances were of "moochink a hand from headquarters." I said we hadn't got a girl yet but would let him know as soon as we did. We got on the general subject of secretaries and their idiosyncrasies, and von Pantz recalled for our amusement one he'd had in Leipzig who could only take dictation directly at the typewriter, though her speed made the method very nearly feasible. As he talked, I studied him with my usual interest.

He was part schnauzer, though the strain would have been more marked had he let his hair grow and his mustache friz out a bit. He clipped his mustache and cut his hair close to the scalp — so close that the top of his flat head looked like a carpet sample. It matched absolutely the pewter rug on the floor of his office. He represented the return to orthodoxy, and was said to believe in the Devil.

"Still she was quite a pretty girl," he mused in conclusion. "I hated to leave her behind."

"Her what?" I said.

"Behind."

"Now you're doing it!" I exclaimed, pointing at him. "Listen to von Pantz, everybody. He's getting off some good ones!"

He looked blank, but a little exegesis of what he had said

soon established his skill at *double entendre*. Von Pantz rose, stomping to his feet, and shook his finger over me.

"I will not be dragged into zis!" he said. "I will not be made party to zis awful thing you are in the grip of. Now I don't care." There were tears in his eyes, and his expression was not one of anger so much as a kind of violent petulance. Somebody rose and put an arm around him, to quiet him.

I am always amazed at the infantilism one encounters in supposedly adult people. They are those whom the rest of us must make up for; must "carry," so to speak, in the round of social transactions that go to make up mature human life. Add to which mountainous enough hazard, never kid a kraut.

I apologized and he was calmed down. But the other committee members, three in number, pointed out that this fresh incident clearly revealed the gravity of my "trouble" which they had come to discuss, and before departing they repeated their ultimatum. If there was a repetition of this sort of thing at morning service next Sunday, they would have no choice but to demand my removal to the clinic for an indefinite rest and observation.

I stood at the window watching them get into their cars. I shook my head. It was obvious which way the wind was blowing, and what pretexts were being resorted to. By the time they got through with Mackerel, Knopf wouldn't have a leg to stand on.

If the church had been crowded last time, this time they turned them away. People seemed to have come not only from all over Avalon but from surrounding townships and even from outside the state to hear the new sensation, because a few New York license plates were seen among the endemic station wagons and convertibles parked on the lot and both ways along the road. When Mackerel rose to deliver the sermon, a profound hush fell over the audience instantly. A strategy had apparently been agreed upon with which to meet any emergency. Four large, muscular orderlies from the clinic were posted with conspicuous nonchalance at different points in the worship area. They were all in aisle seats and all within sight of von Pantz, who was to give the signal to rise and move down to the platform on the first sign of fireworks. This was obvious from the way they kept glancing over at him.

"Our text for this morning is from the Gospel according to St. Matthew, the twenty-sixth chapter, verse seventy-three," I began. "It is the scene outside the palace of Caiaphas the high priest, where the bystanders say to Peter, 'Surely thou also art one of them; for thy speech bewrayeth thee.'"

I took a swallow of water and set the glass down again. I drew the paper clip from my manuscript. It was a manuscript there had been none to retype for me, besides being wreathed in late marginal interpolations, from which fresh impromptus might supposedly flower . . .

"I would like to consider with you this morning, dearly beloved, the subject of oral diction, not merely as a surface trait but as an expression of national or racial character, dwelling particularly on the long-labored distinction between British and American speech, and the argument as to who best uses the language we allegedly share.

"I know it's customarily assumed that the English pick up the marbles here — marbles being what the cisatlantic mouth is supposedly full of. But I wonder. I mean I wonder if that's all there is to the argument as to who best uses the mother tongue as laid out for us in Webster's dictionary.

Has it ever struck you, hearing an example of so-called impeccable British diction, that while the diction is precise enough, it is in the service of noises curiously at variance with the official spelling? I have given a lot of prayerful consideration to this matter, and I think that the difference, dearly beloved, lies in this. That Americans mumble correct pronunciations while the British clearly articulate faulty ones. Let us take a few examples of what I mean."

There was a resolving stir among the audience, as of relief that Mackerel was adhering to his prepared text, and confidence that everything would be all right this morning.

"The American — be he from Manhattan, Brooklyn, Chicago or Texas — knows that the letters p-o-e-t-r-y, for instance, spell the word poetry. He may slur that word or he may in some other way fall short of giving it its due. But he does not say 'paitry.' That he does not say. He says poet, not pate. He will not read to you from his paims; he will read to you, however miserably, from his poems. His conversation may be as dull as ditchwater, but he will not, immaculately delineating each syllable, refer to something as 'doll as ditchwoetuh.' *That is not what those letters spell*. He answers the phone, not the fen; takes planes, not a plen; goes to a play, not a pleh. Why envy or emulate this gabble! The letters p-l-a-y comprise, I submit to you, the word play. They will not, though the American empire last a thousand years, ever constitute a sequence of characters calling for the sound 'pleh'!"

"Hyah, hyah!" cried an educated but feverishly nationalistic Harvardian named Yates from the third pew, in spontaneous approval. Others nodded and beamed theirs. I was inspired to go on.

"Let Americans square their shoulders against the canard under which they have so long groaned, that of British superiority on this as other scores. They may lack what labial and glottal grace it takes to say, 'To you, my dear,' but they don't, raising their glass, say 'Chew my dim.' The Yankee may mangle the language, but at least he opens his goddam mouth!"

The congregation was deeply moved. They had not heard such a ringing affirmation of faith from an American pulpit in a long time. Two people did get up and walk out, but they were the Árbuckle cousins who did so out of protest at what they considered to be anti-British sentiment. The rest sat and beamed. Not solely, of course, out of pleasure in the message, inspiring though that was, but also because they were glad for Mackerel. It looked as though he was going to make it — get to the end of his sermon without mishap. No digressions lured him; no temptations rose in his path in the form of words offering *double entendres* and other appeals to the base nature. I sailed along through eight minutes, nine, ten.

With sixty seconds to go, I peered to make out a penciled emendation at the end of a paragraph. "Thus we see that such slight matters as vocal inflection mirror what are deeply rooted traits. The American's brash unconcern for nuance indicates a young and vigorous country, the Briton's clipped speech an ancient, proverbial reserve. The difference comes equally into customs and —" Was that the word "folk" or "fond" or "food" or what scribbled in there? Folkways? Fond ways? I was thrown off my stride. I scratched my head and tried to connect the paragraph in thought with the next.

"Folkways," I said, raising my head. "Nothing gives us more keenly the sense of novelty than someone else's. I recently had dinner at the home of acquaintances in Norwalk," I went on, ignoring my manuscript for a moment to recall the incident. "As we finished our coffee I saw that the ladies alone were rising from the table and being shepherded into the drawing room while the host remained behind with the men. I perceived that here in Fairfield County, Connecticut, far in space and time from the Victorian London where it had once flourished, we were observing the custom of the fairer sex separating themselves from the men while the latter remained behind over their port and walnuts. The hostess, perhaps noticing the impression the maneuver made on guests accustomed to less quaint patterns of conduct, said apologetically aside to one or two of us, 'I hope you don't mind. My husband's English, and he likes to withdraw.'"

Von Pantz nodded to the waiting orderlies. They rose quietly and without any ostensible connection with one another, and took lounging but alert positions against the walls. Their faces were impassive, but the audience's? Their eyes implored me not to. "Don't succumb," their collective gaze entreated. Many leaned forward, gripping the pews in front of them, or sat with hands clasped tightly in their laps. Hester bowed her head. Old Meesum was inscrutable, but watchful. Charlie Comstock wet his lips. The temptation in whose grip I writhed had for him its own clear and terrible parallel. The *double entendre* that beckoned was like that glass of whiskey round which the drinker has but to close his fingers to end the struggle and start a fresh cycle of degradation. "Don't touch it," Comstock's eyes begged. "Hold tight. We're all with you." A man mopped his brow. A woman prayed.

I moistened my own lips. I reached for the glass of water and took another gulp, seeing the bruisers move another inch closer to the platform stairs, ready to spring like the powerful cats they were. I put the glass back, and stood shifting my weight from one leg to the other. The cable of self-control stretched; frayed; raveled to a thread; held. My voice was but to be heard stepping on to the next thought, or better yet returning to the prepared text from which it had wandered, and it would be like a foot safely planted on the far bank of a pause now intolerably prolonged.

I raised my head and grinned out at them.

" 'That, madam,' I replied, 'strikes me as carrying Anglo-Saxon restraint a little *too* far.' "

Fifteen

It was a warm, cool day in early spring. The leaves hadn't begun to bud yet, though, so I had a view through bare treetops of the countryside on at least two sides of the high ground on which I strolled. It was sunny and bright, and as I idled up the gravel paths with that double sense of another fresh day and a newly minted season, I flicked a switch I had cut from one of the willows that grew at the far limit of the grounds. Except for a handful of people promenading, singly and in pairs, and a few sunning themselves in Adirondack chairs near the main building, I was pretty much alone outside this morning. Perhaps it was still early. Ten o'clock, I saw by my watch.

On the highest point on this landscaped knoll, and of Avalon as well, I stood a moment gazing off into the blue distance. Of the several houses visible, two were those of members of P.L., and I had therefore been inside them in happier times. One was said to have a ghost. The place was a converted barn haunted, apparently, by a horse, said to be an old plug who had lived there before it was torn down for remodeling; the last animal, in fact, left in it, who had been taken out and shot to make way for construction. The rat-

tling chains and thumpings at midnight attested to by the
present owners suggested a four-footed rather than human
revenant, come to plague those who had done him in and
taken his home. The other was a spanking new modern job
designed by Marcel Breuer. It was so new that the price
tags were still on the shrubbery with which it was landscaped, though the explanation of the couple who lived
there, Marian and Freddy Residue, was that on the reverse
of these were the names of the various plants, by which she
would identify them when they bloomed. Just over the flat
roof I caught a blue haze, a dim translucence of water, and
I thought I made out a thin line of beach and even the
bridge that spanned the tidal river there. It was a bridge de-
serted now, but on which, in summer, girls in bathing suits
strolled all day and men loitered eating hot dogs and drinking soda pop, to watch them parade. It was a local institution known, consequently, as the Bridge of Thighs.

My eye was jerked to the right by a figure of quite another sort.

Emerging from a black sedan and walking purposefully
toward the office of the main building was a man in a tan
suit and checked vest whom I knew I knew. Then I remembered. It was George Chance, chief of detectives. He was a
portly number who had all through his schooldays been
nicknamed, inevitably, Fat Chance. He was trying to live it
down now, from what I gathered of him — the few times I'd
met him and even from what I could sense in his bearing
now. Rotundities fore and aft made him resemble, from the
side prospect, a pair of parentheses that have slipped out of
line. He marched into the front door and disappeared. I
knew where von Pantz's office was in the line of first-story
windows visible through the shrubbery from here, and

watching, sure enough, I caught a dim stir of motion behind it, which would be von Pantz rising to let Fat Chance in.

I turned and after a last comprehensive gaze of the kind we give a panorama we are taking leave of, a kind of visual gulp, I walked back to the bench on which I had formed a habit of sitting in my few weeks' stay at this plaisance. I had left a *New York Times* on it, and setting my switch aside, I opened it up. I had not been reading long when voices near the building, now at my back, made me turn round. Young Evans, the bright-eyed, clean-cut bore from the Yale Divinity School, who was occupying my pulpit during the rest I was taking, said a last word to a nurse in the side doorway and struck out across the grass in my direction. I quickly lay down on the bench, drawing the *Times* over my face.

He had a distance of two hundred yards to come, so it was some moments before he arrived. I heard his footsteps when they reached the gravel walk, twenty yards back. They grew louder, and stopped. He was standing over me, hesitating no doubt. I was safe under my cover. In the interval in which he stood there I reviewed the defects which unfit him for civilized ministry. First was a "solid" Scotch Presbyterian background which he found it possible to pride himself on not having shaken off. Next was the oppressive earnestness with which he went about his work, carrying a pocket Testament on his pastoral rounds and speaking of a Crusade for the suburbs, in which everyone would come in for a complete spiritual check-up. Next was a resort to bland euphemisms in personal conversation, such as his first greeting to me, "Taking your vacation early, are you?" Add to these a tendency to little informal homilies about how radar, jet propulsion and such modern things had always existed in nature, and you can see why he was not long for this community. You can bore all of the people some of the time, you can bore some of the, et cetera.

My breathing was regular. I even turned on a light snore I had developed to discourage visitors and even those sibilant ministers of mercy known as nurses, indoors and out. At last Evans turned and walked away. When I felt it safe to leave my cocoon of newsprint, it was to find he had left a calling card on the bench at my feet, with the jolly penciled inscription, "Hope you're feeling better, old chap!" Shredding this moodily, I watched the approach of a pair of strollers. They were both men, one a fellow named Jackson whom I liked very much. He had confided in me that his tongue was too big for the floor of his mouth. It lay upward against his lower teeth like the edge of a rug against the wainscoting of a room too small for it. "Great architect!" he said. "Huh!"

I heard another footfall; this time one I knew well. I looked up and was not surprised to see von Pantz.

I sat up and swung my feet over the bench. He sat down and joined me.

"Spring in the air," he said.

"I almost could," I answered, appreciating the chance for one of those fancies that grieved his tedious Teutonic heart.

"What? Oh, yes, I see. Quite amusink." He hiked up a trouser leg to cross his knees, and settled himself for one of his talks. He wore the same blue serge he always did, and those bulbous-toed shoes that are known, I believe, as bluchers. His clothes were all of good quality, except for his neckties, which seemed to have been bought at the Army and Navy store. His eyes were large and brown, and looked like boiled chestnuts. I was used to a roundabout approach, supported by transparent indirections and heavy German subtleties. But this time it was a frontal attack.

215

"So your idea is to feign incompetence in hopes that you won't be held responsible," he said.

"For what?" I answered. I spread my arms along the back of the bench and crossed my legs.

"You know what."

"Is that what Fat Chance told you to come out here and try?"

Von Pantz looked away and shook his head.

I said, "At least in the Middle Ages they piled the faggots around you and had done with it. Today they're more civilized. They turn you slowly on a spit."

"How do you account for your behavior in the pulpit if it wasn't to give that impression? It all fits perfectly as part of a scheme — crazy like a fox!" Von Pantz sprang to his feet and began to pace a limited area of the gravel path in front of me. "A man sees ze evidence closing in, and he gives ze wildest possible account of himself in a frenzied attempt to beat ze rap." It was when he most strove to affect slang Americanisms that his Viennese accent oftenest crept from its lair to do him in.

"What did Chance want?"

"He said ze film has been found and ze evidence is damaging." Von Pantz turned away and stood stock-still a moment looking into the distance, as though helping imbibe, on my behalf, great drafts of natural beauty I would not long be here to share.

"Then why doesn't he come and collect me?"

Von Pantz swung round to me again. "Because you are now under my jurisdiction, and I give you sanctuary here." He was tense, almost hysterical. He stood directly in front of me gesturing with both hands. A single gold tooth at the back of his mouth flickered like a firefly as he talked. "I am trying to help you, to save you, but I cannot do it medically

216

because I do not think the trouble is medical. It is spiritual. Oh, yes! I use zat word. I am not ashamed of it. I say that you are in the grip of sin — zat word too. I know it isn't fashionable today but we are coming back to it, mark my word. Because we have done away with the concept of sin, yet never has a generation been more obsessed with guilt. It is part of every modern man's equipment." I remembered Turnbull's having said something of this sort, and wondered if he had got the thought from von Pantz. "Wait. Please do not give me zat here-we-go-again look. Jung used to say to me, 'Hugo, some people can't be cured — they can only be saved.' There is a way open to you, a young intellectual with something missing in his life. A tortured young man for whom there is only one salvation" — here he drew a deep, defiant breath — "to make a decision for Christ."

A puff of wind had blown a page of the *Times* to the ground and I bent to pick it up.

Von Pantz straightened and tightened his stance. He fixed me with a look at once dramatically hard and infinitely gentle.

"I'm going to put this question, this choice up to you now," he said. "Reverend Mackerel, do you now, and before God, accept Jesus Christ as your personal savior?"

I shook my head with a friendly little laugh. "Look, von Pantz, there's really no point in this. We've been through it before. We just don't see eye to eye."

He raised his voice. "Let's forget about seeing eye to eye, it's not an intellectual matter — let's try to see heart to heart!"

"Oh, rubbish," I said, bouncing to my feet and raising my own voice. "Let's knock it off. You don't have any use for my viewpoint and I don't have any use for yours, and certainly not for your godforsaken theology!"

He became livid, and seemed to rise up and down on his heels. "There's something evil in you; why don't you recognize it and call it by its name! It's something you should fear and hate."

"There's only one thing I fear and hate," I said, shaking my face in his, "and that's people shirking the obligation to evolve! Which I consider god-given, if all our sweating history up from the muck on this rotten ball and up into something resembling human grace and wit and beauty means a goddamn thing!" I shouted, in one of those bursts of profanity whose roots lie so close to those of reverence. "I'm sick of this nursery room pie-in-the-sky backsliding revivalism! And I'm especially sick of seeing the clock turned back by people who should know better! Now how do you like that?"

"I like it!" he shouted back, so close to me that I could feel his breath, which smelt of some not disagreeable commercial lozenge. "It proves what I'm saying, that something has got you in its grip. Do you think you set a good example to people I might try to help with Christian therapy? Is it nice of you to badger servants of God in public?"

"There are times when anything else is wrong, by my standards. A little less Christian charity with such boobs and sucklings; a little more Christ-like irritability please!"

"By God, you've got a messianic complex," he said, turning away again.

"I thought you said I was sane," I reminded him. He said nothing, just shook his head, one method of filling a discomposing gap. "You want to know what happened in the pulpit and so on. I'll tell you. There are plenty of Freudian terms for it, but I haven't time to bring you abreast of developments in that field so I'll just use Edgar Allan Poe's term for it — the Imp of the Perverse. A part of you that you don't want to take over but does. Call it an island broken off the mainland and floating away by itself, or trying to if it isn't fetched back. Or perhaps I can explain it to you in another way. Under these stresses and strains, one part of the personality 'separates' from the other precisely like the cream in a bottle of milk. Your job — homogenize me."

I sat down on the bench again. We didn't look at one another for a minute or more. Then an almost involuntary glance on his part brought my own eye toward the front of the main building. On a corner of the portico there, Fat Chance stood leaning against a white pillar, watching us. Some gesture from von Pantz, which I am assuming because I didn't actually see it, brought him down off the portico and across the intervening ground toward us.

"Zis dick wants to talk to you," von Pantz said. He spoke rapidly, so as to finish what he had to say in conclusion before we were joined. "We have no more to say to each other, I am sorry to say. I can't do anything for you, in any way. I can't certify you. There is nothing for me to do but turn you over to the authorities who want you."

I reached into my pocket for a cigarette and lit it.

"I guess we both lost our heads," I said. "Surely we can talk about all these things that interest us later. I was thinking I'd have myself voluntarily committed . . ."

"Committed! You must be crazy," von Pantz said. "No, I'm sorry, Mackerel. I've done all I can, and I regret all too keenly that it's so little. I have no choice but to release you and let you take your chances with the law."

Chance had a dozen yards or so to come, time enough for me to answer: "All right, keep your not very satisfactorily run establishment. And I'll report my impression of it too — all the racket and what-not going on among the help at all hours. I'm still a trustee, remember." I lowered my voice, remembering that it was my belief that I was a trustee of this place that most of the inmates took to be my malaise. "I'll have plenty to say. Hello, Chance."

"You know Inspector Chance?" von Pantz said. "Reverend Mackerel." After a word or two he took his leave, bowing curtly and striking off diagonally across the lawn to his office.

I offered Chance a cigarette, which he declined with a shake of his head, effected with no disturbance of a measuring gaze on me.

"What do you want?" I asked.

"We found the film, Mackerel," he said, narrowing his eyes in the accepted idiom of his trade, "developed it, and I guess maybe you know the rest. Know what we found. I thought maybe you'd like to come to headquarters and make a full confession."

I gathered up my *Times* and retrieved my tweed hat which had fallen behind the bench. I slapped it against my knee and put it on.

"I'm going to pack now. I'm leaving. So if you'll excuse me," I said. I started across the grounds, leaving him standing there. Not for long. Fat Chance was really pathetic, I thought, with his hat shoved back and his hands in his pockets and coat open to reveal the Tattersall waistcoat in which he tried to encase that tummy. The attempt to look like a sleuth, not helped by a bow tie more suited in size to a circus comedian than for normal human society, was so forlornly lost a cause that I wondered angrily, as I heard him trotting abreast of me, whether it was Sprackling who was coaching him in this bluff or whether he was pushing it on his own. Sprackling was just the type to wait in the background, to let Chance make a fool of himself if the bluff fizzled and to jump in and take political credit if it paid off. I let Chance sit in my room and watch while I packed. I wanted to befriend him, so listened tolerantly while he talked.

"You know what the negative shows, don't you?" he asked, more as one whining for co-operation than acting out the stratagem with anything like the brisk tone the role called for.

"Sure, Fat, sure," I said, tucking some shirts into my bag. "People splashing in the water and eating fried chicken on the beach. Perhaps in the distance a background shot of the Bridge of Thighs."

"Would you like to see it run off? Would you dare to face that?"

"Anything you say."

"You want to come along to headquarters?"

"If you like."

"You're not very co-operative," he said. He rose and walked to the window. He stood looking out of it, hands in pockets again. There was a rattling of carts in the hall, and a sound as of two of them colliding; then words of some altercation between the floor superintendent and a mainte-nance man working, too slowly, it seemed, on the elevator.

"This place is a madhouse," I said, throwing in my bath-robe. "I'll be glad to get out of here."

"All right. We don't have the film. We can't find it. And the reason we can't makes us *really* suspicious. You see, we got in touch with the Waldo Hale boy by telephone, and he told us where it was. It was still in the camera, where he'd left it, undeveloped. He said the camera was stored with some other stuff in the barn behind their house, in a big box near the door marked 'Movie Stuff.' He gave us permission to get it and told us where we could get the key to the barn — from an aunt of his who had charge, and had rented the house for him and all. But when we got there the barn had been broken into and that box rifled. The camera was gone. Looks like somebody else had some use for it and got there first. It was general knowledge that the Hale house was rented and almost general knowledge, in the neighborhood at least, that stuff was stored in the barn." Chance turned from the window and looked at me keenly. "What does that sound like to you, Mackerel? What would you think if you were me?"

"Why, that I took it, Fat," I said, closing the suitcase, and eager to get home and ask a few questions of my own.

"Right. And if this particular person were a murderer, what would he do with it?"

"Destroy it," I said, glad to help him enliven his no doubt drab existence.

"Right again. Unless," he said, coming over closer round the foot of the bed on which I was packing, "unless it held a deadly fascination for him, so much so that he couldn't help sending it to the Eastman company and getting it developed. So he could run it off in the secret of his house behind drawn shades."

"Well, it so happens that I do have a projector stored away in my own basement," I laughed. "You have a good imagination."

He nodded. "Enough to have alerted the Eastman Kodak Company and got an order through impounding the merchandise. It takes several days to develop films, of course, so it wouldn't be back yet, but we're ready if and when. I'm afraid we're monitoring your mail, Mackerel."

I smiled tentatively over at him as I bent to squeeze down the lid of the suitcase and raise the locking hasp. That done, I secured the other side. I gave the grip a last pat. "Well, you can't kill a man for trying," I said, looking away from him toward the closet on which I was advancing for my topcoat.

"No," he answered in a level voice, "but you can try a man for killing."

Hester was fixing lunch. I had phoned to tell her I was returning, and she was whipping up a favorite of mine in celebration, a German pancake with Preiselbeeren. I had little appetite for it now.

"What have you done with the film?" I said, coming right to the point in the kitchen.

"What film?" she said, attending the skillet.

"Come now, let's stop this huggermugger, once and for all. Fat Chance — I think you know who he is — just told me it had been stolen and I remembered you had a 'plan.' Did you go over and snitch it? Of course you did, because I certainly didn't. Well, now you've got me in worse soup than ever because they obviously think I did it, and must have a motive. I can't see your expression, but in case you sent it away to be developed, they're watching my mail. When it comes back they'll nab it."

"Why should you care about that, Andrew?" she said, turning the stove off.

"What did you do with it?"

"I burned it."

I swung away with my hands in the air and my eyes to the ceiling. "So you've destroyed the evidence. The only evidence there was."

"Of what, Andrew?" Hester had gone to the icebox and now stood with one hand on the open door for so long without reaching in to take anything out of it that she resembled one of those girls who advertise refrigerators on television; though with a smile strainedly unlike those suited to the delivery of commercials. "Of your guilt?"

"Of course not," I said, resenting the grotesqueness of

223

having to make the reply at all, "my innocence. Now I'll have to live the rest of my life under a cloud."

"Not with me, Andrew."

"You're damn right not with you," I said, deliberately mistaking her meaning.

"Don't you see, this is what I've been waiting to hear from you?" She now had three eggs in one hand and the jar of Preiselbeeren in the other, a combination which hardly corresponded to the sequence of manufacturing a German pancake, the one neither of us was going to eat. "I can tell from the way you say it that it's true. I knew all the literary talk about being done in by forces leagued against you was all right, but it was because you could think deep down that you were safe, physically I mean. Actually if it came to a showdown about the other part of it — the police part — you were quite scared. And I was quite scared that . . . that . . ."

I watched her close the refrigerator door and set the eggs and jam on the table.

"That I was really guilty?" I came over and shook her by the shoulders. "That I could really do your sister in? Come on, tell me! I'd like to know what's going on in that head of yours once and for all!" I shook her more vehemently, till an earring dropped from her ear and I could smell her perfume like a scent shaken from a flower. It was some expensive, not unpleasant odor, that made my own head swim, what with the variety of developments being visited upon it this morning.

"Well, she must have been hard to live with. I knew what it must have been to put up with at times. Andrew, was it really awful?"

I stood back, reeling from this further bolt. I simply didn't know what was going on here. The floor seemed to be sucked from under me like the sand from under your feet by a receding wave.

"I have been through three theories about this whole thing," I said, speaking with ghastly calm. "First that you loved her. Second that you just more or less hated me, and wanted to keep me bottled up. Next — God forgive me — that you were in love with me. Don't let it bother you because others urged that one on me. My fourth hypothesis better be right, because I've got time and strength for only one more. It's that you felt, for her, such a deep, bitter, abiding —"

"No, not that. I didn't hate her. It's not that. But I did feel a certain aggressive tendency toward her that knew no bounds when — when she married you." She jerked her head away toward the icebox with such an apparent aim to lay her brow against it that she might now have been enacting a role in a drama sponsored by the maker of that product. "When she was the one who got you."

"Sweet Christ in the morning," I said, dropping like dung into the nearest chair. I loosened my tie and collar. I drew a few much-needed breaths, then asked, "If that's the way you felt about her, why go to all this trouble to keep her memory green, as you call it?"

"Because it's the only way to cover up the awfulness." She had whipped about, and spoke in such a tone of pent-up feelings released that I thought of dams bursting, of powder kegs erupting. "The awfulness of what I felt, and of not being able to feel any more love for her than I knew I did, and probably feeling guilty about that too — No, not guilty. Just hating the fact of how things were. Of how she didn't deserve any more love, not that any of us do in the long run. So I had this overwhelming need to — to heap the awful truth over, to bury it as deep as possible, smother it the way we

225

do death with flowers anyway. It's the same as your drive to *believe* when you know there really isn't anything to believe. Like in that awful poem of MacLeish's where the top of the circus tent blows off and there's nothing — nothing, nothing at all. Well, let's *make* something. Let's bury the awfulness and the nothingness with somethingness we've made with our own two hands. Let's make the lie so big and so convincing, and worship it so bitterly, bitterly much, that it becomes a truth."

I rose and staggered past her, as though there might be some virtue or advantage in occupying another part of the room than where her revelation blazed, but at the same time heading efficiently for the bar. There was a throbbing in my ears as though my brains were being squeezed out through them by some vise-like pressure exerted at the crest of my skull. I thought again of the term "warped New England house" as I poured and drank my whiskey.

"Was she pretty bad to live with, Andrew? Tell me. You can speak to me frankly. Was it hell living with her?"

"Of *course* she wasn't awful! Where do you *get* all these romantic notions about marriage?"

"You had fights. I used to hear them."

"Of *course* we had fights. Don't you ever go to the *movies*, for the love of God? Don't you ever read books? Do you think we'd have spatted in front of you if they were serious. They were good spats too, if I say so myself — we were perfectly matched." I gulped another whiskey and asked, "How did your mother feel about her? Let's get this all cleared up."

"Mother always said a very interesting thing." I steeled myself for another bromide, but I was surprised. "She used to say, 'I guess I love Ida May most because, of all my children, she's the hardest to love.'"

"Well, I loved her," I said resentfully, "and I want to tell you she was good company. I liked *especially* that waspish tongue of hers. She was entertaining partly because she *was* so malicious. These people often make the best humanitarians, because it's out of the pain of limitation that the ideal is often best apprehended . . . Just coffee if you've got it. I don't want anything to eat."

She'd had it brewing in an electric percolator we'd recently got. It was ready, and she poured two cups. We sat in the kitchen drinking it in silence. When one of us spoke, it was I, and as one thinking aloud.

"This is something all right. Molly thinks I'm innocent but deserts me. You think I might be guilty but stick."

Hester drank the last of her coffee and carried the cup and saucer to the sink.

"I didn't say I thought you might be guilty. I just said I was glad you weren't. The way you responded when I said I destroyed the film. The relief I felt."

I shook my head. Not to her, or even very much for my own benefit by way of elucidating a reaction: it was just a man sitting in the middle of a kitchen shaking his head. It was his own kitchen, and he had a right to. There was another silence. In a listless tone I said, "Do you want to marry me?"

She opened the refrigerator door again to put away what she had taken out of it. She did some more tidying up. She removed her apron, folded it, and set it over the back of a chair.

"Excuse me, I'm going upstairs," she said, and did.

I went into the living room and settled myself with pencil and paper in an armchair to jot some notes. The trustees of the church had given me three months for a complete

227

rest, and I was using it to work on the book. I was deep in a new chapter on Religion and Art. I wrote:

"We want shelter equally from death's darkness and life's glare. Religion is an umbrella that protects us from the rain, art a parasol with which we shield ourselves from the sun. But let us not forget —"

I looked up to see Hester coming down the stairs banging two grips.

"What are you doing?"

"I'm leaving," she said.

"Because of something I said?"

"You could put it that way." She set the grips down in the vestibule. "I didn't know you felt that way about me, Andrew."

Having said what I didn't mean, I was faced with the alternative of meaning what I'd said. At least of construing it in some fashion with which I could honestly align myself.

"Well, you aren't unattractive," I said from the chair. "After all you're a woman and I'm a man, Hester. You're a person of considerable charms. Your hair is like cornsilk," I continued, after an absurd pause in which there was nothing to do but go on, "your breasts are like brioches . . ."

"You see? Everything's changed between us. I couldn't stay in the same house with you now," she said, lowering her eyes. "It wouldn't be — right."

"But damn it, I thought you were going to stick by me." I put my writing things down and went into the entrance hall.

"I'll stick by you, but I won't stay with you. I can't, not under the same roof. Everything's changed between us now. You wouldn't want me to — you wouldn't want that kind of a girl. I'm taking what I need now. I'll send for the rest of my things later. I'll probably stay at the Chelsea

House until I — until things get settled. Would you call me a cab, please?"

I did. When I finished the phone call, I said, "But this is so sudden. Who'll take care of the house for me?"

"You can get somebody. You can get a housekeeper easily enough. The agencies will find someone for you."

"Just the way they did a secretary. All right," I said angrily. "Go ahead. Good-by and good luck!" I tramped on upstairs, leaving her to wait for her cab alone.

To say that a man never knows what a woman is going to do next isn't to say very much, because neither does another woman. Seeking clues to female motives is like fishing in a whirlpool. Molly wouldn't have made head or tail of Hester's maneuver, nor would Hester have made head or tail of Tabitha Twitchet's next. It is my story that not an hour after the house was empty (except for me, who evidently didn't count) the doorbell rang and it was Mrs. Calico, holding a present. It was a blue crock, more or less wrapped in foil, in which reposed a custard she had baked for me.

When I expressed confusion, she explained, "I appreciated the way you behaved about Molly. Not trying to keep her. Oh, I don't mean just giving the devil his due. You were true blue."

"Well, thank you very much," I said, both for the compliment and for the custard, which I set on a table in the living room. "How is Molly?" I asked, waving her to a chair.

"Why, she's in Florida, with some stock company which I believe Todarescu will soon be down to direct." She regarded me from her chair. "I hear you haven't been well," she said with her own kind of cherubic severity. "I took that to the hospital, but they said you'd gone home. How are things?"

"All right, except that I have no housekeeper," I said. "Do you know where I might get somebody — even part-time?"

In a twinkling she was at the phone calling a woman with a domestic for whom she had only partial use and who might be willing to take on other jobs. That was just the way it turned out. The woman was a client of our very own clinic. The clinic had a free employment agency which got jobs, part-time or full, for out-patients based on their aptitudes as gauged by the social workers, and that promised to be more or less therapeutic. Mrs. Calico handled the whole thing beautifully, and that was how it came about that, within twenty-four hours, I had a cleaning woman with a washing compulsion.

The caseworker had been right in her belief that Mrs. Vobiscum would sublimate at this job. She scrubbed for an hour at one floor plank, she rubbed for an hour at one piece of silver. She left with one corner of her domain spotless but the rest the shambles she had found it. She picked dirt out of the cracks between the floorboards with a toothpick; she wiped the wires of the telephone with a damp cloth. She spent a quarter-hour buffing one of my shoes, another quarter-hour on the other — I timed her from a corner where she did not know I was watching. Dishes accumulated in the sink while she vacuumed the living room drapes; then the tie-backs went up the tube and had to be fished out and washed over. When she saw what was inside the vacuum cleaner, she got at that. When she reached the dishes, each plate was given like attention. All this was bad enough (considering that I had to cook my own breakfast and go out for any other meals I didn't want to bother with myself) but when I walked into the parlor one morning and saw her on a stepladder, shampooing a moose over the mantel, I blew my top.

"Don't you realize you're a sick woman?" I said. "Didn't they explain what this is all about to you at the clinic? That this is a compulsion? It's what they call a washing compulsion. You understand what that is, don't you?"

She dismounted the ladder with compressed lips and folded it and set it against the wall. "You mean I'm thorough?" she said, tersely.

"Oh, Mrs. Vobiscum, this is no use," I said. "I'm sorry. What I need really is a full housekeeper. I'm afraid I'll have to let you go."

"That's O.K. with me," she said, and left.

I advertised in every paper around for somebody. Several days passed, and I had despaired of getting anybody when the doorbell rang and it was Mrs. Calico.

"I heard about your trouble and I've seen the ads," she said, entering. "I've come to offer my services."

"Oh, but . . ."

"No, I must." She fled into the living room. She stood with her back to me with an odd tension, then sat down abruptly on a sofa. "I owe it to you."

"Owe it to me?"

"I've wronged you. We all have." She rose and walked nervously to a sofa, tweaking her nose, I saw, with the same or another lace-bordered handkerchief. She lowered her head. "One night after that call I paid on you, I overheard Molly talking to you on the telephone, and knew from what she was saying that it was she who went to the hotel with you. I was in possession of this fact when I brought you the custard. I suppose I was sorry. But in my heart of hearts I knew that for *either* of you marriage under the circumstances would be bad. The scandal was there and why fly in the face of it. I didn't want you both tarred with the same brush, to use your own very original phrase, Mr. Mackerel. And now—"

She broke off and bawled into her handkerchief. Standing miserably off, I noted that she literally said "Boo hoo." She raised her head and, drawing a fresh breath, brought out in a mounting wail, "Now she's married Todarescu down there and he's tuh-tuh-taken her still farther south, because the shuh-shuh-show's folded, and she's got a job in a Miami night club *singing underwater through a snorkel!*"

She screamed out this last and, bending over, began pummeling the fat of the sofa on which she was sitting. I took a step closer but other than that could think of nothing to do. The only method by which I had seen hysteria successfully dealt with was the slap in the face that is invariably administered in the movies, and I could not bring myself to undertake that. I watched her flail the upholstery for perhaps a minute more while she emitted further wails of despair and further declarations that I was true blue and "a knight in shining armor" and the like. I finally did shake her briskly and pour her a glass of brandy.

"Here, take this," I said with a touch of masterliness.

She shook her head after smelling it and gasped, "No. Too strong. Something milder perhaps."

I went back to the cellaret, before which I squatted calling out its contents as consulted. "Benedictine?" I said. "Kummel, cherry Heering? No? How about a spot of *crème de menthe?*" She nodded and I poured some into a glass, downing the brandy myself. She sipped the *crème de menthe*, raising her eyes in appreciation as though to say, "Good."

She was soon quite herself again, and I in possession of a crackajack cleaning woman. For she would not hear of my declining her kind offer to "pitch in." She pitched in right then and there, and had that awful house in apple pie order with a vigor and dexterity that made my head swim. I smiled to myself as I thought that *this* ought to make Hester come running. I was in a position now to make her return, not me go begging to her.

After three weeks of coming on alternate days, more or less as a living-out maid, as she put it herself, Mrs. Calico said to me while she was fixing my dinner one night, "Mr. Mackerel, it's really more inconvenient than I thought. This coming and going I mean. Of the two houses, I've got more to do in this than my own, and so I was thinking — only if it's suitable to your mind — if I lived in here and trotted over *there* to give *Toits Rouges* a lick and a promise now and again, it would make so much more sense."

I was mentally deep in a chapter of *Maturity Comes of Age* and hardly heard what she said or, hearing it, took it in. "Sure, that's O.K.," I said. "Anything that's convenient for you, Mrs. Calico. I appreciate your doing this. And I must say this is a terrific chicken pot pie."

"Oh, thank you. And of course it'll mean having Fatima here with us. But she'll give you no trouble. Not a meower and a scratcher."

She was gone soon after doing the dishes, and back again bright and early the next morning, suitcase in one hand and puss in the other. I blinked at the speed with which houses could be opened and shut, and transferences made by determined women. Watching Fatima make her sniffing tour of the interior, beginning with my own person, I said worriedly, "Are you sure this is all right?"

"Of course. Glad to do it," Mrs. Calico said. "I have no ties back there any more." She jerked her head in the direction of *Toits Rouges*. "I'm a widow, remember?" She heaved her two arms into the air and drew a pin from her hat. "An Enoch Arden widow to be sure, but a widow, nonetheless. In other words, a free and available woman."

Sixteen

IT WAS warm for April and then it was warm
for May. Not a breeze had blown for days, but, more serious, not a drop of rain had fallen in months. Newly sprung
lawns had already withered and died, and though any vege-
table crops were still young and tender, farmers in many
parts of the country were anxious for them, remembering
last year's dry spell. Sprinkling had been discouraged by
the local hydraulic company, now forbidden by city ordi-
nance. The northeast was in the grip of its worst drought
in seventy-five years.

"The governor has declared an emergency and asked all
churches to observe a day of prayer," Mrs. Calico read to me
from the paper at breakfast. "Next Friday. P.L. is joining,
I see. Special services at eight o'clock sharp, all over town.
The idea is that all of the congregations, thousands of
people all over the state, will be praying at once."

With the tine of my fork I produced a lesion in the yolk
of a fried egg and watched it bleed slowly across the plate.
I munched a piece of toast and remembered the shower in
which I had been caught under the awning after a night of
hot iniquity in Chickenfoot. That was very likely the last
rain we'd had since the beginning of the year. Chewing,
I studied a full-page ad on the back of the upheld paper

across the table. It showed a movie actress with breasts so magnificent as to comprise a deformity, enjoying a much-prized lager with friends. I moved my eye upward to take in Mrs. Calico. She was wearing a crisp plum-colored dress and her glossy brown hair, symmetrically undulant on either side of a straight part, was drawn into a bun secured with tortoise-shell hairpins. The result was someone who looked like an elevator starter from the neck down, and above that, like a trade mark for a line of home-style relishes. I had more than once been on the point of urging hexagonal spectacles on her to complete the prototype, but had not yet acted on the impulse. I had so far limited myself to daily inclusion in her focus, to give freest possible play to that uniqueness and individuality which was nearly always hers, and to sustain and feed that fascination which was certainly always mine. I played, that is, the interlocutor.

"Look, there goes another one," I said, pointing out the window, from which the sidewalk was visible. "Nothing but shorts and a halter. In town."

"Yes," she sighed, shaking her head, after censoriously taking in the sight. "Well, if that's what we want, walking around half naked, with our stomach button showing in broad daylight, even with some of those midriff dresses I've seen, all right. But then we pay the price — rape, whistling and irritability."

It was pleasant, cozy, playing interlocutor for the sake of the archaic spell she spun around me. We lived in a pocket of time, safe from the world's way, from the harms which had pursued me, but which, like dogs called off or at least momentarily off the scent, seemed briefly in recess. We were suspended in a cocoon of words and ways and nostalgic allusions. We never called curtains drapes, nor a shawl a stole; we said not scram but skidoo; on the phone we asked for central; we drove to market in my machine. I made a trip to New York, this time spending three hard days in the public library, and on my return told her about all the dry goods stores I had been in — Lord and Taylor, Bonwit's, Bergdorf Goodman and Saks Fifth Avenue — browsing on my lunch hour and picking up this and that for future Christmas presents and for myself, and a wool jersey shawl for her.

One afternoon at lunch — I believe it was the day on which she had read about the governor's proclamation — she said:

"The Shenstones have asked us over some evening."

"The Shenstones?" I said, looking up from my plate.

"The people who moved into that old Johnson house up the block. I met her on the street this morning. She's a very pleasant, well-spoken woman. She referred to her husband as Doctor Shenstone, so I guess we have a doctor on the block. They seem very desirable people. I was thinking maybe we should have them over, because they're the ones who just moved in. Welcome them. I think that's such a nice custom, don't you, Andrew?"

"Yes, but — do they think we're —? Oh, well, we'll see."

Here began the rude summons from my dream. A slight sensation had gone up my spine that ended in the roots of my hair. It had successors of greater duration and severity. That afternoon I complimented her on her efficiency as a housekeeper, particularly as to letting my books and papers where I had left them. "It's a rare woman who does that, Mrs. Calico," I said.

"Call me Pippa," she answered.

I choked on some cigarette smoke and said, "I'll try."

"We do seem to hit it off."

It was the cursed result of playing interlocutor; she felt us compatible, no doubt. I was not without a current of emo-

tion for Mrs. Calico, but only as an instrument in my strategy
— to make Hester jealous of her place in the house. I had
not imagined a greater scope for her jealousy than that. The
task of downgrading myself to drive still another woman off
the premises was one I hadn't the strength to contemplate
even the thought of, even allowing for the fact that Mrs.
Calico would give shorter shrift than her predecessor to un-
punctuality, messiness and filth, whether of mind or body.
Why didn't Hester let me hear from her? What the devil
was the matter with that girl? Did pride disallow her to make
the first move? Well, I had pride too. I could sweat the war
out a little longer, despite the ominous turn things seemed
to be taking. A little longer, anyway . . . But I was glad to
see Turnbull's figure come up the porch steps and interrupt
the passage with Mrs. Calico in which she spoke of our com-
patibility. He had the virtue of making Mrs. Calico scuttle
for the kitchen. She must have thought him quite an ogre
indeed, judging by the way she always broke for cover when
he came.

It goes without saying that Turnbull now viewed me with
new eyes. The scandal, while demoting me in public esteem,
elevated me to peerage with himself as a possessor of sexual
background; if half the stories were true, I could a tale un-
fold, and he was forever asking me if I "cared to talk about
it." He urged this purgative on me again this muggy afternoon, and again I declined it. Instead we talked about the
drought and the forthcoming prayer meeting.

"Will you be there?" he asked me.

"I don't go to rain dances."

"Well, it's a good thing Evans ·is here to handle it. . . .
Otherwise he's a bore, though. . . . Do you hear anything
of Hester?" I shook my head. "I saw her on the street in
front of the Chelsea. She's staying there."

He switched the radio on to hear the two o'clock weather report. I excused myself after a moment, pleading work, and went upstairs, leaving him there to listen and urging him to make himself at home. "Fix yourself a drink if you'd like." I often had to do this with him, and he never minded. From upstairs, I heard the radio off and on for two hours or more; and when I came down for a drink about half-past four he was still there. I asked him to stay to dinner, as he frequently did, but this time he said he had an engagement and left.

At table, Mrs. Calico looked up from the roast lamb and said, "I think we ought to cancel our subscription to *Life*."

" 'We'?" I said in very nearly a falsetto register.

She nodded. "It's rather an uncouth magazine in many ways. And why can't people read? Is that all they can do any more is look at pictures?" She took a very firm and cultured line, calculated to impress anyone at all classifiable as an intellectual. "I wonder why I haven't been receiving my *Scribner's* lately."

"Maybe because they folded twenty years ago."

"Oh, yes. Well, that might explain it." She poured herself some claret from the bottle, did the same for me, then sat studying the label with interest. "This is an excellent year. 1628."

"No, that is the year the bottler was established."

She drank three glasses in rather rapid succession. Having finished the last, she sat back in her chair as one who has fulfilled the aim of fortifying herself to bring up a delicate subject, regarded me across the table, and said, "Andrew, do you think a difference in two people's ages is a hindrance if they are matched in other ways?"

I rose and, feeling twice my normal weight, dragged myself into the living room with the posture of a man toting two enormous but invisible units of luggage. "I don't know anything about those things," I said. "But by and large, yes. Emphatically yes. It does make a difference."

"How old are you, Andrew?"

"Thirty-five. I was a kid in high school when *Scribner's* folded. I remember my teacher mourning its passing." My voice raised itself in both pitch and volume as we called to one another across the length of two rooms. Mrs. Calico seemed far away as though seen through the wrong end of a telescope, her brown paw curled like a sweetbread around the stem of her glass.

"Perhaps you are too young to know about these things," she answered. "I am older than you are."

"I know that."

"Why don't you sit down and finish your dinner?"

"I've had enough," I said. "Quite enough. Who is this — who are these people you're talking about?"

"The man has shown every interest, the two seem well matched," she said, lowering her eyes, "at least I *think* he has shown interest, judging from his attitude and presents he has given me, and I am not going to let his misgivings about the age difference interfere with what can and will be a happy union."

Again I had the sensation that the contents of my skull were being extruded through my ears, but this time as an alternative to the pressure lifting off my scalp like the cap on a freezing bottle of milk. I staggered toward the vestibule stairs hearing her cry behind me, "Andrew, what is it? You look ill."

"I am," I threw back, plunging up the stairs to my room. "And I have to go out." I gained my bedroom, where I set to work getting into a clean shirt. I was tying the tie with

239

vibrating hands when there was a rap on the door and she came in.

"You mustn't go out if you're sick," she said. She felt my brow. "You're quite flushed. You've probably caught the flu that's going around. We'll dose you with something, then to bed with you and off to sleepsin-bye. You need a good night's rest."

"Breach of promise, that's been done away with, hasn't it?" I said, tying the tie. "Women can't get a judgment any more just by taking it into their heads to wave what they think are tokens of esteem around in a courtroom? Hasn't that been laughed off the books along with alienation of affections?"

"Not in Connecticut, it hasn't," Mrs. Calico said, sweeping something down the front of her dress. "It's one of the states that still has it if I'm not mistaken."

I thought of sliding the knot up my tie till my blood supply was cut off, my eyes popped from my purple face, and I breathed no more.

"Now you do look sick, and you're going to bed, I don't care. Come on," she said efficiently, "off with it and in with you. I'll be back in a jiffy with something to bring you round."

I was glad enough to comply with this line of thought, and I was in bed when she returned with two aspirin and a glass of hot lemonade. I drank the latter with lots of ice cubes and after its equipment with gin, to which she agreed on the ground that the potion was medicinal in purpose. When I had finished it, I felt better though weaker. She beamed at me, taking the empty glass from my hand and setting it on a table. She was sitting on the bed. She continued to beam, as though expecting me to show some sign of emotional or physical life.

"Have you said anything to anybody else?" I asked, folding my hands on the coverlet and looking away. "About what you were just talking about?"

She shook her head, still smiling beatifically. "I thought maybe you would make the announcement."

Mackerel made for the other side of the bed, like those semi-defeated figures crawling on their bellies for ammunition in action movies. He was hauled peremptorily and with tender skill back into a supine position and organized snugly under the blankets. She tucked the foot end in with a bounce of the mattress. "Now off to sleepsin-bye."

"Wait," I said when she started out of the room. "This is serious."

"Shall I call a doctor?"

"Yes," I said, grasping at any diversion. "Doctor Chaucer's my regular one but he's out of town now."

"He's mine too. Who else could we call?" She paced the room, a thumbnail to her lower teeth.

"Hey. This guy who lives down the street — the new one. Shotwell or Fontaine or something like that."

"Doctor Shenstone! Of course."

Shenstone came bounding up the stairs two at a time in answer to her summons, so breathless was her account of my condition, which was certainly by now ghastly enough. "What seems to be the trouble?" he asked. He was a lean, pale, rather wild-eyed man, though perhaps in less frenzied circumstances his air might be simply one of preoccupied timidity.

"Well, my heart is pounding so, and I feel so — so —"

"Flushed," Mrs. Calico put in from the foot of the bed.

"Flushed, yes, that's it."

He lowered his ear to my chest and listened. I don't know what he heard but I could certainly hear his own thumping, which struck me as an odd lack of detachment in a man of science. I also thought it funny that a medical man should be conducting this kind of examination without a stethoscope. The situation was almost immediately cleared up when he suddenly raised his head in answer to a remark one of us made.

"I'm not a physician," he said. "They call me doctor because I have a degree. I'm a Ph.D."

I hitched myself up on one elbow and gave him a glare. "In what?"

"Egyptology."

"I see."

I bundled him out the door without any further formality and in my pajamas, overriding his apologies and protestations of concern by assuring him that I would in all likelihood live, for what that was worth.

"Sorry about the misunderstanding," he said, casting me a wild glance, his thin gray hair flying. "We must get together some time . . ." His departing aspect belied that any initiative in such a development would be taken by him. Perhaps he had heard of my criminal background? That gave me my strategy.

It came to me in a flash how I must disencumber myself of Mrs. Calico, but I was two days of careful thought in planning it in detail. The evening of the second day, I sat in a living room chair with a highball. She was knitting in the corner, with Fatima snoozing at her feet.

"Pippa?" I said.

"Yes, Andrew?"

"Do you have any life insurance?"

She looked up and adjusted her glasses.

"Why do you ask that?"

"Why do I ask that? Because a man likes to know how a woman he is going to marry is fixed. Financially."

There was a pause, broken by the sound of her needles clicking, albeit at a slower rate, and another dollop of bourbon going into my glass. I drank this off and, plowing ahead, said:

"Did you plan to change the beneficiary?"

"Change the beneficiary?"

"Yes, change the beneficiary." The colloquy seemed to be proceeding on the antiphonal lines developed by vaudeville comedians for arriving at payoffs. "Well, you might think about it." I yawned artificially and went to bed, taking my glass with me.

It was the next day but one that she came upon me in the basement, examining a shotgun. "Thing needs oiling," I said.

"What are you going to use that for?" she asked.

"You never know, do you?" I said, licking my lips and ogling like Barrymore in his prime. I tramped upstairs to find her sitting in the living room with a feather duster in her hand and a preoccupied expression on her face.

"Do you know what I like about you, Pippa?" I said, with a smile neither too maniacal nor insufficiently so for my purpose. "You're a realist. You're willing to let bygones be bygones. You know what I mean? About a man's — past?"

"What do you mean? Mr. Mackerel, I don't think I quite —"

"Follow me? Ah, but you're way ahead of me, I can see that." I flicked her nose with my finger, leaning over her. "You know what I mean. It's not for nothing they call me a lady killer."

She rose with a gasp and tugged at her bodice. "Are you

implying," she gasped, "that there actually *was* something to those — those charges?"

"Don't worry," I said, "they can't pin anything on me."

She turned and fled tentatively to the foot of the stairs. She surveyed me, breathing heavily, her hand on the newel post. "Why are you chattering away like this? Are you drunk, Mr. Mackerel?"

"Naw, I just don't think two people should have any secrets from each other. Do you? What in Tophet is the matter with you, Pippa?"

"This is not a subject to joke about!"

I walked over to her, my fists in the pockets of my bath-robe. "On the contrary," I said, "I'd say it's something not to get too serious about. I want you to remember that. Because if you turned out to become a bore about it, you'd be wrong. *Dead wrong.*"

She fled up the stairs. I went back to my chair, in which I was having a quiet brandy when I heard the thump of luggage upstairs. Fifteen minutes later she was gone, Fatima with her, and I sat, brandy in hand, savoring the quiet of an empty house.

"Would you like to talk about it? Go on, tell me about some of them. I'd like to hear."

Turnbull and I were slouched in easy chairs on the screened porch. It was Friday night, the night of the prayer meetings. A good day for it, or the reverse, according to how you looked at it. The air was dead, like a damp vestment clinging to one's skin. It had been ninety-three all day, and the mercury still stood at ninety, though the sun had set. There wasn't a cloud in the sky. No precipitation was foreseen by any eastern weather bureau for as far ahead as they dared look. A real challenge to believers like Evans, whose contingent of the community rain dance could already be heard gathering in the nearby church. Turnbull was going to the rain dance but had dropped over early to see if I couldn't be persuaded to come along, a vain remonstrance, of course, and we were having a drink and a quiet chat before he went on. As he pressed me to open up, it occurred to me that I probably owed him something in exchange for his own regalements.

I pushed an ice cube down with one finger, as though experimenting with the possibility of its remaining submerged out of sheer discouragement after it had been poked enough times.

"I've never told you about a little interlude I had in Innsbruck, have I?" I said, striking up that tone of prudent indiscretion suitable to club chair narrations of this kind. I was fabricating, but that seemed of little importance. I knew at least one Italian episode in the other's repertory to have been fallacious, in that Turnbull had had Mussolini in Rome a good two years before the Fascists had marched on it, and in an English summer also dear to his memory, he claimed to have had an affair with a woman whose name I remembered as that of a character in one of Galsworthy's novels. "Well, sir, I was detained by engine trouble on a motor trip through that part of the Austrian Tyrol in 1947 — no, perhaps it was '48 — when, rolling up in a Daimler to the door of this little inn on which I had luckily chanced, was the most . . ."

I saw soon enough that he wasn't listening. I laid this to some fault of improvisation on my part, but that wasn't the reason. He had something on his mind, I presently found out. He moistened his lips and rubbed his palms together between his knees.

"What is it, Turnbull?" I asked.

245

"I'm thinking of getting married again."

"Wonderful!" I leaped to my feet with honest delight. "That's great, old boy, I'm glad to hear it. This calls for a drink!" The exclamation was rhetorical, since we were both supplied with fresh ones. I raised mine and quaffed his health. He took a perfunctory sip of his. "Who's the lucky lady?" He glanced over his shoulder toward the kitchen. "Don't worry about Mrs. Calico. She left my employ yesterday. Come on, who is it? Anybody I know?"

"It's her. Mrs. Calico," he said. "She's the one."

When I had finished wiping the rattan porch rug, I refilled the glass I had spilled on it. I came back from the living room where I'd gone to replenish myself.

"Well, well. I'm delighted to hear it. How long has this been going on?"

"Oh, since she's been here. Didn't you notice anything?"

"Ahh, well . . . That accounts for why she skittered out of the room every time you showed up, and then you'd go sneaking back in the kitchen, making time for yourself while I was up there with my nose in a book."

"Sorry." There was a disturbance in the even line of his mustache that could only be construed as a smile. "I haven't actually popped the question yet because, well, I have a feeling she may be worried about the difference in our ages — or may think I am. But I'm not. By God, I've got a few years left in me yet and she's jolly well welcome to them . . . Didn't she let on to you anything was up?"

"Well, ahh, not in so many words, but I could sense there was something on her mind, and I wasn't so far wrong was I you old rascal there's somebody at the door excuse me."

I was grateful for deliverance from *that* passage. But scarcely ready for the one that followed on its heels. It was Hester at the door.

"Why, Hester," I said. "Hello, hello, hello. Come in."

"Hello, Andrew."

We stood in the vestibule, nervously prolonging greetings and inquiries as to how we were and remarks on the heat. Then she paused and said, "I thought I'd come and see you tonight because — well, it's a big night for you. Oh, I don't mean that," she laughed. "That's ridiculous. I was thinking of the prayer meetings going on all over and you alone in your stubborn corner. When I said a big night I was thinking of something like election night. Waiting for the returns to come in — or not come in."

"There won't be any returns," I said. "The whole thing is absurd, and, as you know I'll add, an insult to God through a debauch of the use of prayer. The conditions are meteorologically impossible for rain. The only thing that could bring it on would be a miracle."

"That's what they're praying for, isn't it?" She looked down at the floor and laughed self-consciously again. "And it's you against them. That's why I thought I'd come and keep you company. But it was a silly idea, wasn't it?" She turned and started out again.

I took her by the shoulder. "No, no, of course it isn't. It's very sweet of you." A car had stopped in front of the house and I drew her away from the screen door, aware that somebody emerging from it was listening to us. "Come in and sit down."

She came in but she remained standing in the living room. She took it in. "It looks pretty clean."

"I do all right," I said. I immediately repented this churlish remark. "No, I've had a housekeeper. She's gone now. None so good as you."

"Sent her packing, did you? I —" Hester turned, open-mouthed, at a knock on the front screen door. As I went to see who it was, the bell in the church steeple began to ring out the call to prayer. I could hear others in the distance take it up, and the air was suddenly a sweet jumble of golden peals.

The figure on the porch was that of a stout man wearing a soft black hat.

"Mr. Mackerel?"

"Why, Fat Chance, come in." I opened the screen door for him. Over his shoulder I saw another man leaning against the back door of the car. "You know Inspector Chance? This is Miss Pedlock."

"I believe not," Hester said, offering him her hand.

"Pleased to meet you, Miss Pedlock." Chance glanced meaningly at her and then to me. "I'd like to see you alone if I could."

"No, it's all right. You can speak in front of her. What is it?"

"I'm sorry to say it is my painful duty to arrest you on suspicion of murder."

"On what new evidence?" I asked. As though I didn't know.

"Testimony of your former housekeeper — Mrs. Calico. She claims you blurted out you did it in her presence. I'd like to ask you to come to the station and make out a statement concerning these charges. I must warn you that anything you say may be used against you."

"I can explain everything," I said. "I just said that to, er —" I saw Turnbull materialize from the porch where I'd left him. "Maybe I'd better tell you at headquarters at that."

Hester had turned away to the front window. Now she wheeled around and at the same time drew something from her bag. "Here's the film," she said. "Let's have this business settled once and for all. This ought to put an end to it one way or another."

She thrust it into Chance's hand. He hefted it in his palm, looking at it, as though weighing it might weigh the merits of what she had suggested. I snapped on a light, for it had grown dark. The box in Chance's hand was a yellow square one, of the sort in which negatives are mailed between customers and the factory. "All right, we'll have this developed," Chance said. "Thank you for this evidence. The law appreciates it."

"You don't have to get it developed. It's already been developed. I got it and sent it in and got it back and there it is. So you don't have to take it in either, or impound it, or whatever you call it. We've got a projector. Sixteen millimeter, just like this."

"General Delivery, Bridgeport," Chance said, reading the return address. "That's how you escaped the mail watch. You're a very clever girl, Miss Pedlock."

"I know," Hester said, meekly. She turned to me and said, "Andrew, get the projector. You haven't used it for years but it's probably still good, and I'm anxious to —"

"Why, I don't believe I know where it is offhand . . ." I said.

"I do," she said, putting her bag down on a table. "It's back in that basement bin among all that stuff I've been trying to get you to sort out. You wait here. I think I can dig it out without any trouble."

We stood watching her walk out through the dining room and then the kitchen, to descend the cellar stairs. "Well, here goes," Fat Chance said, opening the package.

I noticed, with a wave of emotion I didn't quite understand at the moment, that he had to break the seal on the lid.

Seventeen

WE ARRANGED the chairs in the living room so as to face one wall. The screen couldn't readily be found, but the wall was white plaster and would serve the purpose, after a picture, a Dufy reproduction, had been removed and set to one side. Hester dusted the projector off with a cloth in the kitchen and Fat Chance carried it in. He took charge of getting it set up on a table, and also offered to run it, being experienced with his own home movies. "Should see the ones I take," he said with humorous self-deprecation. Turnbull had stayed, skipping the church service, and sat in the rear of two improvised rows, in a deep chair, steeped in funk, his chin in his hand or drumming his fingers on the arm. Chance had called in the henchmen he'd had with him in the car, who turned out to be two in number. He referred to them as Fred and McIver, and did not formally introduce them, out of politeness. They seemed rather keyed up, or at least self-conscious.

"O.K., we're ready now," Chance said at last. "Would somebody turn the lights off please?"

I snapped a switch on the wall beside the vestibule, sauntering on out of the room after I had done so. My free hand was in my trouser pocket, masticating loose change in a way that is habitual with me.

I went into the kitchen and began to slice bread for sandwiches in case I would be starved. I got some roast beef, tomatoes and butter out of the icebox, and put them on the table. I could hear the soft, steady whirr of the projector, and occasionally low voices. A man said, "Who's that?" and another, "Must be his mother. Yes, that's Mrs. Hale." I counted the number of slices I had cut. They were seven. To even it, I cut one more. Then I put the loaf back into its wax wrapper and stuffed it into the metal bin on the counter beside the sink. ". . . playing with her dog. I don't know what good this is doing us."

"Wait. There's the beach."

I saw that the door to the cellar was open and the light on the stairway lit. I went down. I made directly for the storage stall, formerly used for coal, to tidy things up there. I shoved a few things back that Hester had dragged out, a folding table, a half-decayed carton with croquet materials in it, and then swung the door of the stall to without altogether shutting it. Just then the oil furnace, which had been going for hot water, stopped. In the silence, I could hear the voices upstairs much more clearly than I had in the kitchen, because I stood directly under the floor where the group sat. I heard a footstep move out of the living room toward the kitchen, and recognized it as Hester's. The projector clattered softly on. I thought: if I hadn't complained about the Jesus Saves signs, all this wouldn't have happened.

Suddenly I heard Chance say, "Mackerel — he's gone! That's enough for me! He's lit out! Fred, you take the back door and search out the yards. McIver, take the car and circle north around the block. I'll come around the other way and meet you. Radio headquarters to alert all prowl cars. And tell them to phone the state police to issue a general wanted! Hurry!"

There was a great bumping and scraping of chairs, and a thud of footsteps in all directions. When they had vanished out the front and back, and the shouting voices with them, there was silence in the house. Except for the faint whirring of the projector, which somehow only emphasized it, made it more than total. I gave a last look around and walked back upstairs, snapping out the basement switch.

Hester was slicing the roast beef for the sandwiches. "Here, let me do that," I said. I fixed two sandwiches, divided them diagonally on saucers and shoved them away. "Who's out there?"

"Just Turnbull." Hester sat down on a tall kitchen stool beside the sink and crossed her legs. "What's that noise?" she asked. "Not the machine — that other. That funny ticking, rustling sort of sound." She glanced up.

I listened a moment. "Squirrels on the roof again probably." I set coffee to brewing in the electric percolator. Out of the tail of my eye, I saw Hester thrust an arm out the open window and hold her hand a moment palm up. She drew it in and tugged at her dress. It was a white cotton print splashed with red flowers.

A sharp flapping clatter in the living room indicated that the film was finished. It stopped as the projector was turned off. Presently there were heavy footsteps and the swinging door to the kitchen opened. Turnbull came in, groping his way, his hand to his eyes.

"Oh, Andy," he said. "Andy, Andy Mackerel. Why? You shouldn't have. Do you realize what you did, boy?"

"I couldn't have! You never know what you're doing

then!" I said in a shrill voice, gesturing with the bread knife. "Your mind goes blank. I didn't know what was happening then. I don't know. Doesn't that prove it?"

"Risked your life to save mine. That's all." Turnbull dropped into a chair and put his head in his hands. "And you not even any great shakes as a swimmer. Yet you jump in and come to my miserable, unworthy, undeserving aid."

"Oh, that," I said, laying the bread knife by. "It was nothing, old boy. Forget it."

"And then turning back to see what had happened behind you, you dive underwater to try to save her. Till they had to pull you out. Till they damn near had to save you, you're such a lousy swimmer. You can see it all on there. It's as plain as day."

He sat shaking his head, his hands plowing his face. He emitted low, muffled moans, and brushed his eyes, whether at real tears or for dramatic validity was hard to tell. He continued after a moment, "Why didn't you speak up, let me know who my thank offering should be for?" He lifted his head and had another of his apocalypses right there in my kitchen. "It'll just say 'Mackerel Plaza.' No first name. So it could just as well mean —"

"Now, look," I said, taking a stance over him and gesturing with the bread knife once more. "We're not going to open that can of tomatoes again. Do you hear? That's an order, and if you so much as open your trap about any last-minute changes in the script, so help me I'll slit your throat with this knife. Is that clear? Is it!" He gave a vague nod and gestured acquiescently. "Because I don't want to be put through that wringer again. We'll burn the film for sure now. That is, after we've let Fat Chance have a look at it. Poor Fat," I thought aloud. I imagined him scurrying through town and stirring up half the state of Connecticut.

253

A sudden increase in the sound Hester had noted put an end to this line of compassion.

Turnbull rose and lifted his shaggy head to yet another vision. "It's raining," he said. "My God, it's raining! Listen to it!" As we did that, listened to it, pattering on the dry leaves and pocking the dust, we heard another sound joining it — a church bell, distantly ringing in acknowledgment, in gratitude. Other bells took up the sound, till presently it threatened to drown out that of the rain. P.L.'s belfry was silent, but we could hear singing: Evans was leading them in a hymn of praise.

"I'm going over. I've got to see this," Turnbull said. "Come on!" He ran bareheaded out the front door toward the church.

Hester got cups and put them on saucers. She poured us both coffee when it was done and set the kitchen table for us. We had the sandwiches together there. "I'm starved," I said, picking a little at mine.

"I haven't had dinner either." Hester bit hungrily into her sandwich and took a sip of coffee. She was still sitting on the high stool, and not across the table from me but around the corner of it, near me. "Patter of rain on the roof is nice."

"It is?"

She smiled and reached a hand through my arm, scratching the back of my wrist. There was a low growl which was not my stomach, having issued in the distant west. I smiled back at her. "Jehovah's wetness," I said.

She twisted about on her chair to look into the dining room, through whose open windows the curtains were billowing into the room. "It's working up into something," she said, rising. "Andy, don't you think you ought to close

254

the windows? Please do. I'm afraid of electrical storms." There was a flash of lightning and a crack of thunder. "Please."

I put my sandwich down and went about the house as bade. A spat of wet caught me in the face as I lowered one parlor window. "Good God," I said, looking upward through a thrashing maple bough. "Really."

Hester went about pulling electrical appliance plugs from their sockets, in the belief that their connection invited currents from the storm. Toaster, percolator, radios, everything came loose. "Now upstairs," she said, dashing up the staircase as another more deafening crash and a blinding glare ended in a ring of the telephone.

The house was now being battered like a drum. The windows rattled, the roof rumbled, the very floors throbbed beneath us as the heavens emptied. It was a cloudburst — without there having been a cloud. It was not a question of its raining cats and dogs, sheets and pillow cases or anything else familiar to popular conception: we were *in water*. We were as solidly underwater as that fabled city which was "removed from the steadfast foundations of the shore to the coral floors of ocean." And it was now, racing up the stairs after Hester, that I had my apocalypse.

It occurred to me on the instant of my realizing that the accumulating churchbells, rather than drowning out the sound of the rain as they a moment ago had, were now in the reverse position of being drowned out by it. Oh, it was quite definitely that. They were no longer, as might be said, in it. Then it came to me in a flash — flash of lightning quite, if you will. God was not answering their prayers by sending them the rain they had asked; he was telling them what he thought of this gimme use of prayer, this debauch of its purpose of simply seeking communion with him — which was what I said prayer was for and why I had refused to join the rain dance — he was telling them what he thought of such medieval goings on by sending them more than the rain they had asked for. This wasn't a blessing, it was a judgment! This wasn't just a storm, it was a flash flood! I could see it all now. After soaking the crops, it would wash the crops away. Having drenched the ground and glutted the drains, it would flood the streets. Thousands would be rendered homeless as buildings were evacuated, houses and storefronts crumbled. The Red Cross would send a relief corps to stricken Avalon, and down from Greenwich and New Canaan and wealthy Westport would come the foodstuffs gathered in *other* congregations: cans of vichyssoise and cheese straws and smoked pâté and tomato juice for bloody Marys; onion soup and canned fruit and vegetables and *babas au rhum* and tinned oysters and Miltown and dexamyl and bundles of old clothes, Brooks Brothers suits and Hathaway shirts and hand-me-down ascots for victims of the flood area.

"Evidently an object in the vicinity has been struck," I said hysterically, sprinting down the upstairs hall after Hester as a shattering crash was heard. I had jagged glimpses of her fleeing form in the now almost continuous flashes. I followed her into her old bedroom and pulled the windows down. The front of my shirt was sopping. I turned back and saw her standing rigid in the middle of the room, her hands in front of her face. I went over to her and put an arm around her. "There, there," I said, in a thick voice. "You can stay here tonight."

She whirled around to me and seized and held me in a shivering embrace.

We stood that way for two or three minutes. Then as suddenly as it had come, the electrical storm drew off. The rain settled down to a quiet, steady, drenching fall.

"Just what we need," Hester said, moving away from me.

I took a shower and got into bed. The house was shut up. I opened my bedroom window and lay in the cool fresh air that came through it. It rained steadily. I could hear sounds of retiring in Hester's room. A little glow came into mine from the light in hers, for both our doors were open. Then hers went out and I heard her bed creak. A faint illumination still fell across my bed from the streetlamp between the church and the parsonage. I lay staring up at the dark ceiling, on which the shadows of foliage dimly fluttered.

Presently I heard a sound gentler than the rain, on my open door. A deferential tap, repeated.

Hester said, "I have no nightgown."

I laced my fingers on the pillow and settled my head in the hollow of my two palms. "In what sense?"

"I'm still frightened."

"Come on in."

I heard, rather than saw, her advance through the cool dark. She drifted, a pale slim shape, across the foot of my bed. She stood at the window with her arms folded, shivering as she glanced out. I patted the side of my bed and she slipped over and sat down.

"I have no more faith," I said. "That's gone. That's all over now. And what I'm wondering is, what have I lost? If it was just an illusion — a workable illusion — then its removal mightn't matter so much. I mean it's not such a tragedy. Like losing a wooden leg in an accident."

"Dearest Andrew." She laid a cool hand on my bare shoulder. "A rout for the liberal forces — that what the election returns amount to?"

"It's not that I resent finding there is a God after all who answers prayers," I said, speaking up to the ceiling. "That kind of personal God whose nonexistence was the mast to which I nailed my flag, and said Let's get on from there. It's not just having to face up to that possibility (as an alternative to pure fluke), it's that my position is no longer tenable. If this is his answer, I'm just not his sort. Because who were at those prayer meetings? All the bores, dullards and bigots in town — not a person of civilized sensibility was there. If that's the lot he gives aid and comfort to, so be it. But I cannot worship him. I can believe in him. But I cannot worship him."

"Poorest Andrew." With one deft motion her feet were under the sheet with mine. The sheet came only up to our ankles. Her hand slipped round me and stroked my back.

"When I was young, a student I mean, we used to debate whether Christ was the son of God. Now the question is whether God is the father of Christ. Is there a family resemblance, if this is the way he proceeds? We would argue long into the dormitory nights about the divinity of Christ. Now the question is the humanity of God. No, I have lost my faith."

She stirred somewhat against me, with a caress of impatience. "They'll say it was a weak thing, that not even a miracle could save it."

"It's just the other way around. It was so strong it took a miracle to crush it."

She seemed to move her head a little and laugh. "Quite a Calvinist."

I was so incredulous that I sat up in the bed. "*What?*"

She sat up too and, gesticulating, we argued there for a brief bit.

"Of course. This all-or-nothing idea. Whole hog. It's got to be one thing or another, splitting hairs right down to the finish. All right, not hairs — essentials. This intolerance with other points of view, Dutch Calvinist stubbornness with people who don't agree with you. Even your anti-Calvinism is the most Calvinistic thing I've ever seen. Certainly a resemblance to *your* father."

I simply let this pass. I dropped back on the pillow and lay with my arms folded over my brow. She parted my arms and peered to engage my vision.

"You don't need a god," she laughed, "you'll *be* one. By the time Turnbull gets through with you around here."

"Not quite."

"They'll give you your pulpit back, if you want it. They'll forgive your sins."

"It's the least they can do, seeing I didn't commit any."

"How about this one?"

"This one won't count, because I expect we'll be legalizing it as soon as possible."

"Ah, Andrew," she said, her arms going around me as mine sought hers in the cool dark, "the answer is yes."

Her body against me was like a bursting star.

With the loss of my faith, I threw myself into parish work. It was the only way to forget. If there was Nothing, what did it matter what you did? If there was Nothing, so much the more need to tend your own visions of truth, beauty and goodness. If there was Nothing, it didn't matter from which direction you drew your validities. For a while there it was Nitchevo, though I knew that in time I would probably be my old self again.

The next day, I noticed a half-written sermon lying on

my writing desk. I shrugged. There seemed no point in not finishing it.

At breakfast, of course, seeing Hester all bright and fresh there in the kitchen with an apron over her dress, I thought of the passage in *Through the Looking Glass* where everybody had to run as fast as they could to stay in the same place. That's how it was with me. I had been running as fast as my legs could carry me for a year, to stay in the same place. With a difference, of course. I thought of how Hester hadn't ever let an argument drop, once it had been taken up.

"You go around Robin Hood's barn with your intellectual arguments, generation after generation, you men," she said, pouring us coffee, "and there isn't a religion anywhere in the world that can't be summed up in a phrase my mother was always fond of."

"Let's have it," I said, bracing myself as ever. "What did your mother used to say?"

" 'To be as humane as is humanly possible.' That was the way she often put it. How we should try to be with one another."

Was that it? Was all the back-breaking, skull-cracking thought of the ages to be summed up in that absurd piece of unconscious irony? Was that the fruit of human wisdom? Maybe so, I thought rather sadly.

"And you *can't* say that there isn't *design*," she went on, gesturing with both hands. "You can't say you don't see that everywhere you look, everywhere in the universe. You can't say there isn't such a thing as a designing intelligence."

"Well," I said, looking across the table at this woman, "I'd be a damn fool if I denied that."